MASTERING THE MARCHIONESS
CAVERN OF PLEASURES

Published by WIND COLOR PRESS
Copyright © 2017 by Em Brown

Printed in the USA.

Cover Design and Interior Format
© KILLION
THE
GROUP, INC.

Mastering the Marchioness

Cavern of Pleasures

BESTSELLING AUTHOR
EM BROWN

A GENTLE WARNING

These stories contain BDSM elements, themes of submission and dominance, and many other forms of wicked wantonness.

GOT HEAT?

"Ms. Brown has written a tantalizing tale full of hot sex…a very sexy and sometimes funny read that will definitely put a smile on your face."
~ *Coffee Time Romance* review of AN AMOROUS ACT

"Darcy's fierce, independent spirit and unconditional loyalty to her family will win readers over, and Broadmoor is a romantic hero to swoon for."
~ *RT Book Reviews* on FORCE MY HAND

"Sometimes you just pick up the right book that just hits you and makes you really love it. This was one of those books for me. I just got so into the story and never wanted it to end."
~ *Romancing the Book* review of SUBMITTING TO THE RAKE

"This one made me go WOW! I read it in a few hours which technically I probably should have gotten more sleep, but for me it was that good that I deprived myself of sleep to finish this most awesome story!"
~ Goodreads reader review of MASTERING THE MARCHIONESS

"HOT AND FUN TO READ!!!!!!!!"
~ Reader review of ALL WRAPPED UP FOR CHRISTMAS

"…sex was intense…thrilling…."
~ Goodreads reader review of CONQUERING THE COUNTESS

"I loved this book. Clever dialogue that kept me laughing, delightful characters and a wonderful story. I am not generally one who likes historical fiction but this book carried me along from page one."
~ Goodreads reader review of CONQUERING THE COUNTESS

CHAPTER ONE

H ANGING FROM A HOOK, HER toes barely touched the floor. Instead of the mask worn by many of the other guests at Madame Botreaux's Cavern of Pleasures, the young woman wore only a silk red blindfold. The rest of her was laid bare for all to see.

Vale Montressor Aubrey, the third Marquess of Dunnesford, circled around her like a predator examining its prey, occasionally running the tip of a riding crop languidly over her nipples. Once or twice he pulled the riding crop back and flicked it against a breast. She gasped, then groaned.

"Please...please, Master..." she pleaded.

Peering at her thighs through his black and silver mask, Vale saw the telltale glisten of moisture at her mons. This one never took long.

"Your punishment has hardly begun, m'dear," Vale told her.

"Please...forgive me...I was weak."

Suppressing a sigh, Vale pulled back the crop and lashed it at her buttocks. It was unfortunate. Her body was beautiful—with full ripe breasts that quivered when punished—but she had indeed proven weak.

"I leave you to contemplate how you can do better," Vale said with another swat of the crop.

As he headed toward the stairs, past a number of men and women engaged in various forms of coupling, a masked woman threw herself at his feet.

"Take me—I would be a far better submissive than she," the woman declared.

Vale looked down at her. His half-mask did not cover his frown or the hard set of his jaw, and she crept away in shame.

"Pray tell that is not boredom writ on your face?" asked Lance Duport when Vale joined his friend and Madame Botreaux in the balcony from where they could view the activity below, much like patrons in an opera box.

It was the favorite spot of Penelope Botreaux. She rarely ventured onto the floor of the *Cavern of Pleasures*—so-called because the large assembly area existed practically in the basement of her residence. Unfinished walls left the ground rock exposed. As there were no windows, only the dim glow of a few strategically placed candelabras penetrated the darkness.

"I let you have the beauty when I could have made her mine," Penelope declared from the settee upon which she lounged like a Grecian goddess, wearing a thin transparent gown over a body that time and a few too many glasses of ratafia had made plump in various places.

"I regret your generosity is wasted on me," Vale replied, removing his mask and looking over the balcony to where he had left the young woman. "Perhaps I am too old for her."

Penelope snorted. "I am over forty and hardly consider myself old. You are barely five and thirty."

"And you could best any of the younger men here," added Lance as he raked an appreciative gaze over Vale's body.

An active life of riding, hunting, fencing, and an occasional bout in the ring kept Vale's physique in admirable shape. His stockings encased calves that were the envy of his peers. His simple linen shirt opened to reveal a broad, strong chest. His tight breeches covered muscular thighs and left little to the imagination.

Lance turned to Penelope. "You know half the women here—and men—would give their right buttock to be partnered with Vale. He needs more than a neophyte."

"Would *you* give your right buttock?" Penelope returned.

Lance curled his thin lips into a salacious grin. "I would give *both* my buttocks. Do you remember Demarco?"

"Ah, yes, how can I not? He was a beautiful brute. A Samson with that lush head of hair."

"And cocky as hell, but Vale had him writhing in submission within the hour. After such a conquest, I wonder that Vale should wish to trifle with the weaker sex."

Vale smiled. "Despite all appearances, women are not the weaker sex."

"Well, what the devil are you looking for?" Penelope prodded. "Apparently not men, nor women of unsurpassed beauty. You have spurned *both* novice and skilled submissives. Only Lovell Elroy has had more partners than you."

Vale pressed his lips into a grim line as he looked over the balcony at a man wearing a red mask flogging a woman. "Lovell is malicious. He cares nothing for the women he is with. I wish you would throw him out, Penelope."

"But the women flock to him—especially those whose hearts you have broken."

"Lovell breaks more than hearts, Penelope."

"Ah well, like you, he is a beautiful specimen to behold, and I do enjoy beauty." Penelope held up her quizzing glass and blatantly directed her gaze at Vale's crotch.

"Egad, Vale," Lance interjected. "Nearly forgot: felicitations to you on your recent nuptials."

Vale started. He had nearly forgotten that he was now married.

"Indeed," Penelope said. "Where are you hiding this wife of yours?"

"We arrived in town but yesterday," Vale answered. "She is with my cousin Charlotte at the moment."

He was not particularly interested in pursuing the subject. Though he was sure that Charlotte would prove better company for Harrietta than he, he nonetheless felt a stab of guilt for pawning his wife off on a relative for the evening.

"And will you be introducing us to her?"

"Good God, no," Vale shot back. "She is a simple girl from the country."

"Hardly sounds like the sort of woman you would choose to marry after all these years," Lance commented.

Vale shrugged. "Dunnesford needs an heir. Does it really matter whom I marry?"

"Yes, but of all the beautiful and wealthy women setting their caps at you, why a chit for whom you seem to have ambivalent feelings?"

"Her brother and I were the best of friends before he died at Yorktown in the service of His Majesty. We served in the same regiment for some time together, and I owe my life to him. At the age of ten, I would have drowned in the lake at Dunnesford but for his efforts." Vale put back his mask. "I should return to the beauty. Her arms must be sore."

"Even if her constitution is weak," Penelope attempted, "her arse must be a delight. I almost wish I were a man that I might experience the feeling of being inside her."

Her arse should have been delightful, Vale thought as he recalled how easily his cock had slid into the woman due to the immense amount of wetness that had dripped from her cunnie into her sphincter earlier. But there had been something missing with this one—as there had been with all the others. The women were more and more beautiful, yet his drive, his passion, continued to diminish. Perhaps it was only natural once one had experienced all there was to experience, tasted all that a feast could offer.

"Ah, we have some newcomers," Lance noted of a few people who had just walked onto the assembly floor. "Damn me, that brunette looks like Charlotte, but who is the one next to her with the lackluster brown hair and emerald necklace?"

Vale narrowed his eyes at the three emeralds separated by two small diamonds and laced together with silver. At first, he paled. Then his jaw hardened as he answered, "My wife."

CHAPTER TWO

FOR HARRIETTA DELANEY, NOW MARCHIONESS of Dunnesford, the eye holes in her mask were not large enough to accommodate her wide-eyed stare as she followed Charlotte onto the floor of *Madame Botreaux's Cavern of Pleasures.* There were men and women about her in all states of undress, and yet she, clothed from head to toe in a modest evening dress, felt like the naked one.

Not only were these men and women openly naked *in public* but they were engaged in all manner of...activity...*in public.* It hardly seemed real. Only in her fantasies—deep, dark fantasies that she had never shared with anyone—had she envisioned such possibilities. Only in London could such a place exist. Certainly not in the small town where she had lived for all four and twenty years of her life. The prospect of living in the City had been the one bright part of marrying the Marquess of Dunnesford. It was a marriage that made her among the luckiest women in England. And the biggest fool.

"He has wealth and breeding and a title *and* is pleasing to the eye," Bethany, Harrietta's junior by four years, had cooed after the Marquess had finally accepted one of their mother's numerous invitations.

"*Exceedingly* handsome," Marianne, who had yet to have her come-out, had sighed.

Even Jacqueline, the youngest Delaney daughter at twelve, had agreed. "He looks like a *prince.*"

Harrietta had to admit that King George himself was unlikely to have produced as grand an entry as the Marquess, arriving in his gilded carriage pulled by a team of four with gleaming white coats and footmen who appeared to possess more expensive garments than the wealthiest of the bourgeoisie. The Marquess was also perfection, from the finely powdered hair to the elaborate cravat tied at his throat, the rich velvet coat that flared from the hips, his delicately embroidered waistcoat, and down to the jeweled high-heeled shoes. He was elegant yet commanding. Powerful but refined. Regal and sensuous.

Nine long years had passed since she had last seen Vale, and she no longer recognized him. She had dreamt of him, still flushed when she remembered their last encounter, and had heard much about him—especially about the many mistresses he had kept in those years. At the time of her marriage to him, he had been most recently rumored to be with an Italian countess. A family friend who traveled in the same social circles as the Marquess had described him as an aloof and arrogant rake—not the sort of man Harrietta had ever envisioned herself marrying.

The Marquess was a stranger to her. He was not the Vale who once preferred the company of the Delaney family to his own, who had been Harold's best friend, and who had been like a second brother to her. She resented this magnificent Marquess for failing to be the man she had fallen in love with as a girl. But Mr. Delaney had three daughters with no dowries. That a man of Lord Dunnesford's stature would offer for Harrietta—poor and plain—was, according to Bethany, nothing short of the most miraculous gift Fate could bestow.

Dear God, Harrietta thought to herself as she glimpsed a woman whose breasts were being serviced by the mouths of two different men, *surely I belong in Bedlam for wanting to see this place?*

What she saw next answered her question affirmatively. A naked young woman was hanging from a hook like a slab of meat in a butcher's shop while a man wearing a silver and black mask was circling around her—and striking her with his riding crop. Harrietta had never seen such tight breeches as those worn by the masked man. She flushed on his behalf. Her gaze traveled from his loins to his finely sculpted chest. The sinews of his strong arms revealed themselves as he pulled the crop back and lashed it against the woman's backside. Harrietta eyed the planes of his pectoral muscles, the ridges that filled his torso, and the rugged hardness of his belly. She had not thought the naked body of a man could be so... captivating. The man would have made an exceptional model for Michelangelo.

"Masterful, is he not?" Charlotte whispered.

"What is he doing to that poor woman?" Harrietta asked, appalled yet intrigued.

"Punishing her. She has displeased him in some way."

The young woman groaned…in pleasure. Harrietta felt warmth spreading through her body. Her own carnal experiences had been limited to a few encounters with the footman and the squire's son. There had been groping—a few playful swats on the butt that she had surprisingly enjoyed—but nothing on the order of what she now witnessed. But she had imagined a world of greater possibilities ever since she had found a copy of *Fanny Hill* that Harold had hidden beneath his bed.

"He is the most desired master," Charlotte explained. "Only the most beautiful and practiced are selected to be his submissive."

"Have you ever been with him?" inquired Harrietta as she followed the hard set of his jaw. "I should think it rather terrifying."

Charlotte closed her eyes and a small smile played upon her lips. "I would be unworthy."

Harrietta studied her companion, who seemed to be reveling in a daydream. She liked Charlotte—and not because the woman was her only friend in London at the moment. Widowed two years ago, before she had turned thirty, Charlotte Kensington possessed a worldliness and self-assurance that Harrietta appreciated. It therefore surprised her that Charlotte would want to submit to a man like the one in the silver and black mask.

When she saw the man leave the assembly floor, Harrietta felt relieved, though she was also curious to see what he might do next with the woman he had left hanging.

"If you wish to leave, you have only to speak it," Charlotte said.

Harrietta contemplated the suggestion. She had seen more tonight than she had ever thought possible. Her mind whirled and she needed time alone to digest all that she saw. And yet, she felt a part of her awakening, a part of her that desired to see more, a part of her that was not merely curious.

"Does everyone wear a mask?" Harrietta asked, stalling.

"Mostly," Charlotte replied.

"Do you know anyone here?"

"No, and that is part of the fun."

They walked past a row of semi-private alcoves occupied alternately by two women licking each other, a group orgy, and a ménage-a-trois.

"Are there no private chambers?"

"Where is the thrill in a private chamber? Ah, it is the time for presenting," Charlotte observed of a number of men and women who had begun forming a line in the middle of the assembly. "Did you wish to present tonight?"

"Present?" Harrietta echoed. Her pulse began to quicken.

"Those new to Madame Botreaux's must first present themselves. Those of a certain seniority here are allowed to choose among the new ones."

"What happens if you do not like the person you are with?"

"If you find you do not enjoy your initial encounter, you may request to present again upon your return."

Harrietta's heart was pounding in her head. For a brief moment she wondered what her new husband would say or do if he ever found out what she had done. He had made it quite clear before they married that he would not interfere in the life she wished to lead if she would afford him the same consideration. The coolness of his tone as he spoke had surprised her. In truth, she had felt a little stung by it. She knew full well she was not the sort of woman to merit the attentions of a man of his wealth and stature. That he had offered for her hand had mystified her. She could only guess that he had felt some obligation to her brother to care for his family.

He was certainly not interested in *her*. That much had become clear as crystal to her when he had chosen not to consummate their marriage on their wedding night. Instead, he had adopted a fatherly tone, assuring her that he would not press his privileges upon her but would wait until she was ready. What the bloody hell could he have met by that? The only answer that came to her was that he had no desire to bed her. Her lack of beauty had never bothered her before—Harold had often told her how he would sooner be in her company than all the Helens of Troy in the world—but on her wedding night, she had felt the pain of her plainness.

It was possible that despite the understanding that she and the Marquess had not to interfere in each other's lives, this would be too much for him to accept. *But why should he have all the fun?* Harrietta found herself reasoning as she thought of the Marquess with his mistress. Moreover, her identity was protected by her mask, and she trusted Charlotte not to divulge their illicit tryst. He would never know.

The man in the silver and black mask had returned and released the young woman from her bonds and her blindfold. He said something to her that made her cry. At first Harrietta thought he was telling the woman how much more she would be punished, but then he gently wiped away the tears from her face, and his lips formed what seemed to be the word *adieu*. The woman departed with obvious reluctance, casting one last look of longing at him before she left.

What would it feel like to want to be with someone that much? Harrietta wondered.

"If you worry that Vale—" Charlotte began.

Harrietta was quick to dismiss the suggestion. "Not at all. One of the maidservants mentioned that he is likely to be at the home of his mistress, the Countess D'Alessio. I suspect he will not return for some time."

"Does that mean you wish to present?"

For some reason, the thought of her husband with his mistress spurred her courage. "Yes—for tonight."

"Very well. I will wait for you when you are done."

I have lost my mind, Harrietta said to herself as she stepped into the line formed by four other women and three men. She could not deny that her body felt warm from seeing all the bodies of men and women writhing in pleasure, but she had not expected that she might be one of them tonight. From the corners of her eyes, she saw the man in the silver and black mask, his arms crossed over his chest as he looked over the line of men and women presenting. She wanted to flee.

But then she saw him move. He was coming toward her.

CHAPTER THREE

VALE SAW LOVELL ELROY, A man equal to him in physique and dominance, saunter toward the line of newcomers. It was unlikely that Lovell would select Harrietta—if the man selected anyone at all. Not all newcomers merited a partner. And Harrietta, with her square shoulders, petite breasts, and common features, was not the type of woman who would catch Lovell's eye. But Vale couldn't take that chance.

Damn Charlotte, Vale thought, when I lay my hands upon her...

"You," he said to Harrietta in a hoarse whisper to disguise his voice. "Come with me."

Lovell looked over. The rivalry between him and Vale was understated but obvious. Vale knew that Lovell was wondering why he was bothering with someone like Harrietta.

Vale began walking away. The sooner he removed Harrietta the better. What the devil was Charlotte thinking bringing her here?

He realized he was not being followed and turned back. Harrietta had not moved. Instead, she simply stared at him dumbly.

"I will assume you did not hear me," Vale told her. Heads around them began to shake.

She glanced over to where Charlotte was standing. Charlotte nodded her head encouragingly.

"Come with me," Vale repeated and turned once more. This time Harrietta followed. He led her to the farthest and most private alcove. It was also one of the darkest, allowing him to reside in the shadows of the faint candlelight.

"Stand there," he directed her, pointing to the center of the room with his riding crop. He surveyed her evening dress. It was a simple gown of violet damask that was part of the new wardrobe he had purchased for her as part of her wedding gift. The corset had managed to push her petite breasts up to form faint contours above the décolletage. She wore her hair curled, but loose and pulled away from her face. The blue half-mask covered what he knew to be a pert little nose but not her full lips, which formed a slight frown in their state of rest. Vale shook his head. Why did she bother with a mask when her emerald necklace—a family heirloom he had presented to her on the day of their wedding—flashed around her neck like a beacon?

"That is a striking necklace, ma petite," he said as he ambled around her slowly.

She realized her error and stammered, "I—it belongs to a friend. She lent it to me for the evening."

An adequate lie, Vale thought to himself. He wanted to sigh and run his hand through his hair. But he continued to circle around her as she watched him cautiously. Why had she come? And what was he going to do with her now that she was here?

"You don't belong here," he pronounced.

She lifted her chin. "Indeed?"

"You had best return home with your friend."

"I will leave when I am ready."

Vale pressed his lips together in displeasure. He was well acquainted with her stubborn streak—one that she shared with Harold—and it seemed time had not diminished that quality. God, but she looked so much like her brother, Vale thought to himself as he studied her. The memory of his best friend tugged at his heart with fresh vigor in her presence. He could feel the guilt in every cell of his body. He should have tended to the Delaney family immediately upon learning of Harold's death. Or at least when he had assumed the title of Marquess and had come into his full inheritance. The Delaney family had provided him with the warmth and affection that he lacked from his own family. He owed them the courtesy of a visit and so much more. But each passing year only strengthened the inertia. The guilt grew until he could ignore it no longer, and he had thought to absolve himself by marrying Harrietta; a posthumous apology to Harold for not having taken better care of his best friend's family.

"This is no place for you," he told her.

"Who are you to judge?"

He stepped toward her. She jumped a little but remained where she was. He stood behind her and leaned in toward her ear.

"Did you think I could not smell your apprehension?"

"That is merely because I am unfamiliar here," she responded.

Vale raised his brows. "You have been to similar establishments before?"

A smile tugged at the corner of her lips. "You seem to know all. You tell me."

Vale stepped back to better observe her. Was she lying or possibly telling the truth? If the latter, he had greatly misjudged the country girl he had married. She was staring at him, and he stepped once more into the shadows.

"In the Cavern, you will always direct your gaze in front of you," he explained. "You are not to meet my gaze or look upon me unless I direct you to. You shall always address me as your 'lord' or 'master.' Failure to do so has consequences."

Why was he telling her this? Vale wondered to himself. Best to get her on her way. But her response stunned him: she laughed.

"And what have you done to merit such a title?" she asked.

Insolent chit. Vale could hardly believe he was having this conversation. "You…are clearly a novice or you would not have the audacity to question me. I have no patience for greenhorns."

"Then why did you choose me—my lord and master?"

He would have preferred she not have added those last words, spoken with such mockery. Never had Vale encountered such impudence in the Cavern. He was almost tempted to punish her.

"Because others would not be so kind as to advise you of the prudent course, which is to return from whence you came."

"Kind?" Harrietta echoed. "And were you kind to that young woman you hung from the ceiling?"

A flush spread through Vale. So she had seen him with the beauty. How much had she seen? But it didn't matter. It wasn't as if she knew who he was. Not even Charlotte knew. "She was being punished," Vale explained. "And perhaps you noticed that she was not exactly complaining."

Harrietta seemed to consider the matter, but returned with, "And who gave you the authority to punish her?"

"She did. The source of authority always comes from the submissive. All that I do is what she desires me to do."

"She desired for you to strike her with your riding crop?"

"Yes. With an experienced master, even acts that she fears, resents, and dislikes are ultimately ones she wants to happen."

"What was she being punished for?"

"Spending without permission."

At last he was able to silence her. Her brows were knit in thought.

"An experienced submissive would know to do what she was told," Vale continued, "and would not forget to address her master as 'my lord,' as you have done—repeatedly."

Her voice wavered every slightly as she asked, "And what will you do with me—my lord?"

This time the words were spoken with more respect.

"Send you home," Vale answered.

She seemed disappointed.

"Madame Botreaux's is not a place for the faint of heart," Vale told her with the tenderness of a parent explaining what was best for a child. "It is understandable to be curious, but in here a person needs to be committed and possessed of a certain level of … ability."

"What kind of ability?"

"That you need ask shows your lack of understanding. Return home, ma petite."

He began to walk away.

"Where can I obtain the requisite ability?" she asked.

Damn it, Vale swore. Would she not give up? He had no idea how to answer that question. Many years ago, he had taken the time to work with new submissives, but he no longer had any interest.

"Would you teach me, my lord?"

Vale whirled on his heels and strode over to her. She was more than a head shorter and had to lift her chin quite high to meet his gaze.

"You do not know what you ask, ma petite," he warned.

"Stop speaking to me as if I were a child," she returned. "You know nothing of me, but have conceived some prejudice against me. Why?"

She was beginning to irritate him. If he lifted his mask to reveal his identity, perhaps he could scare her away.

"Because you are a child," Vale said. "Only a child would persist in asking foolish questions."

"And only an arrogant lout would persist in sending me away." She lowered her voice. "I could be better than any submissive you have had."

The quaintness of her delusion made him laugh, which made her cheeks redden in anger. "I do not mean to deride you, ma petite, but you have no notion of the challenges you face."

"Show me," she insisted.

"As I said, I've no patience for neophytes."

"Then tell me who has. Will the gentleman with the red mask—"

"No," Vale returned with such vehemence that she jumped back. "He has less patience than I."

"And perhaps less arrogance," she muttered.

Vale caught her jaw between his thumb and forefinger. "You tread in dangerous waters, ma petite. You have courage only because you are unaware of all that you do not know."

"I know more than you think."

"Do you? How many men have you lain with?"

"Is it breadth or depth that matters?" she countered.

Vale would easily have wagered that she was still a virgin. "And how deep does your depth extend?"

"Deep enough."

"I will be the judge of that. Have you ever been fucked?"

Her eyes widened behind her mask, and her breath quickened. "Often."

Liar, he thought to himself, but decided to let it go for he had another question he could ask. He stepped away from her and pointed to a ring on her finger with his crop.

"You are married. Have you lain with your husband?"

"If I was interested in fucking my husband, would I be here?"

Vale nearly choked. The ungrateful little chit. He could have married any number of women—women of unsurpassed beauty or breeding or wealth. She could not have done better than a tradesman or perhaps a wealthy but aging merchant.

Containing his own feelings, he remarked, "You do not regard your husband highly."

She hesitated. "Once… now I find him indolent and useless."

"Is he old and homely?"

"I understand many find him attractive, but he is old."

Devil take it, Harrietta, thirty-four is hardly old. Vale collected himself and continued. "Do you think him attractive?"

"His countenance is not displeasurable, but his beauty is marred by the lack of beauty in his soul."

Vale stared in disbelief. He had never heard himself spoken of so harshly—and certainly not to his face.

"As bad as that?" he asked.

She winced. "I did not mean to…well, he is not the man I would have freely chosen to marry."

For the first time, Vale wondered if he had done a disservice in offering for her hand. "Is there someone you would have preferred?"

"No."

Relief washed over him.

"We have a convenient arrangement in which neither is to intrude into the life of the other," she added. "We are civil to each other."

"Does he know you're here?"

"He would not care, I think."

Vale suppressed a snort.

"He has himself a mistress," she supplied.

His heart sank. Though her countenance remained stiff and she straightened her shoulders, something in her tone belied her stoicism. He felt an odd compulsion to assure her that all was not what it seemed.

"If you've no wish to instruct me, my lord," Harrietta continued, "it is of no consequence to me. I will find another who can."

Vale began to pace the room. He could not let her go about her own devices and risk her landing in the hands of someone like Lovell.

He held out his riding crop and with its end, kissed a nipple through her gown. Pulling his wrist back, he made to strike her in that same spot. She gasped audibly, but to her credit, she did not shrink from him. The chit was determined.

"Very well," he relented. "I will give you one night and one night only, but I have three conditions. Failure to meet any of them will indicate that you are not suited to be my pupil. Indeed, you will not possess the mettle to be a member of Madame Botreaux's if you cannot perform these simple tasks. First, you will arrive alone. No friends, no chaperones, and certainly no husbands or lovers."

"Your second requisite, my lord?" Harrietta prompted.

"Your impatience displeases me. The second condition is that you will meet me no later than ten o'clock tomorrow night—"

"Not tomorrow night!"

"Interrupting one's master merits a sound punishment," he informed her. "I recommend against it in the future."

He smiled to himself, knowing full well that tomorrow night would prove difficult for her, for he had offered to take her to her very first opera, Le Nozze di Figaro by Mozart. Harrietta had been thrilled, for the Austrian composer was her favorite.

"I can do any night but tomorrow."

"The choice is not yours."

She bit her lower lip in thought. "Very well."

Taken aback, he stared at her. Surely she did not mean it? He continued, "You will come clothed in no other color but red."

"That were impossible."

"The punishment for failing to address me properly will be three lashes. I can assure you already that your first lesson will not be an easy one."

Her lips curled in a frown, and Vale felt satisfied. "Those are your conditions. Unless you are able to meet all of them, I suggest you think no more of this place. There are other diversions in London that will better suit you, ma petite."

He left her to her own thoughts, satisfied there was little chance that she could succeed. But his plan did little to address another concern of his: what had prompted her to come to Madame Botreaux's—and wish to stay? He thought about their wedding night and wondered if he had offended her somehow. He knew plenty of husbands who would rape their wives and consider it no offense. Surely she would consider him kind for not forcing his attentions upon her? He did not think he could even if he tried. For God's sake, she was Harold's little sister. Though she had grown much in the nine years since he had last seen her—no longer a girl but a woman now—he could not resist the urge to protect her.

They would have to mate as husband and wife at some point. Dunnesford needed an heir, and it was the passing of his father a year ago that had finally forced the matter of marriage upon Vale. He had lived most of his life with little to regard for his father and had joined the army to spite the domineering old man, but his father had surprised him.

"Forgive me for the poor father I have been," the former Marquess had said on his deathbed. "I would not reproach you for refusing to honor me with a grandson."

For a man who had developed a keen sense of the desires of women, Vale had neglected to consider that his wife had certain needs as well. Lustful needs. For a moment he considered all the young men he knew, but quickly dismissed each and every one of them as an unsuitable partner for Harrietta. He shook his head. What other husband would find himself seeking a paramour for his wife? But he had to find another means to satisfy her. One that did not entail Madame Botreaux's.

God, what a bloody mess.

CHAPTER FOUR

Ⳕ

D ESPITE THE COOL NIGHT AIR wafting through the window of
her bed chamber, Harrietta felt flush and warm. Her pulse had raced
like never before upon leaving *Madame Botreaux's,* and though over an
hour had passed since she took her leave of Charlotte, her body still felt
unable to calm itself. Harrietta could only recall one other time in her life
when she had felt such a mixture of intrigue and agitation: when, at the
age of six and ten, she had seen Vale naked. He and Harold had decided to
take a swim in the lake at Dunnesford one early summer morning. They
had disrobed, not realizing she had stolen from the house with the same
intention. Hiding behind the bushes, Harrietta had watched Vale strip off
his shirt and breeches, baring his arse. She had felt the heat in her cheeks
as she admired his naked form before he disappeared into the water,
wishing that she could join him.

Tonight, however, her mind was filled with the image of her "lord" and
the feel of his riding crop upon her body. Harrietta shivered. She touched
the nipple that he had attended, fingering it until it hardened.

"How fortunate you are, Harrietta!" Charlotte had gasped when they
had returned to their carriage. "To be chosen by his lordship on your first
present! But why the pensive look, my dear?"

"I'm not sure I like him," Harrietta had answered. There was something
oddly familiar about his lordship. As if she had met him before. "I found
him terribly condescending. He wanted me to leave the *Cavern.* He told
me I did not belong there."

"He must have been testing you. Oh, Harrietta, any woman there
would have died to be in your place. You should be delighted."

Harrietta had worked her lower lip—a habit her mother had derided as
most unbecoming in a young woman. She was quite confident his lord-

ship had not selected her out of desire, but his parting conditions were
indeed a test. One that she did not intend on failing. But could she pass
his other tests? And what would those other tests entail? The prospect
excited and alarmed her.

"I found the gentleman in the red mask rather interesting," Harrietta
had confessed to Charlotte. Indeed, that man would have been her first
choice had she the liberty of choosing. The way he stood, the way he
moved indicated power and confidence.

But there was definitely a thrilling quality to his lordship as well. He
was familiar and different all at once. Unlike any man she had ever known.

She heard movement in the hallway and through the door she could
hear male voices. Vale was back? She had expected him to spend the
night with his mistress. Perhaps he and the Countess D'Alessio had had
a quarrel. Harrietta found herself hoping but then reminded herself that
she was not to care what the Marquess did in his private life. They had an
understanding not to interfere with each other.

In the quiet of her bedroom, Harrietta reached a hand down toward
her pussy to find herself moist. Purring, she stroked her clitoris with one
hand and teased her nipple with the other. She imagined what it would
feel like to have his lordship's crop against her nipple again, imagined how
it would feel to have it flicked against the hardened nub. Would the pain
be little or large? Would she find it stimulating? She pinched her nipple
to test her tolerance, but try as she might, she could not pinch herself
hard enough for it to hurt. She needed the hand of another…of a master.

She fingered her clit more vigorously until she came. Lying in her bed
as she absorbed the relief of her orgasm, Harrietta smiled to herself.

London was a new world to her, and now another was about to open
as well.

C

"I ENTRUSTED HARRIETTA INTO YOUR CARE for one evening—one evening, Charlotte," Vale began as soon as the butler had
shown him into the garden where Charlotte had set up an easel and was
painting, "and you took her to *Madame Botreaux's*?"

Charlotte nearly dropped her paintbrush and kept her widened eyes on
the canvass. "Who told you?"

At least her voice quivered with some semblance of guilt, Vale thought.

"It matters not who told me or how I came to find out. Suffice it to say that you could not have done worse had you taken Harrietta to a cockfight in St. Giles."

Changing her tactics, Charlotte shrugged and resumed her portrait of a naked man. "You asked me to befriend her. If you doubted my ability to play chaperone, you should not have left her with me."

The faint breeze wafting through the serenity of the lush garden should have calmed him, but Vale found himself particularly aggravated. Despite the cool air, he felt warm in his embroidered waistcoat and gold brocade coat. "I had no notion that you were a patron of *Madame Botreaux's.*"

"It has been years since I was there," Charlotte admitted, "but when your wife asked me to take her, I could not refuse. She can be rather persuasive."

"My wife requested it?" Vale asked incredulously. "How does she even know of *Madame Botreaux's?*"

Her cheeks reddened. "She saw a painting of mine. One I had done upon my last visit to the *Cavern.*"

Vale put a hand to his temple. The fact that Harrietta had prompted the visit to *Madame Botreaux's* was not encouraging.

"You need not fear," Charlotte reassured him. "She came to no harm."

"In the future, you will refrain from taking her to *Madame Botreaux's* or any establishment that in the slightest should resemble it."

"Hardly seems fair," Charlotte grumbled. "Wives are expected to sit home with their broidery or some such while husbands gallivant about with their mistresses."

"Since when have you ever stayed home embroidering?" Vale returned as he glanced from her painting to the nude model reclining on a bench before the lily pond.

A grin tugged at her lips. She turned to look at him frankly. "I like Harrietta, Vale. I may even become more fond of her than I am of you—and you know how fond I am of you. If you can entertain your Italian mistress, why cannot Harrietta have her own source of amusement?"

"She can have all the damn amusement—or paramours—she wants. I take no offense at being a cuckold, but it will *not* happen at *Madame Botreaux's.*"

He held her gaze until she looked away and mumbled a petulant, "Very well."

Vale was unsure whether or not to trust Charlotte, but he had other plans to put into place where his wife was concerned.

C

THAT MORNING, HARRIETTA AWOKE AND the rush of the evening before quickly returned. Throwing aside her coverlet, she bounded out of bed and rang for her maid. She wondered how she could possibly wait until the evening when she felt such anticipation?

"Will your ladyship be joining the Marquess for breakfast?" asked Sarah, her new maid.

"He told me yesterday that he would not be able to," Harrietta replied.

The Marquess of Dunnesford apparently sought to spend as little time with his new wife as possible. They had barely arrived at his home in Grosvenor Square before he had cast her upon his cousin and trotted off to see his mistress.

"What shall your ladyship wear today?" Sarah asked.

"Anything will do," Harrietta responded. The daunting collection of gowns, undergarments, headdresses and jewelry made Harrietta's head spin.

A knock drew Sarah to the door. It was the Marquess's valet.

"His lordship requests the presence of your ladyship at breakfast," Sarah informed Harrietta upon returning.

Harrietta sat at attention before the vanity, pleasantly surprised, though she had told herself a thousand times that she cared not what Vale did. Nonetheless, she took more pains with her attire than she was wont to, selecting an elegant chiffon gown with a green sash.

"Ah, Harrietta," Vale greeted her in the dining room, "you look lovely."

He gave her a kiss on the forehead before leading her to the table. She could not help but feel the kiss was one that Harold might have given her. She glanced over the long table at him and thought how terribly handsome he looked in his gold-embroidered coat and perfectly tied lace cravat. Once again, she felt rather plain in comparison, but even had she the most magnificent gown, she would be considered plain next to her husband, who no doubt should have had a prized beauty as a wife.

"Did you enjoy your time with Charlotte?" he asked with interest.

"Very much," she replied, hiding the sudden flush in her cheeks by staring intently at her plate of eggs and ham. "Charlotte is most agreeable company."

"And how did you ladies choose to pass the time?" he inquired casually as he spread butter on his toast.

"Oh, the idle chatter of women." Harrietta waved a dismissive hand. "Naught that you would find of interest."

"On the contrary, I am greatly interested."

His cool grey eyes staring across the table unnerved her.

"We talked of her paintings," she answered. "Charlotte is quite skilled with the brush."

"Yes," Vale murmured wryly. "I have seen her artwork."

Harrietta wondered if he had ever seen her private collection, but she wanted to turn the conversation as far from herself as possible.

"And you?" she asked. "Did you pass a pleasant evening?"

She almost wondered to add *with the Countess D'Alessio*, but that would have been impolite, especially given their understanding.

"It was not the evening I expected to have. Did you spend your entire evening talking of art?"

His eyes seemed to bore into her. Harrietta stuffed her mouth with more ham than she could chew comfortably and made an affirmative sound. It wasn't exactly a lie if she did not actually speak a coherent word.

"I shall be ready for the opera tonight early, shall I, that we shall not be late to arrive at the theatre?" Harrietta asked. "I should have liked to have seen a performance with the great David Garrick. I understand he was quite impressive in *Richard III*."

"If you like Shakespeare, The First Haymarket Theatre will have a production of *All's Well That Ends Well*. If you wish to attend—"

"Oh! Very much so!"

"Then I shall secure a box."

He smiled warmly at her, and Harrietta felt if they were not separated by the length of the table, she would have thrown her arms about him.

"I think there will not be hours enough in the day to see and do all that London has to offer," Harrietta said.

"Good. We must attempt every site and every activity your heart fancies."

His words took her breath away. She hoped he meant that he would join her in these pursuits, then reminded herself that the Marquess had more important matters to tend to than escorting her about the city. And some of those matters included the Countess D'Alessio, no doubt.

As if reading her mind, he said, "I have an engagement to attend, a meeting of shareholders at my bank, but I shall leave you in the capable hands of Mrs. Stewart for the day."

Mrs. Stewart was the stern housekeeper who had served the previous Marquess of Dunnesford.

"The library. I saw it yesterday," Harrietta said to the stout matron during their meeting after breakfast. "It faces southeast and receives such beautiful light, I wonder that lighter colors might not suit it better? Perhaps we can have the curtains drawn daily from the windows to allow more of the sun into the room?"

"That room has not changed since the *first* Marquess of Dunnesford," Mrs. Stewart replied with a defiant lift of the chin. "Bringing in more sunlight would cause the tapestries to fade."

"Perhaps we can find another place for the tapestries?" Harrietta asked, hoping her sweet tone would soothe the woman's disposition.

It did not.

The silent frown that prevailed was answer enough, and Harrietta decided not to pursue the matter. She had more important items to attend to: such as finding her way to *Madame Botreaux's* and satisfying the requisites of her "lord."

⁕

VALE SAT BACK AND WATCHED as Harrietta, perched on the edge of her carriage seat, commented on nearly everything they passed on their way to Covenant Garden. Harrietta was not among the loveliest women he knew, but the glow in her face was exceptionally charming. The sparkle in her eyes warmed him—and reassured him. He was convinced that she would not be able to draw herself away from the opera to return to *Madame Botreaux's*.

When the carriage drew up before the stucco façade of the theatre on Bridges Street, her excitement had penetrated him, and Vale found himself looking forward to the performance, though he had already seen *Le Nozze*. Her response to his suggestion that they take in as much of London as possible had made him feel *purposeful*. Contrary to Harrietta's enthusiasm for London, he had become rather bored of the city. The ennui extended to much of his life. The start of it, years ago, was what had prompted him to become a regular at *Madame Botreaux's*, but even that establishment interested him less lately.

"How grand," Harrietta sighed as they entered the amphitheatre.

"This must be the new Marchioness of Dunnesford."

The voice made the hairs on the back of his neck stand on end. Vale turned around to see Lovell Elroy. He was with his sister, the Lady Falconet, whose husband rarely ventured into the City. The pair were fraternal twins and resembled one another in all but body shape. Both had golden hair and blue eyes of such brightness that they might glow in the dark. Lovell had a touch of the feminine in his countenance but was still strikingly handsome to the women.

"Harrietta, I present you Lord Elroy and Lady Falconet," introduced Vale with reluctance, angling his body as a shield so that Lovell would not think to step too closely to Harrietta.

"Alexandra," Lady Falconet supplied. "We women have no need for such formalities."

"Harrietta. Though I am known by family and friends as Hetty. Indeed, I am more at ease with it than I am being addressed as Lady Dunnesford."

"What a delightful sobriquet," Lovell remarked.

Alexandra curled her lips in a broad smile. She reminded Vale of a vulture seeking a kill.

"Dunnesford," Lovell addressed Vale, "you will be showing her properly about society, I hope?"

"We would love to see more of you, my dear," Alexandra added. "Perhaps you can join us in our box during intermission?"

"Perhaps," Vale interjected upon seeing that Harrietta was about to accept the invitation. "This is but her second evening in London, and many have yet to make her acquaintance."

He steered Harrietta away and settled her into their private seats opposite the stage.

"You do not seem fond of them," Harrietta observed.

"And they are not of me," he replied, adjusting himself uneasily in his chair.

"Indeed? They seemed quite friendly."

"Who could not be gracious toward you, Harrietta?"

He could tell his response did not satisfy her in the least, but he could not tell her the truth: that he had broken one of the unspoken rules of the *Cavern* and only his deep friendship with Penelope had prevented his being thrown out. Unless invited, no interference between a master and his submissive was accepted. And yet, after witnessing Lovell flogging his submissive, who was sobbing hysterically, until her skin bled, he could not resist intervening. Lovell had shoved him away and meant to continue his flogging, but Vale had intercepted the lash. With the cat-o-nine tails wrapped about his arm, Vale had wrenched it from Lovell's hand. He remembered well the hatred in Lovell's eyes.

Harrietta did not pry, and Vale was reminded that he was often surprised by her maturity.

The curtain lifted, and Harrietta was enraptured. If she leaned any further forward, she might tumble out of the balcony. It pleased him that she took such pleasure from the show, and she smiled her gratitude toward him between acts. As rich as the set and the costumes were, and as exquisite as the music was, Vale found himself more absorbed in his wife than in the opera. Years had passed between them, and she was at once the girl he remembered and a woman he did not recognize. Last night had been the first evidence that she might not be wholly pleased with their marriage. He had assumed that, given her lack of beauty and dowry, she would have been, well, grateful to be his wife. That apparently was not the case. He wondered what else was still to be revealed about this little wife of his.

As Act II drew to a close, the footman delivered a note to Vale. He glanced at Harrietta, whose gaze had not drifted from the stage for a second, before opening the note. It was from the Countess D'Alessio, apparently in attendance as well. Act II ended with the character of the Countess fainting in distress.

"What superb performances!" Harrietta exclaimed. "What beautiful voices! It were an experience beyond what I could have imagined."

"The arias in the final two acts are even more lovely," Vale told her, then excused himself to pay a visit to an old friend and promised to bring back refreshments.

But he returned to an empty box. He asked the attendant where the Marchioness had gone.

"Her ladyship felt ill of a sudden and thought it best not to stay," the man informed him. "She asked me to convey to your lordship that there would be no need to worry of her and to enjoy the rest of the performance."

At first Vale thought that perhaps Harrietta had seen him with the Countess D'Alessio and become upset, but he felt the blood drain from his face when he realized the truth. Harrietta was headed to *Madame Botreaux's*.

CHAPTER FIVE

"THERE IS A WOMAN WAITING for you in the last alcove," Vale was informed by Lance upon his arrival at the *Cavern*.

Vale cursed. He had hurried from the opera as fast as he could, shedding his silken clothes for his customary attire at the Cavern: linen breeches, black boots, and his black and silver mask.

"Is she not the one—is she not your wife?" Lance asked, confused.

"We shall see the last of her here tonight," Vale told him before striding down to the assembly floor and toward the alcove that he and Harrietta had occupied the night before.

She may have found her way here, but it was doubtful that she could have undressed in time. His own undressing had been no easy task. With her stays, corset, petticoats and stockings, she would have required more time and certainly could not have undressed on her own. And even were she to have contrived to remove the gown she had worn to the opera, red was an extremely rare color for clothing. It would be impossible for her to satisfy his third condition.

"Good evening, my lord," Harrietta greeted.

Standing barefoot in the middle of the room, she was clothed entirely in red.

He stood stunned as he took in the odd garment, draped over her body like a toga from Roman days. He narrowed his eyes. It looked familiar.

"Is that—?" he asked, then quickly assumed the hoarse tone he had adopted previously to disguise his voice. "Is that a *drapery?*"

"You did not specify the material, only the color, my lord," she answered.

She must have had help from someone. Her maid Sarah, perhaps? Vale clenched his jaw. Damnation. He had not expected to find himself here—

and just as he was starting to enjoy the opera. He paced around her, trying to sort his thoughts. He had to put an end to this.

"You did not think I would come," she observed, a small triumphant smile tugging at the corner of her mouth.

"Do not speak unless spoken to," he responded, irritated by his lack of preparation for this situation while impressed that she had managed to satisfy his three conditions. But she would see this was no place for her. She did not understand the world of the *Cavern*. He had but to show her a glimpse and she would want nothing more to do with it.

"Disrobe," he commanded.

She hesitated.

"Failure to comply will merit you the crop." He slapped the riding crop into his palm for effect.

Wordlessly, she looked about the curtain for the pins and unhooked as many as she could. The garment fell off her shoulders, exposing her breasts. She quickly covered them with her arms, but with his crop, he nudged her arms away. In the dim candlelight of their alcove, he saw the luster of her skin. He suppressed the urge to feel its silkiness.

"Continue," he ordered.

Her hands rested on the pins about her waist. She paused.

"Do not keep me waiting, *ma petite*," he warned her.

With a surge of resolve, she discarded the remaining pins. The whole of her garment fell to the floor, and all of her was laid bare. Her hips flared in womanly fashion, her arse was arched high, her thighs supple, and the patch of hair above her mons charming. Vale wondered if this was the first time she had stood naked before a man. If so, that man ought to have been her husband.

Her chest rose and fell with quick breaths. Her unease was palpable, and Vale made no effort to relieve it.

"Caress yourself," he instructed.

Her voice waivered. "My lord?"

"Arouse your nipples."

She hesitated.

"Now!"

Startled, she put her hands to her breasts and flicked her forefingers about her areolas until her nipples hardened into pebbled points. She stared down at herself as if astonished that her body would react in the way that it did.

I can help you discover more than you ever thought possible with your body,

Vale said silently, then pushed the thought from his mind. He had a task to execute.

"Do you pleasure yourself?" he asked.

Her cheeks burned. "My lord?"

"If I am to repeat every word, our evening here together will not go well. Do you bring pleasure to your body?"

"Yes," she mumbled.

"Yes, what?"

"Yes, my lord."

"How?" He stepped nearer to her and said in a low voice over her shoulder into her ear. "How do you pleasure yourself?"

"I…I touch myself."

"Where?"

"I reach between my legs," she murmured reluctantly. The heat in her face was rising.

"Where between the legs, *ma petite*?"

"The pubis area."

"Be more specific."

She grimaced, then forced out the words. "There is a nub of flesh…"

"Ah, you mean the clitoris."

She nodded.

"And what do you do to it?"

"I stroke it."

"With what?"

"My fingers."

Vale took in a deep breath. It felt warm in the *Cavern* tonight. He pulled over a bench and set it before her. The bench was unlike any other, so thin one had to straddle it. The back was simply a cross upon which one's arms could be affixed.

"Demonstrate. You may sit if you wish."

Her eyes widened beneath her mask, but she made her way to the bench and sat down upon it gingerly as if it might come to life and bite her in the arse.

"You are a quick study," he said approvingly when she made no protest.

Leaning his back against the wall, he folded his arms and waited. She shifted about restlessly but eventually parted her thighs. Vale glimpsed the supple folds of her pussy and watched intently as she slid a finger down toward her clitoris. She stroked herself there a few times, then looked up at him as if finished.

"Can you make yourself spend?" he inquired.

"I think not…it is a most private act, my lord."

"Try."

She looked about herself helplessly, though what she expected to find to assist her in the sparse alcove he could not guess. Again her finger slid down, and she stroked herself some more.

"Spread your legs wider."

He could sense her humiliation and felt a pang of regret, but he had to persist. She had to leave in fear or disgust if she were to never return.

She obeyed and even leaned against the back of the bench. He gazed at the whiteness of her thighs. They were among his favorite parts of the female body. A quick flick of the crop against the inner thigh usually drew a gasp from the subject. Its proximity to that ultimate prize of womanhood made it rich with possibility.

He waited patiently—longer than he had waited for anyone, but he could tell Harrietta was no nearer to spending. He wanted her to spend, wanted her to enjoy her body. There had been women who could practically bring about their orgasms with thoughts alone, and here he was with a novice who might as well have been reading her catechisms for all that she was accomplishing at the moment. He yearned to help her, and not just because he was reminded that she was Harold's sister.

"Desist," he told her before removing from the wall a collar and leash.

"What is that for?" she asked.

"Did I ask that you speak?"

Standing before her, he attempted to clasp the collar about her neck, but she shied away.

"I will not wear such a thing," she declared.

"You are trying my patience, *ma petite.*"

"For what purpose would I wear a collar and leash?"

"Here in the *Cavern,* you will abide by my dictates. If you cannot, you are free to leave. You always have that choice."

She knit her brows. He waited, hopeful that she would choose to leave. But she did not. She straightened herself and lifted her chin to allow him access to her neck, almost defying him to put the collar about her. No matter, Vale thought to himself. He was about to test the limits of her tolerance and propriety.

"Come with me," he said.

HARRIETTA FINGERED THE COLLAR WITH reservation. What had she placed herself into? She found some consolation in remembering that Charlotte had been a frequent visitor to the *Cavern* and had said no one came to any harm despite appearances. Especially in masterful hands. And the man in black and silver was supposed to be among the most masterful. She followed him into the general assembly area.

This was even more humiliating than fondling herself in front of him, Harrietta decided, being led about on a leash as if she were a bitch. She wondered that she had chosen to be here with this man when she could have been listening to the beautiful strains of Mozart with her husband. She had been enjoying her time with Vale. He had entertained all her questions during the carriage ride and before the performance began, explaining points of interest and the history behind the theatre. As curious as she was about the ways of the *Cavern*, its appeal had diminished in her time with Vale.

Until she had seen her husband in the box of the Countess D'Alessio.

During the intermission, Lady Falconet had stopped by to mention a little soirée she was hosting.

"I should very much like to extend you an invitation," Alexandra had said. "You strike me as quite a kindred spirit, and I do pride myself on my judgment of people. I can tell by your *milieu* that you are someone with whom I wish to become better acquainted. I fear, however, that Dunnesford may not approve."

She scanned the amphitheatre with her quizzing glass. "Ah, there he is with the Countess D—"

Alexandra paled and quickly switched the direction of her gaze. "There is some history, alas, betwixt your husband and my brother. But I do not see that that should thwart a friendship between the two of us."

But it was too late. Harrietta had seen the box of the Countess D'Alessio and Vale was indeed present there. The Countess was a beautiful woman with raven hair, large sparkling eyes, and an enviable figure. It should come as no surprise that Vale would have such a mistress. Harrietta was no comparison, and it was at that moment she decided she would return to the *Cavern*. She had already put in place her plans with the aid of Charlotte's maid, who apparently knew all about her mistress' proclivities and escapades. Charlotte's carriage had been waiting on Drury Lane with the draperies she had pilfered from one of the unused bedrooms, and with a heady triumph she had arrived at *Madame Botreaux's* with minutes to spare.

"You asked the purpose of the collar," he said. "It is to show that you are my submissive, and I your master. No one else is allowed to approach you lest I grant them permission. You belong to me."

She stared at him, her heart hammering as his words sunk in. She was his submissive? His property? Was that meant to be appealing? Charlotte had thought so. Harrietta understood it from a corporal sense. The man was a striking specimen of the male species. His tight breeches molded to his buttocks and thighs. He looked like one of the nudes that Charlotte liked to paint. But a master—or, rather, her master? She was unsure she could tolerate that, for she believed not any man deserved complete dominance over a woman, not even a husband over his wife.

"What you are about to witness," his lordship continued, "will do much to determine if you are suitable for *Madame Botreaux's.*"

He walked over to another alcove where a woman was on her knees and hands, her head bent over the boot of a man. She lapped his boot like a grateful dog.

"You frown," his lordship noted of the distaste in Harrietta's countenance, "but everyone here chooses to be here of his or her own free will. Not a one is forced into submission."

Harrietta glanced at his lordship. Would he make her lick his boot? Somehow she didn't think he would. She could not explain why, but she sensed a generosity of spirit in him.

They walked to the next alcove where one man was chained to a post in front of him. He had on a strange contraption of steel about his cock. A masked woman wearing only a corset and shoes wielded a flogger upon him.

"Thank you, mistress," the chained man said after the woman had struck at his crotch.

That must have been hellishly painful, Harrietta thought to herself, remembering the time that she and Harold were playing cricket and the ball had been hit straight into his groin. Harrietta shivered for the man being flogged, yet her body was growing warm.

As if reading her mind, his lordship said in a low voice near her ear, "Pain and pleasure can often be one."

She had fantasized about the possibility but was unsure whether she could handle it. Was it only for deviants or could she, too, experience pleasure from such things?

"Would his lordship care to sample my submissive?" the mistress asked upon seeing them.

The small gasp that escaped from Harrietta seemed to determine the mind for her 'lord.' He walked over to accept the flogger from the mistress. The flogger landed on the bound man with a sharp sound that split the air. The submissive groaned in agony.

"Thank you, master," the man said between clenched teeth.

The mistress came to stand next to Harrietta.

"No one brandishes a flogger or crop as well as your master," the woman said, then ran her tongue along her lower lip as she watched the flogger land on the brawny buttocks of her submissive.

Harrietta watched in astonishment as her 'lord' reached in front of the submissive to grab the man by his scrotum. The submissive roared as his balls were twisted and squeezed. More astonishing was the pulsing she felt between her legs. She wished the lighting were better, but she could tell from the silhouettes that both men had splendid bodies. The nakedness of one and the near nudity of the other, their bodies so close together, was more provocative than she could have imagined.

Her 'lord' administered the flogger without relinquishing his grip on the other man's sac. It was hard to tell in the darkness, but Harrietta thought the bulge between her 'lord's legs had grown.

"Beg him to take you," the mistress commanded.

"Take me, I beg of you, take me," the submissive croaked, pulling a little at his chains.

Her 'lord' unbuttoned his breeches and a long thick cock sprung out. He spit into his palm, rubbed it along his shaft and pushed himself into the arse before him. The submissive wailed at being impaled upon her 'lord's cock. His mistress strode over, grabbed him by the jaw, and pushed her tongue into his mouth. Harrietta watched the three bodies writhing, feeling her own body flushing from head to toe, content in her role of voyeur yet wishing she could be a party to their bacchanal somehow.

The submissive groaned into his mistress's mouth as she continued to lap at him. His legs shook and his body began jerking between the post and the equally hard body behind him. He bellowed as he spent. When the twitching of his body had subsided, her 'lord' pulled away from him, his cock still hard. He pulled up his breeches and directed his gaze at Harrietta. Her flush intensified under his stare, wondering if he had other plans for that formidable erection of his.

"I hope you will pay us another visit," the mistress purred to his lordship as she ran a hand down his bare chest. She stared at his crotch and licked her lips once more. "I should be happy to be of service to you."

His lordship smiled but made no comment. Instead he motioned for Harrietta to approach. They walked back towards their own alcove, past an area where a woman had a cock buried in her mouth while her cunt was being serviced by another woman.

"Have you ever tasted or been tasted by another woman?" his lordship asked her.

She felt prickles on her skin. "No."

He touched the riding crop to her leg.

"No, my lord," she added hastily.

"Ever wonder what it would be like?"

"I...I read a passage once in *Fanny Hill*."

"You read *Memoirs of a Woman of Pleasure*?" he asked in disbelief.

"I came upon a copy my brother had hidden in his room."

"How would you feel if I asked you to lick the cunnie of another woman?"

The flush filled her cheeks and went down her neck.

"I know not—my lord."

"Then we must find an answer for you."

He led her back to their alcove and bade her sit on the bench once more.

"Pleasure yourself," he commanded.

Wordlessly, she leaned back, spread her legs, and began to finger her clitoris. The area about her quim was already warm, and it was not long before she provoked that gnawing tingling sensation both pleasant and frustrating. She looked at his lordship, but she could read no expression upon his face, could not tell if he approved or disapproved. And yet his intense gaze was...titillating. She felt wanton, defiant, and free. She would never have thought it possible to be so bold as to masturbate in front of someone—a stranger, no less.

And her climax came. Upon that hard narrow bench, her body quivered. She closed her eyes and allowed the glorious feelings to wave over her body. When she felt her body settling back into a normal state with a contented sigh, she opened her eyes and waited for his lordship's response.

CHAPTER SIX

⚭

A SMILE CURLED ABOUT THE CORNERS of her lips. She was relieved—and perhaps a bit proud. Vale felt proud for her as well. She had more fortitude than he had expected, and yet, if he were to recollect her when she was younger, he should not have been surprised. He knew full well that she was here tonight to satisfy a curiosity—it was quite obvious she was a novice. But how far would she allow him to take her?

No. He was not to entertain such questions. It was best that she not return. She was looking at him expectantly, waiting for his instructions.

"We are done for tonight, *ma petite*," he told her.

She seemed disappointed. "What time shall I return tomorrow—my lord?"

A presumptuous question, Vale thought. "You wish to return?"

"Yes, my lord."

"Not tomorrow," Vale said. "In a sennight, you may return, but know first that I indulged your inexperience tonight. The next will not be as easy."

"My lord?"

"The rules are simple. The consequences are as follows: three lashes for failing to address me properly, five lashes for speaking out of turn, ten lashes for failure to obey without hesitation, and twenty lashes for arriving late. You will always stand at attention, your eyes to the back wall, waiting for my instructions. You will be clothed in nothing. Madame Botreaux has a maid who can assist you in your wardrobe. If at any time, you miss our appointment, I will assume you to have concluded your association with *Madame Botreaux's*. Is all that clear?"

"Yes, my lord."

He unclasped the collar from her. "Now be gone. And take your robe with you."

After she had left, Vale let out a haggard breath and sat down on the bench she had occupied but moments before. He put a hand to his forehead. This was not how he had envisioned his marriage. Granted, he had once sought a mate who shared the same proclivities he did in the bed chamber, but while he had met many such women at the *Cavern*, he could not find one that he could sustain a fondness for, and so he had given up his quest for the perfect match.

Harrietta's distaste for their marriage had surprised him, especially since he had taken the precaution of not forcing himself upon her on their wedding night. As it had been nine years since they had last seen one another, he had thought to ease her back into acquaintance. He had sensed that she had not been particularly eager to marry him, though he did not understand precisely why. She had been attracted to him once. He was sure of it.

They had been much younger. Harrietta had been no more than six and ten. Vale, in search of Harold, had come upon Harrietta and her sisters in the garden at their home. Harrietta was to have her come out, and her sisters were speculating about the men she would come across and what courtship entailed.

"Will you let a gentleman kiss you?" Bethany had asked.

"Only upon the hand, but If I am fond of him, I may let him kiss me on the cheek," Harrietta had responded.

"And not the mouth? What does the lady do when kissed upon the mouth?"

"Why, kissing is quite simple," Harrietta had said with all the authority merited by being the eldest sister. "You but have to pout your lips a bit like this, and press it like so."

She demonstrated with the back of her hand.

"With your mouth closed like that?" Jacqueline inquired.

"Of course," Harrietta answered resolutely.

Vale could not help but laugh at the quaint conviction in her tone.

"Pray, what is it you find so amusing?" Harrietta demanded, her cheeks reddening upon realizing he had heard their conversation.

"Not all kisses are the same," he explained.

She raised an eyebrow.

He sat down next to her on the garden bench. "Some kisses are better with an open mouth....like this."

Lifting her chin, he kissed her fully on the mouth, and when he parted his lips, hers opened of their own accord.

When he had disengaged, he could feel that her breath had quickened. Her eyes seemed unable to focus. He remembered the smell of flowers that blew about them, saw the blush in her cheeks deepen. She was still leaning in toward him, as if ready for more, and he wondered if he had parted prematurely. He would have kissed her again had he not noticed the mouths of Bethany and Jacqueline hanging agape in shock.

But that was then. He might have been Harrietta's first kiss, and an easy source of infatuation.

This was entirely different. Harrietta was not in the bloom of youth. *Madame Botreaux's* was not a bucolic garden. And the lips...the lips involved were not those of the mouth but of a more intimate place.

The image of her quim flashed before Vale. Pink, supple, swollen. Her clitoris extended. Her finger working it furiously. The moisture glistening, the color deepening.

Vale unbuttoned his breeches and pulled out his hardening cock. He rubbed his hand up and down the shaft as he wondered how she would have reacted to his touch. He remembered her short little breaths as she neared her climax. The sound of a woman in pleasure was more melodic to him than any opera. Vale circled his hand around the head of his cock and pulled at it until he felt his balls clench. With a grunt, his seed spilling over his hand, he spent in the very chair in which Harrietta had spent.

He was glad he would not see Harrietta at the *Cavern* for another seven days. For the first time since he had become a regular at *Madame Botreaux's*, Vale felt unsure of himself.

&

HARRIETTA TOOK HER BREAKFAST THE following morning in her room. It would not do to appear in good health after she had left her husband at the opera the night before. She gathered he knew it would have taken quite an illness to tear her away from Mozart. For a moment she felt a cringe of remorse for being deceptive, but then she remembered the beautiful Countess D'Alessio. If he could have his little *divertissement*, why could she not have hers?

Last night had been an experience that had no equal. She had no idea such guilty, sinful pleasures could be so arousing. She felt a side of her, ere hidden, now exposed. It was frightening and exhilarating. Back in her bed, she had pleasured herself again to the memory of what she had done earlier in the *Cavern*, but most of all, she remembered *him*. She knew nothing of him, and yet he attracted her. She wondered what sort of countenance he had hidden beneath that mask of his. In the darkness of the *Cavern,* it was difficult to see details. Was his physiognomy as magnificent as the silhouette of his body or was he a hideous toad? But she had no need for his face. His body and even the harsh whisper of his voice was alluring. The huskiness of his voice was forced, but she found it oddly comforting.

"Did my lady enjoy the opera?" asked Sarah, who had brought up her breakfast tray and was now drawing aside the curtains.

"It was wonderful," Harrietta responded as she ate readily of her toast and jam. She stole a glance at Sarah, who was quite pretty with her pert little nose and soft tendrils of hair curling out from beneath her mobcap.

"He is a most handsome lad," Harrietta commented.

Sarah whirled around, alarm in her eyes. "My lady?"

"The tall one who held your hand last night."

Harrietta had seen the pair kissing upon her own return late in the night. "Worry not," Harrietta assured Sarah, finishing her plate, "your secret is safe with me."

Sarah clasped her hands tightly. "Oh, *thank you*, my lady, *thank you*. Mrs. Stewart would be most upset if she knew Johnny had come calling."

The poor distraught thing, Harrietta thought to herself. Sarah seemed ready to throw herself at Harrietta's feet in gratitude, but a knock at the door drew their attention. Sarah went to open the door and admitted the Marquis.

How debonair her husband always looked. This morning he was richly dressed in a dark blue coat. The ruffles of his sleeves fell delicately over his hands, and he carried with him an ivory handled walking stick. His hair was perfectly pulled back with a dark bow, and the buckles of his shoes gleamed. Adorned from head to foot in layers of garments and accessories, Vale contrasted sharply to the barren dress of her lordship of the *Cavern*.

"I came to see how you were faring," Vale said after Sarah had left the room. "You must have been quite ill to have left the opera so abruptly."

"Yes," Harrietta said, busying herself with drinking her hot chocolate.

He strode over to her bed. "What manner of ailment was it that afflicted you?"

"I...a disorder of the stomach," Harrietta answered. "It was nausea."

"How terrible. I should have sent for a doctor."

"Oh, no need for a doctor. I am feeling much better now."

Vale looked down at her empty plate, where barely a crumb of her breakfast was left. "I see. I am glad to hear it. But you must allow me to accompany you home in the future. It is not wise for a woman to traverse the streets alone at such an hour."

"You were...occupied."

It seemed Vale straightened his back a little at that, but then his features softened. "I worried about you, Harrietta."

Had he really? Harrietta wondered. Now she felt doubly bad for having lied to him.

"Did you leave the opera early then?" Harrietta asked a little nervously.

"I could not stay if you were ill."

"I took to my bed immediately," Harrietta lied, avoiding his gaze. "I think the respite did much to improve my state. I am sorry that you could not enjoy the rest of the opera."

"We shall have to make a point to see it again so that you may see it in its entirety."

She smiled at him. "I should enjoy that very much."

"Yes, well, it will have to be in a few days. I am off to a coffeehouse this morning to meet with investors and will be taking a trip to view the properties they wish me to consider. I will be back in a sennight."

Harrietta nodded, though she felt disappointed that she would lose his company for so long.

As if reading her mind, he added, "Charlotte will prove better company for you than I."

He leaned down and kissed her on the top of her brow and turned to leave. He stopped.

"You would not happen to know what has become of the draperies in the bedroom upstairs?" he asked. "Mrs. Stewart notified me of their absence."

Harrietta shook her head. "Perhaps they were taken down to be cleaned?"

"Perhaps," Vale said, his brows knit in thought, but then his face cleared. "Au revoir, my dear."

When Vale was gone, Harrietta sank into her pillows. Perhaps she should not consider returning to *Madame Botreaux's.*

"How can you not?" Charlotte pressed later that day as they were riding through Hyde Park.

It was a warm afternoon and anyone who was anyone appeared to be in the Park.

"It is no easy task to get to *Madame Botreaux's*," Harrietta responded. "The servants seem quite loyal to Vale. If they should talk…"

"Of course they will talk if they find out, but the worst they will assume is that you have a lover. And if Dunnesford is not concerned, why should you be?"

Harrietta pressed her lips into a grim line. "Vale would be indifferent to my taking a lover?"

Charlotte hesitated. "Well, there be flaws to my cousin's character, indeed, but unfairness be not one of them. In that regard, he is quite exceptional for a husband. It shows a generosity of spirit, I think."

"He said as much to you about the prospect of my having an affair?"

"In passing."

Vale must be more devoted to the Countess than Harrietta had previously thought.

"Pray, do not think me disloyal to my cousin," Charlotte continued. "I have great affection for Dunnesford, but he and I are both of free minds and a mutual understanding."

"Would he be indifferent to my association with *Madame Botreaux's* then?"

"No. A lover is one thing, *Madame Botreaux's* another."

"I have six days to think on it," Harrietta said.

They turned their horses around and came upon Lady Falconet and another woman.

"My dear Hetty, what a pleasant sight you are," Alexandra greeted. "My compliments to your dressmaker. Normally, I am not much fond of the color green, but you wear it well."

"You are too kind, Lady Falconet," Harrietta thanked.

Alexandra gave a curt nod to Charlotte, who returned with a tight smile.

"I am hosting a dinner tomorrow evening and would be much pleased to invite you. Mrs. Windleton will be in attendance, and she plays a marvelous spinet. And you as well, Charlotte, you are welcome to come."

"I should be delighted," Harrietta replied.

"Wonderful. Six o'clock in Berkeley Square."

They exchanged further pleasantries. Alexandra introduced her companion, and then they bid adieu. Harrietta looked at Charlotte.

"You do not seem pleased," Harrietta noted to Charlotte, wondering if her friend was upset Alexandra had invited Charlotte as an afterthought. "Is it because of Vale and Alexandra's brother?"

"In truth, yes, but I have never felt warmly toward either Lord Elroy or Lady Falconet. I cannot specify why, and will decline her belated dinner invitation to me."

Harrietta found Charlotte's sentiments interesting. She understood Charlotte's loyalty toward Vale, but she herself thought Alexandra and Lovell rather amiable. And she was determined to ascertain the reason for the coldness between Vale and Lord Elroy.

CHAPTER SEVEN

⊙⋈⊙

THERE WAS SOMETHING FAMILIAR ABOUT Lovell Elroy, though Harrietta could not put a name to it. She and Lovell were paired together in a game of whist at Lady Falconet's dinner. He was quite a striking man, Harrietta thought to herself. She had never seen eyes so blue. And his dress was as impeccable as Vale's. The silk brocade coat seemed quite commanding on his broad shoulders. The lace cuffs of his shirt served to make his large hands appear more masculine. It was little wonder, then, that the ladies flirted openly with him.

He was polite to Harrietta but not nearly as attentive as his sister.

"Has London treated you well thus far?" he asked her in between sets, filling her glass with port.

"Exceptionally well," Harrietta replied. "There is all the world in London, as Doctor Johnson says. The museums, the arts, the music, the history, the parks…I cannot imagine ever tiring of living here."

"For oldtimers like myself, it takes a refreshing new view such as yours to make us appreciate what we have come to take for granted. Did you enjoy *Le Nozze di Figaro*?"

Harrietta colored. "I, er, I took ill during the intermission and could not complete it."

"That is a shame. I hope your recovery was quick."

"Very quick," Harrietta acknowledged and took a sip of her port to avoid Lovell's piercing gaze. Those blue eyes seemed to miss very little. "We may attempt another performance so that I may see the second half. Mozart is my favorite composer."

"Ah, mine as well," Lovell said, surprised. "The six quartets he dedicated to Haydn are masterful."

"I heard that Haydn himself considers Mozart the greatest composer in a hundred years."

"Yes. Bach would come in a close second for me, but a second nonetheless."

Harrietta enjoyed her conversation with Lovell and became increasingly mystified that Vale should have conceived such an aversion to the man.

At the end of their cardplay, Lovell remarked to Harrietta, "You are a marvelous whist player. I do hope we may be partners again. I think I have never had such a successful run at whist, but you must keep the entire winnings for yourself. You merit them more than I."

Harrietta shook her head. "I could not take them from the brother of the hostess."

"And I could not from an honored guest. Please. I insist."

He deposited the pieces in a pouch and handed it to her. Rising, he bowed to her and the other players, then took himself to visit with others in the room.

It was no small sum of money—more than Harrietta had ever won in her lifetime. Most of her games of whist had been with her sisters and Harold, in which the bets were paltry in comparison. Indeed, she had been unsure of participating in a card game here at Lady Falconet's when the stakes were first voiced. She had not much money upon her, but Lovell assured her that he would be happy to loan her any sum she required. But she had played a good game, and proudly decided that she would donate the winnings to the parish orphanage.

"Felicitations to you," Alexandra congratulated her afterwards as they were sitting at the sofa listening to Mrs. Windleton at the ivories. "I understand you have quite a way with cards. You must come again. Tomorrow night we feature vingt-et-un."

"I am not as familiar with that game," Harrietta said.

"I am sure you will become quite adept at it."

"Thank you for your invitation, Lady Falconet. Yours is the first I have received in London. You have been most kind to me."

"If I may be bold, I do hope we can become as sisters, for I have always wanted a sister, and there is a quality about you, Hetty, that I find suits me exceptionally well."

"I do miss my sisters and family, and understand they will not be visiting me for some time. I should very much like having a sister here in London."

Alexandra smiled broadly. "That is wonderful to hear. I only hope…."

"Yes?"

"Well…you may have discerned there is no love lost between your husband and my brother."

Harrietta took a deep breath and decided to ask the question that had been burning in her mind. "Indeed, what has caused the rift?"

Alexandra looked away. "My brother would not wish me to speak of it to you."

"Oh."

"But I suppose if we are to be sisters—you must not breathe a word to Lovell or Dunnesford. Lovell would be quite cross with me if he knew I told you. He was quite surprised I had invited you. I believe he has taken a liking to you despite his inclination not to be partial to any wife of Dunnesford's."

"I won't tell a soul."

Alexandra looked in Lovell's direction, and, assured that he was out of earshot, proceeded. "Many years ago, they were in love with the same woman."

Harrietta nodded. That explained the animosity.

"She chose Dunnesford over my brother, and though Lovell was quite heartbroken over it, he wished her only happiness. It was no fault of Dunnesford that she preferred him over my brother. But then Dunnes-ford cast her aside, choosing not to marry her, and instead took a mistress. She died unexpectedly a few months later. Lovell is convinced she died of a broken heart, and for that he holds Dunnesford responsible and has said as much to your husband. I had advised my brother against it, as I am sure Dunnesford did not appreciate hearing such words. But my brother was quite filled with agony, especially when he learned the woman he had loved had died heavy with child. A letter she had written to her sister before her death said that Dunnesford had denied he was the father and said he had found another mistress."

Harrietta felt her insides crumbling within her. How could Vale have done such a thing?

"Was that mistress the Countess D'Alessio?"

Alexandra looked uncomfortable but eventually nodded.

Harrietta sighed. She tried to think of reasons that might justify his behavior, but she found none satisfactory. It was hard to imagine Vale could have been so coldhearted, and yet she understood him to be quite dedicated to the Countess. Her heart ached for the poor deceased woman.

"I have caused you misery," Alexandra said, distressed. "I should not have spoken."

"No, I would rather know than not."

"Then you are a stronger woman than most."

Harrietta spent many hours in the following days with Lovell and Alexandra, whose favorite pastime was cards. Vingt-et-un did not come as easily to Harrietta as whist, but she was only in debt to Alexandra a few guineas at the end of it all. No more was said of the history between Dunnesford and Elroy. True to her word, she kept the knowledge to herself, and did not even speak of it to Charlotte, though she did try to ascertain what Charlotte knew.

"I only know it involved a woman," Charlotte had said.

Harrietta decided she needed no further confirmation and berated herself for ever having had tender affections for Vale. In marrying him, she had executed her obligation to her family. Vale, in turn, had himself a wife who would not ask more from him in marriage than he cared to give. Thus, there was no reason why she should not return to *Madame Botreaux's* if that was her inclination. Indeed, she counted the days till her next assignation with the man in silver and black.

&

VALE COULD NOT UNDERSTAND WHY Harrietta had greeted him with such curtness upon his return, which was quite in contrast to the warmth and friendship they had shared before his departure. Something clearly seemed to weigh upon her mind. Was she regretting their marriage? Was she thinking about *Madame Botreaux's*? He shook his head. He had married Harrietta precisely so that he would not have to trouble his mind over such matters in the manner of a typical husband, but here he was disconcerted by the state of his wife.

The report from his most trusted footman, Francis, whom he had assigned to keep watch over Harrietta without her knowledge—if she was reckless enough to travel the length of Covenant Garden to *Madame Botreaux's* unaccompanied, he needed Francis to ensure her safety—made his displeasure worse.

"Her ladyship made no visit to *Madame Botreaux's* but has spent the majority of her time with Lady Falconet," Francis told him.

Vale cursed openly. He wondered if Alexandra or Lovell had aught to do with Harrietta's sudden change in demeanor toward him. Regardless, the pair was not safe companionship for Harrietta. He should have said something to Harrietta when they had first encountered them at the opera, but he had hoped not to draw attention to the twins. Little did he think that Lovell or Alexandra would want much to do with Harrietta. Now he knew they clearly had some design upon her.

He found Harrietta in the library, curled before the fire, reading a book.

"I regret to have left you alone for so long when you are yet new to the city," he told her.

"I am capable of seeing to myself," she assured him, then turned back to her book.

"I have been meaning to present you more properly to my friends and acquaintances. Many of them are quite impatient to meet you. Perhaps we can host a dinner here."

"If it pleases you," she replied without looking up.

Vale frowned, but forced himself to remain optimistic. "I am sure you will make many new friends...and will have no more need for the company of Lord Elroy or Lady Falconet."

She looked up sharply. "Did the servants....?"

"It matters not how I know." He sat down near her and said in a gentle tone, "They are not worthy of your friendship."

She raised a brow at him. "I know you do not regard them highly, but they have been naught but amiable to me."

He felt a muscle ripple in his jaw. "I would rather you did not associate with them."

"Why?"

The bluntness of her question caught him off guard.

"The past is best kept in the past," he replied.

"It must be an unsavory past for you not to be able to give voice to it."

Vale narrowed his eyes. "Did Lovell say something to you?"

"No, he did not."

She sounded convincing, but he remained unsure.

"Harrietta," he said, attempting his best to be patient, though his blood always boiled where Lovell was concerned, "I have known them for much longer than you. You may trust that I would not dispense such advice lightly."

"I am not a child and can form my own judgments."

"I doubt it not, but in this, you would do best to heed my counsel."

"Will my association with Lord Elroy or Lady Falconet cause you harm or dishonor your name?"

"No," Vale answered, a little taken aback by her query. He had not expected her to contest him on this with such fervor.

"Then I do not see why I should stop seeing them. We had an understanding, you and I, not to interfere with one another."

Astonished, he rose to his feet. "You would deliberately defy my wishes?"

"Defy your wishes?" she echoed. "Are you attempting to be my father? I already have one, thank you."

Vale could hardly believe her words—or the tartness of her tone. "I may not be your father, Harrietta, but I am your husband. And I forbid you to associate with Lord Elroy or his sister."

Her bottom lip quivered, and Vale wished his words had not come out as harshly as they had. She stood and said through clenched teeth, "You are not my lord and keeper."

Whirling on her heels, she left the room. Vale let out an oath. He had always respected Mr. Aubrey as a progressive man who raised his daughters to be independent, but at the moment he cursed the man for having done too good a job with Harrietta. Independence could border on foolhardiness. And reining in his wife was not something he had counted on doing. Inside or out of the *Cavern of Pleasures*.

&

HARRIETTA STOOD IN THE ALCOVE, sans clothing, her chin tilted high, waiting. As he studied her naked form, Vale found she had a nicer body than he would have thought. Although her arms were more slender than he liked, her breasts slightly smaller than the other women he had come across, he appreciated the firmness of her orbs. They would not be as easy to bind because of their smaller size—he once had a submissive who adored having her large overripe breasts tied in a tourniquet till they turned red—but there were so many parts of a woman's body that could be addressed.

That he should now feel his skin warming was no surprise, being that he was a red-blooded man standing before a nude woman—one awaiting him to use her body at his discretion. He was relieved that she had arrived at her appointed time for he had no desire to strike her for being late. Indeed, he felt his nerves on edge, fearing that she would falter and commit him to use his crop or the lash upon her. He had never felt such unease. And yet the darker part of him was curious. Curious to know how she would react to the crop and how she would enjoy it.

"Hold out your wrists," he instructed her, noticing that she obeyed promptly, her arms presented at chest level, straight and strong. Not like the last beauty who had offered her arms meekly.

He wound a rope around Harrietta's wrists and flung one end of the rope over a hook overhead, securing her arms above her. From another hook, he created a cradle with the rope and slid her left leg through the noose. Casting the final rope to a hook on the wall, he wrapped the rope around her left ankle to secure her leg in place and prevent it from moving. He stood back to assess his handiwork. He could see the curiosity writ upon her face, but she held her questions in check.

"The asymmetry of your position," he explained, "keeps you from feeling too comfortable. If you are good, you may merit a more relaxing and symmetrical bondage."

In his early years, he had always bound a submissive symmetrically and one of them had actually fallen asleep in the ropes.

"Your discomfort will sharpen your awareness," he continued. "You will begin to feel parts of your body you had never much noticed before. Tell me, when you are with a man, which parts of your body do you wish him to touch?"

After a pause, she replied, "If I bear him affection, the cheek first—my lord."

"And if you have no affection?"

"Then I should not desire him to touch me at all, my lord."

"What of a man you have a carnal desire but no affection for?"

He could see that her brow furrowed beneath her mask. "I do not think that were possible, my lord. Perhaps for the male sex."

"A limiting philosophy."

"It is less philosophy and more physiology."

Vale raised an eyebrow.

"My lord," she added hastily.

"*Ma petite*, your presence here belies your belief."

She gave him a challenging look.

"Do you bear me affection?" he asked plainly.

"No, my lord."

"And yet you will spend for me—you have already."

"I did pleasure myself, my lord."

Vale smiled. Save for the first time he had lain with a woman—a serving wench in a roadside inn decades ago—he had never failed to make a woman spend. He walked up to her and stroked her cheek with the knuckle of his forefinger.

"If I desired it, you would spend and spend willingly, *ma petite*," he told her softly.

Her chest rose with her quickened breath, but a corner of her mouth curled derisively. "Indeed, my lord?"

"Indeed. But you have yet to earn the right to spend tonight." He stepped away. "What follows the cheek?"

"A kiss on the lips. A hand to the breast. Then the…the part between my legs…my lord."

"You move too fast, *ma petite*. Allow him to savor each part before you allow him another."

Using the end of his crop, he circled one breast. "There is much that can be done here. The flesh can be fondled, aye, but do you not feel an intensity of sensation collected here?"

He touched her nipple with his crop and watched as it hardened beautifully for him. "These are incredible points of arousal. And stimulation by hand is but one means. Have you ever had your breasts kissed? Bitten? Suckled?"

Her voice quivered. "No, my lord."

"Then you are in for a pleasant discovery."

"Will you, my lord?"

Her question stunned him. Surely he had not heard correctly?

"Will you k-kiss my breast?"

Vale narrowed his eyes at her, stared at a breast with its pretty pink nub pointed at him. He felt his mouth water at the thought of taking her areola between his lips. His blood was stirring in his loins. He felt flustered. Bloody hell, this was not how it was supposed to proceed.

CHAPTER EIGHT

H ARRIETTA FELT THREE SHARP BLOWS to her buttocks. She gasped. Had she asked a wrong question? He had never mentioned a rule against asking questions.

"What the devil!" she exclaimed, though the blows had not been overly harsh.

"Failure to address me properly," he informed. "Do you wish three more?"

"No, my lord," she answered but with an indignant flush. Inside, she wondered that she had allowed a man to take his riding crop to her as if she were an errant pup.

He did not leave her time to dwell and ran the crop along the inside of her arm. "Did your lovers not caress your arms? Trace their tongues along your throat? Admire your belly?"

Everywhere he spoke of, he preceded with the lingering of his crop until she shivered, feeling as if he had awakened every nerve that he touched. Her lifted leg began to ache, but even that did nothing to diminish the arousal of the rest of her body.

Then his crop reached her mons, and a groan escaped her lips. He swirled the crop in her patch of hair, then slid it between her legs.

If I desired it, you would spend and spend willingly.

The crop grazed the bottom of her clit, teasing it, increasing the aggravation. He slid the crop to the thigh of her lifted leg, tapping it.

"This," he said, his voice filled with such sensuality that she felt like melting, "is a wondrous part of the body. So close to the pinnacle of pleasure. So sensitive. So aware."

He flicked the crop against the inside of her thigh, not hard enough to hurt, but in an instant her lower body stood at attention. She became conscious of the faint pulsing in her quim.

"Imagine the mixture of pain and pleasure," he said, "when the crop strikes you here while my hand pleasures your womanhood? Will you heed the pain more than the pleasure or will the pain intensify the pleasure?"

She pondered the question, unsure of the answer, but what she did know is that she wanted to find out. And to find out with him, this masked man. He was standing close enough for her to smell his scent. She wondered if he could see her little hair follicles standing on end at his nearness. He probably knew full well his effect on women.

"I should like to know the answer, my lord," she said.

"I do not think you ready, *ma petite.*"

Suppressing a pout, she lifted her chin. "How can I be ready, my lord?"

"There is much to learn."

"I am quite an adept student, my lord."

"An adept student is a patient student."

He stepped away from her, depriving her of his nearness. She liked having his body inches from hers. The air between them seemed to give off sparks like flint striking against tinder.

She took a chance. "I would be patient, my lord, if I had confidence that my instructor was capable of the lessons that needed to be taught."

He whirled around. "Are you questioning my ability?"

"Aside from tying me up, you have demonstrated no specific skill—my lord. I have experienced neither pain nor pleasure from you. I take it pain is not that difficult to administer, but if the end is pleasure, why should I squander my efforts with someone who could not provide what I seek? My lord?"

His eyes blinked in disbelief, then his mouth curled sardonically to one side. "You think I could not bring you pleasure?"

"I know you not," Harrietta responded matter-of-fact.

His smile broadened and he went to stand behind her. He reached a hand around her right hip and stroked the inside of her thigh, sliding his fingers and thumb along its smoothness.

"Ah, soft as a dove's breast," he murmured.

She felt her heart palpitating faster. What was it about this man that could rouse her in such a manner? Though she knew nothing of the man, she felt safe with him. He possessed a quality that was comforting, like a familiar friend. And, of course, a quality that stirred the most naughty thoughts and warmed her loins.

As he continued to caress the length of her thigh, he said, "The journey to what the Greek term *orgasmos* is more important than the end."

"But without the climax, there is no fulfillment, my lord."

"What is your favorite food?"

"My lord?"

"What do you enjoy eating?"

"Plum pudding, my lord," she answered, though she felt an impatience building within her. She wanted him to touch more of her.

"You would not savor the first bite even if you could not finish it?"

As she considered his question, he moved his hand over her mons and fondled her clit with his forefinger. The digit, thicker than her own, felt marvelous against that nub of flesh.

"Did you enjoy that, *ma petite?*"

"Yes," Harrietta replied breathlessly. "My lord."

He moved his hand aside. "Do not rush, *ma petite*. Remember the feeling. Exalt in it."

When he returned his hand, her clit pulsed to meet his finger. He pressed against her, gently swirled her clit. Her head fell back as she gave her body over to the stimulation, the delicious stroking, the desirable ache building in her abdomen. His hand ventured up from her mons, past her belly button, past her stomach with the fluttering softness of a butterfly's wing. Then he cupped her breasts with both hands, weighing each orb as if his hands were scales.

"Charming," he said, a breath from her ear. If she turned her head quickly enough, might she find her mouth on his?

His thumbs grazed one nipple, then the other, sparking the connection between the tips of her breasts and her quim. Harrietta whimpered quietly, wanting his hand at her clit once more.

"Do you doubt my ability now, *ma petite?*"

"'Tis too soon to render a verdict, my lord," she persisted, though her mind screamed for him to take her up to the pinnacle.

"If I put a hand to your quim, tell me that I would not find you wet with desire."

She remained silent. She wanted him to prove his point. And he did. Lowering one hand, he cupped the mound of her womanhood and inserted a finger into her slit. Her standing leg began to tremble. It had been some time since her nerves down there had been touched by a man. She felt almost virginal. Would he like the tight feel of her?

Sliding his finger from her, he presented the evidence to her. She could smell herself upon him, and her head spun with how lewd, how wanton, how provocative she found it all.

"Taste your desire," he commanded.

"Wh—"

But she did not have time to protest. He slid his wet finger into her open mouth.

"Suck it."

Her mind whirled, but she did as he bid, closing her lips about his finger. She had never tasted of her own fluids before, save for the occasional teardrop, and could not say she was enamored of the flavor that knew no epicurean likeness. She did not like his pressing his finger upon her tongue. It felt invasive. Humiliating.

To add insult, he swirled his finger all over the inside of her mouth, then told her to suck harder. She felt like crying, but conceding his doubt of her would prove more humiliating. Thus, she sucked his finger with all her might, until her cheeks were sore. And gradually, her indignation turned provocative. She felt naughty and aroused. Using her tongue, she made love to his finger, and when he pulled from her, she felt satisfied.

And craved more.

☙

VALE SILENTLY CURSED A DOZEN different ways in his head. This—she—was proving much more difficult than he had anticipated. He needed to frighten her or discomfort her into fleeing, to never want to set foot in the *Cavern* again, yet he could not bring himself to fully implement his strategy. Not when her flesh felt so desirable beneath his hands. Not when her soft sighs and whimpers intoxicated his ears. Not when her scent—like the clear freshness of the early spring, before the perfumed heaviness of flowers blooming later in the season—filled his nostrils.

And the way her mouth suckled his finger—may God have mercy—for a moment he was lost. His blood raged in his loins and throbbed in his cock. He had allowed himself to wonder how it would feel to have her mouth wrapped about his erection—especially with the earnestness with which she sucked and tongued his finger. The desire to fuck flared in his body. He could take her so easily. He had but to pull his cock from his breeches and push it into her waiting quim from behind her.

Cursing once more, he willed his mind to concentrate on the task at hand. Palming her breasts again, he rolled her nipples between his thumbs and fingers. He tugged them lightly.

"Have you ever had clamps affixed to your nipples?" he asked.

"My lord?"

Not surprisingly, she had never heard of such a device. He explained, "They fasten onto your nipples. The pinching pain is excruciating."

He demonstrated with his fingers until she cried out.

"And pales in comparison to what you have just experienced," he continued. "A clamp may also be affixed here."

He flicked her clitoris and felt her shudder against him. He pinched the tender flesh of the inside of her thigh. "And here. On the wall to your right you can see a set with weights at the end. Beside it you will find the cat-o-nine tails. It delivers a more diffuse blow. I prefer the crop for its precision, but a good lashing is a nice diversion."

As he spoke, his right hand traveled down to her clitoris and stroked it languidly. Her head fell softly against his chest, and he caught the fragrance of her hair.

"What did your friend tell you of *Madame Botreaux's*? What was it that interested you to come here?" he asked.

"She—she said that all forms of sensual pleasures are indulged here, my lord."

"Did she elaborate on those pleasures?"

"Only that they ranged from playful to perverse, my lord."

Her breath was coming faster. He had heard the sharp inhale when he pressed upon a more sensitive spot on her clitoris, but he was not yet ready to have her spend.

"What do you consider playful?"

"A...a spanking—my lord."

"And perverse?"

"The nipple clamps you described."

He withdrew his hand and waited.

"My lord," she added hastily.

He returned his hand, dipping a finger into the clear nectar of her quim to lubricate his strokes.

"Do you prefer playful or perverse?"

"Playful...but I am intrigued by the perverse, my lord."

"You will find many experiences less perverse when you understand the enjoyment of them. An experienced master will know how far to take you. He will sense and know your willingness, your deep-seated and unspoken desires. Of which, I believe, you have many, *ma petite.*"

There was a pause before she responded, "I have a desire to spend, my lord."

"In good time, my dear."

At that, she strained against her bonds, but they would not allow her to push herself further into his hand.

"As my submissive, you will spend when I allow you to spend, if I deem you worthy of spending."

A snort.

"By coming here, by presenting, you have committed yourself, your body, into my keeping. Your body is mine to use as I please. I may pleasure it if I wish or I may punish you. I may even wish to share you."

He could not see, but he knew her eyes had widened. Building on her tension, he continued, "At my discretion, I may command you to give fellatio to another man. Or to pleasure another woman. Or impale your anus on another man's cock."

"No!"

Vale stopped his caress of her clitoris. The wetness from her quim now glistened on the thigh of her standing leg.

"If you cannot relinquish control to me, then you are not ready for *Madame Botreaux's*. I do not tolerate protests from my submissives. Do you comprehend?"

She groaned in aggravation, then hung her head. She muttered, "Yes, my lord."

"Your pardon?"

"Yes, my lord, I comprehend," she spat.

For a moment he wondered if she would come to loathe him, but the trust she was placing in his hands by uttering those words overwhelmed him. He resumed his stroking, this time with care to strum the spot that made her writhe the most. The feel of her body twisting against him drove him mad, and he thought his cock would burst through his breeches. He should reprove her for her defiance. If he were cruel, he would leave her in her binds without giving her the climax she so desired.

But he couldn't. He wanted to make her spend, wanted to see her spending. And she did. Quivers ruptured gloriously through her body. A beautiful cry escaped her lips. Her quim pulsed madly against his hand. His head spun. His cock tightened further.

When her orgasm finally subsided, he quickly undid the ropes that held her arms and her leg. She slid toward the floor. He gathered her in his arms and held her, knowing the soreness in her limbs would now make itself known. Gently, he rubbed her arms and massaged her leg. His cock was still stiff and he contemplated who he might have to fuck tonight to relieve himself. His first thought, surprisingly, was of his wife. Harrietta. The woman he now held in his arms.

But that would not be wise.

Would it?

CHAPTER NINE

L ANCE GRUNTED, BRACING HIMSELF AGAINST the settee, as Vale continued to pound him from behind. With beads of perspiration glistening on his face and back, Vale thrust vigorously into Lance. From another settee in her expansive boudoir, Penelope watched them with a hand between her thighs. She was the first to spend. Then Lance. And finally Vale.

After Vale had discharged into Lance, he staggered back, taking in deep gulps of air. Lance collapsed onto the settee.

"Damn me," Lance said between gasps, "that were the best fuck I've had in years."

"An absolute vision," murmured Penelope.

Catching his breath, Vale sat down on a nearby wingchair and said nothing.

"My body shall always be made available to you, Dunnesford, as a means to release your anguish," Lance offered.

Penelope raised her quizzing glass at Vale. "Indeed, I cannot fair remember when you have fucked with such vehemence. What, in God's name, transpired between you and your wife?"

"Nothing but my failure to dissuade her from returning," Vale grumbled.

"Why dissuade her if she enjoys it here?"

Vale glanced sharply at Penelope. "She is merely a curious child. She does not understand the ways of the *Cavern*."

"Then why are you so troubled?" Lance asked, folding his arms beneath his head, his knees draped over the arms of the settee.

"I think your little wife would make a fine member of our establishment," Penelope declared.

"That won't happen, Penelope," Vale informed her. He turned to Lance. "If I am troubled, it is because I have been incapable of doing that which I must do to discourage her future attendance here."

She was Harold's sister, Vale remindedhimself as he recalled the first time he had met her. He had been waiting for Harold at the Delaney home so that the two of them could go out fishing. Harold's two-year old sister had wandered into the parlor, carrying a children's book and looking for someone to read to her.

"Read it, this one," she had instructed him, approaching a complete stranger with no hesitation.

He had been caught quite off guard by the imp with her head of motley curls, but there had been such a complacency to her directive, as if it were the most natural order of things that he should read to her, as if his presence in the parlor had been Providence. There was no nursemaid in attendance—he later discovered the woman had wearied of chasing after her charge and left the child in the nursery, not foreseeing the child would open the door on her own—and when little Harrietta had spread the book on his lap, he felt he had no choice but to submit to the child's order.

In the following years, Harrietta was often, though not always, an adjunct to their escapades. She clearly worshipped Harold, who in turn, indulged his sister until they eventually matured beyond the point at which it was acceptable. Vale could tell Harrietta had been loath to conform to the expectations of a proper young woman in society when she had come of age.

That was apparently still the case, Vale thought grimly.

"I could take your place," Lance proposed. "I have no prejudice with your wife."

"No," Vale snapped, gripped with an insane possessiveness, though he knew his friend had only a generous motive behind the proposition.

And even though he himself had suggested to Harrietta earlier that he might share her body, he would not have allowed another to touch his wife. Not in the *Cavern*. Not anywhere.

Penelope raised her brows. "I think it rather hypocritical of you, Vale, to prohibit your wife from enjoying the pleasures of the Cavern when you have partaken for so long."

"You will take her side as well?" Vale asked as he rose to his feet. First Charlotte. Now Penelope.

"I suspect she would make a natural submissive. She only needs the proper instruction, and you are clearly qualified."

"Ironically," Lance drawled, "neither one of you would be committing adultery to boot."

"She doesn't know that," Vale said, his tone tinged with sarcasm—or was it bitterness?

"Posh," Penelope said, "since when do we care of such matters as adultery?"

"True enough," Lance conceded. "All the same, for myself, I am content to remain a bachelor."

Grabbing his clothes, Vale began to dress. The thread of their conversation rankled him, and he had no wish to tarry with Penelope and Lance. Not tonight.

"Off to the Countess, are we?" Penelope inquired. "Beautiful woman. Wish she would make an appearance here."

"Daresay your wife knows about the Countess?" asked Lance.

Vale stopped. He wasn't sure and had made no assumptions. He had simply made it clear before they tied the knot that she had to respect the life that he led, and he in turn, would not question hers.

"Why has my wife, of a sudden, become such a topic of interest?" Vale returned.

"Because if it weren't for her, I doubt you would have buggered me," Lance replied flatly. "And I do hope to have an encore of our performance."

Vale did not reveal to his friend that their buggering had not done much to relieve his disquiet. After taking his leave of the *Cavern*, with the reins of his horse in hand, he was tempted to turn left toward his home in Grosvenor Square rather than right to where the Countess lived. There was no need for him to see her for Francis would usher her safely home. And the Countess was expecting him.

Harrietta had departed from the *Cavern* with nary a glance back at him after he had finally assisted her to her feet.

"Thank you, my lord," she had said, but he could not read the emotion behind her words. What was she feeling? What was she thinking? Had she been disappointed? Overwhelmed?

But what could he—her husband—possibly say or do? Vale sighed and turned his horse right.

_**C**_

T HE SOFA IN THE ANTEROOM to the bed chambers of the Countess D'Alessio had felt particularly unyielding to Vale last night, and
he was glad when the morning put an end to his fitful slumber—if he
had indeed slept. He studied the dust particles illuminated by what little
sunlight had crept through the heavy drapery covering the windows. He
wondered what Harrietta would have done had she not discovered the
draperies in the spare bedroom. A small smile curled the corners of his
mouth. No doubt she would have found a means.

"She must be delightful."

Vale looked up to see Isabella D'Alessio, looking as radiant as she always
did in the morning. Not many women woke up as lovely as they appeared
after their toilette, but the Countess, with her striking black hair, wide
defined lips, and full dark lashes, wanted very little cosmetic adornments.
She was wearing an elegant negligee over an ivory laced nightgown.

"Your pardon?" Vale asked, stretching as he sat up.

Isabella took a seat next to him. "The woman who made you smile ere
now."

"M'dear, there is no woman but you present in my view, and you are
indeed a vision worth smiling about."

After raising her hand to his lips, he reached over and took his waistcoat
from the back of the sofa.

"_Before_ I came into your line of sight," Isabella pursued. "Will you not
tell me her name? Or—I am remiss—there are no names at _Madame
Botreaux's_."

Vale paused before sliding his feet into his buckled shoes. "I know her
name."

Isabella raised two perfectly arched brows. "How splendid!"

He shook his head, and the Countess frowned in sympathy.

"Ah, she is a married woman then?"

His mouth curled in an ironic smile. "Yes, she is married. Have you
rung for breakfast? I am in sore need of a cup of coffee this morning."

"Yes."

"Is Miss Trinidad asleep still?" He glanced toward the closed door of
her bed chamber.

"My sleeping beauty loathes rising with the sun."

He made no comment. The Countess and her lover had not gone to sleep for some time. Despite the closed doors, he had heard the two women all too well last night.

"Your nights may be numbered," Isabella assured him as he worked out the soreness in his neck. "My aunt has of late expressed an interest in returning home. I pray for it nightly that I will no longer have to live under her prying eyes."

"Worry not, Isabella. A night on your sofa is of no great inconvenience."

"Or perhaps my father will finally succumb to old age and poor health. I do not think I will miss him much."

"He is a brute, and I wish him as much pain in his death as he has given to you," Vale said, remembering how the man had struck her upon hearing rumors that his daughter had a female lover.

She looked at him with large grateful eyes. "You are a good friend, Vale. I would that you find a love as fulfilling as that betwixt Honora and me. If you will forgive my prejudice, I do not think you will happen upon it at *Madame Botreaux's.*"

"But I am not in search of it, Countess. I am, after all, a married man," he reminded her as a servant knocked on the door and entered with the breakfast tray.

"Of course," Isabella said after the servant had left. "I saw her from across the amphitheatre during the opera. She is charming. I should like to meet her someday, though I suspect she has no interest in meeting me."

"I would not underestimate Harrietta," he murmured and proceeded to finish his cup of coffee in two gulps.

Unfortunately, it was weak coffee and Vale felt in need of a second dose when he arrived home and dragged himself up the stairs to his chambers. Harrietta was still in hers.

"Her ladyship has not yet risen," his valet, Jacobs, informed him upon seeing the direction of his gaze.

"Have the breakfast table set for two then," Vale told Jacobs.

After a shave and change of clothes, Vale felt much better. Harrietta, however, seemed less than refreshed during breakfast. She seemed to avoid his gaze and asked for the paper but did not seem to read it. He wondered what had kept her from sleeping.

"What diversion has my lady arranged for herself today?" Vale asked after some silence.

"Hm? Oh. I had thought to visit a mantua maker on Ludgate Hill to shorten the hem of a gown I wish to wear to Lord and Lady Granview's ball," Harrietta replied. "And I have accepted an invitation from a Mr.

Winters to visit a new orphanage for girls that has been erected in the parish of St. Giles."

"And who is accompanying you? St. Giles is safe neither night nor day."

"I have Sarah to keep me company."

Vale was quiet, and from her lifted chin he could tell she was about to protest whatever he meant to say.

"Allow me to keep you company," he offered.

It was not what she expected to hear. She blinked several times before saying, "If you have the time..."

"I will make the time."

Vale's secretary was surprised to hear his employer rearranging his day to accompany his wife to the mantua maker of all things, but the man knew better than to question the Marquess.

The gown of forest green with matching feathered cap became Harrietta, Vale thought to himself as he watched her descend the flight of stairs. She had a sense of elegance that he had not expected from a country girl. He offered his arm. She hesitated, eying it warily, but allowed him to walk her out to the carriage. He wondered if he had been too rash with her where the Elroys were concerned. Harrietta was still young enough to have the desire to rebel against authority—especially those who threatened to impose their will upon her independence.

He wanted to apologize for his harshness, but he could not, nor would not, condone her keeping company with Lovell or Alexandra. She had to simply trust him on that. But he knew he had yet to earn her trust. Indeed, if she were cognizant of all the lies of omission that existed in their marriage, she would be less inclined than ever to trust him.

She had trusted Harold, and Vale wished that she had that same faith in him. He remembered being envious of Harold for having sisters when he himself had no siblings. As he grew older, more than enough men and women, filled that void with ease. But Harold had been the brother he had always longed for.

Harrietta kept her gaze out the carriage window. He described some points of interest that they passed, but their conversation remained tepid. It lacked the abandon that Harrietta exuded on the night of the opera.

At the shop of Mrs. Darling, one of the finest mantua makers in London, Harrietta was obliged to don the gown so that the hem might be measured to its proper length. From his chair, Vale observed one of Mrs. Darling's assistants pinning the hem of the dress.

"Is that the finest of the dresses you had made?" Vale asked Harrietta as he eyed the modest gown through his quizzing glass.

"Yes. You disapprove?" she asked, attempting to turn around to see herself in the mirror without losing her foothold on the stool she stood upon.

"Lord and Lady Granview's ball is no small affair. Any number of the royal family may be in attendance." He turned to Mrs. Darling. "Have you the latest edition of the *Ladies' Magazine?*"

"Indeed, your lordship," Mrs. Darling sniffed, affronted that he should even ask.

Flipping through the fashion plates, he found one he liked. "This one will do."

Harrietta gasped. "That would be much too extravagant. I would have to be a princess to wear such a gown."

"You are the Marchioness of Dunnesford. I will not having you dressed as anything less."

"His lordship has a discerning eye," Mrs. Darling approved.

Harrietta examined the drawing of the richly decorated gown with eschelle stomacher and embroidered petticoat, pursing her lips in doubt.

"Let us see your finest bolts of satin," Vale said to Mrs. Darling.

After he had selected a golden peach colored satin and agreed to pay nearly double for the gown to be completed in time for the ball, he ensured she completed the ensemble with the purchase of matching silk covered shoes, embroidered stockings, an ivory handled fan, reticule, and pearl bracelets. Perhaps Harrietta was overwhelmed by the shopping, but he had expected more enthusiasm on her part. All his mistresses had adored it when he bought them things.

From the comfortable establishments of London's finest purveyors of haberdashery, they turned into a parish with rutted streets and the smell of open sewers. Vale held up a perfumed handkerchief to his nose and marveled that Harrietta could do without one. They reached the *Orphan Asylum for Girls*, a two storied building in need of much renovation.

A short but stout gentleman—Mr. Winters, Vale presumed—greeted them. "Lady Dunnesford, welcome, welcome! My word, and Lord Dunnesford, is it? You honor us, your lord and ladyship."

They were ushered into a small parlor to sit down for tea while Mr. Winters described the short history of the asylum.

"As you may be aware there are many efforts to reform those who have strayed from the respectable path," Mr. Winters told them, "and I mean no disregard for the Society for the Suppression of Vice who have labored to save the souls of many a poor woman, but I firmly believe the best way to thwart a life of misery and prostitution is to nurture them before they grow from girls to women. Many of the foundlings we have here are from mothers who ply that trade, and have a propensity toward that same future if no intervention is provided them."

The man spoke in earnest and with conviction. After a few more words on his philosophy for the asylum, he offered them a tour. Vale was ready to decline the invitation and simply offer the man a pledge of monetary support, but Harrietta jumped at the idea.

"I should very much like to see the girls," Harrietta said.

Mr. Winters beamed in return and directed them down a narrow hallway.

"This is the classroom where they learn to read and recite their catechisms," he informed them proudly. "At present, we have but a few books and they must share with one another. We start promptly at seven o'clock in the morning after they have woken, dressed, and had their breakfast. After their morning lesson, they each have chores: sewing, cleaning, cooking."

Vale studied the motley assortment of children, who watched him and Harrietta with large curious eyes. Their attire was worn, but they were groomed and, for the most part, not the disheveled ragamuffins he had expected.

They walked outside to a fenced area in the back. Mr. Winters explained, "Here they are allowed to play."

He left their side to attend to two girls fighting over the only doll. To Vale's surprise, Harrietta grabbed his arm suddenly.

"Does it not break your heart to see them, knowing they have neither mother nor father?" she whispered.

Instinctively, he covered her hands with one of his own. A little black girl of about seven years of age wandered over to them.

"I picked flowers," she told them, holding up three stems.

"They're beautiful," Harrietta replied, crouching to match eye level with the girl. Vale wondered that she was able to do it with all the hoops and petticoats beneath her skirt. It must have been an awkward stance.

The little girl took one of the stems and handed it to Harrietta, then turned to consider Vale and handed one to him as well. Taking the lead from his wife, Vale also bent down.

"Thank you," Harrietta said. "Are you sure you want not to keep it for yourself?"

"I have one," the girl said and showed them the remaining flower that she held.

"What is your name, little one?" Vale asked, noting that the girl had the largest and roundest eyes he had ever seen.

"Mr. Winters said I needing a Christian name and did give me 'Beatrice' for my name, but my mama, she called me Adia."

"Adia. A lovely name for a lovely girl."

She gave him a half smile, unsure how to respond to the compliment.

"You knew your mother?" Harrietta inquired.

Adia nodded. "She was bought and put on a ship to America, but her owner had no wish to purchase me as I was but a child."

Mr. Winters returned and offered to show them the room where the girls slept. Vale was glad to straighten his legs.

"Shall I see you again?" Adia asked them.

As Vale deliberated an appropriate response, his wife answered, "Of course! Perhaps you should like to visit our place? If you like flowers, we have many in bloom in our garden at present."

"Now, now, Beatrice," Mr. Winters intervened. "Run along and play."

Adia brightened. "When, my lady?"

Mr. Winters was about to protest more sternly, but Vale put a hand on the man's shoulder to stop him.

"Harrietta," Vale said gently, wanting to tell her that the asylum no doubt had protocols in place for their wards, and he himself was unsure that inviting an orphan over for a walk in the Aubrey gardens was what the girl needed.

"How about Sunday?" Harrietta proposed.

"We have services for the girls, albeit very modest, on Sunday mornings," Mr. Winters explained.

"Ah, then the afternoon? I shall return in a carriage, shall I? Have you ever ridden in a carriage?"

Mr. Winters protested, "My lady is most gracious, but there is no need—"

Harrietta looked sharply at the man, and Vale could tell his wife meant to have her way on this matter.

"Perhaps two o'clock would be a good time?" Vale suggested. "We can discuss at that time what contribution can be made for the asylum."

At that Mr. Winters' eyes grew larger than Adia's. "Absolutely. Any time that is convenient for your lordship. If I may show you the room where the girls spend the night, you will see the roof is in need of repair. When it rains, only half the room is usable."

Vale smiled at Harrietta over the head of Mr. Winters. The sparkle in her eyes was what he had hoped to see earlier when they were shopping, and he was both proud and thankful to have the means to produce that gleam in her.

His thoughts turned to what he might do with her later that night in the *Cavern of Pleasures*.

CHAPTER TEN

⚭

T HE CONFUSION OF SENTIMENTS SWIRLING inside her in regard to her husband was maddening. Harrietta sighed as she threw a cape about her shoulders and prepared for her furtive journey into the night. His gesture at the orphan asylum had filled her with joy. As she had looked from the hopeful eyes of Adia to the cool but glimmering grey of her husband's, for a moment she had thought to herself that she could love him, and love him with all her heart. But then she had only to remember the Countess.

She remembered that morning, as she lay awake staring at the canopy above her bed, reliving all that had transpired at *Madame Botreaux's*, she had heard Vale's return, had heard the footman informing him in the hallway that his hot water was ready for his morning shave. And she remembered how tired Vale had appeared at breakfast—no doubt the result of a vigorous night with the Countess. She wondered who had the voracious appetite. Was it the Countess or Vale?

Shaking her head, she admonished herself for filling her thoughts with Vale when she was heading to her assignation with *him*. The one in the black and silver mask. Had she truly surrendered her body to him? Allowed a stranger to pleasure her until she spent? His touch had been.... unlike any she had imagined possible. He had seemed privy to that particularly sensitive ridge beneath her clitoris, strummed it to full effect, and she had spent easily and quickly for him. Not till after her mind had finally surfaced from the flood of ecstasy did she realize the pain in her arms and legs. When he had cut her bonds, she could not hold herself erect. He had been so tender with her afterwards that she almost did not wish to part from his arms.

After walking on her toes past Vale's chambers, Harrietta wound her way down the stairs and into the drawing room, which had French doors leading out to the garden. She slid through the doors into the coolness of the night. A lattice of vines on the wall provided her the footing she needed to pull herself up and over the bushes. Once on the pavement, she rounded the corner of the house to head up the street where a coach would be waiting for her.

Once inside *Madame Botreaux's*, Harrietta was greeted by a dressing maid who assisted her out of her clothing. Harrietta remembered being shy in front of the maid upon her first visit, but now she felt quite at ease as if she had been a long time patron of *Madame Botreaux's*. With her mask fixed firmly in place, Harrietta, wearing only a thin silk robe, sauntered down onto the assembly floor.

"This marks your fourth visit to *Madame Botreaux's*, does it not?" a low voice dripping with sensuality asked from behind her on the stairs.

Turning, she saw the man in the red mask that had caught her attention the first night. Her hand instinctively went up to her mask to assure that it was firmly in place.

"You have been counting?" she returned, lowering her own voice to mask her identity.

"I noticed you the first night you came," the man said, stepping closer toward her.

Harrietta inhaled sharply as his body invaded the space around her. He wore tight black breeches and no shirt. His chest was as finely chiseled as that of her "lord" and his carriage as imposing. There was something predatory in the way that he moved and gazed upon her. It quickened her pulse, making her aware of her vulnerability.

She could have said the same of him, but only raised her brows solicitously. Good God, she had come a long way since her first wide-eyed appearance at this establishment.

He did not indulge her with more information and merely smiled. "When you have tired of your current master—as many women eventually do—you are welcome to grace my company. I can assure you a most memorable experience. The loudest screams of ecstasy always emerge from my corner."

After allowing a moment for his words to sink in, he bowed and slid past her down the stairs. Harrietta, blood pounding in her head, watched him, smooth and lithe as a panther, disappear into one of the recessed alcoves. Her curiosity had been piqued, and she wondered what it would be like to be his submissive. In what ways would he differ from her "lord?" What a wanton harlot she had become! Shaking her head, Harrietta quickly descended the rest of the stairs. It was likely past the hour now, but she had not seen her "lord" pass by her. If she hurried, he would not know she was late. Hastily shedding her robe, she hung it on a hook on the wall and took her place in her customary spot.

"You are late."

Startled, Harrietta looked to the shadow from where the disapproving voice had come. Her heart sank when she saw the form of her "lord" sitting on the bench she had occupied her second night with him. He stood up and advanced toward her, crop in hand.

"Do you remember the punishment for a late arrival?" he inquired.

"T-ten lashes, my lord," Harrietta answered nervously.

"A nice but fruitless attempt," he sneered, circling around her like a hawk. "The correct answer is twenty, but I shall add five more to prompt your memory for the future."

Harrietta tried not to cringe. Her "lord" pulled over a strange contraption. It was waist high and resembled an inverted letter V. Iron shackles adorned each leg corner.

"Bend over the gable," he instructed her.

She obeyed, and he pulled her arms toward the ground, clasping the shackles about her wrists. He spread her legs and shackled her ankles. The blood was rushing to her head and she could see only her own legs and those of her "lord" standing behind her.

"Count for me," he said before inflicting the first blow to her right buttock.

Harrietta cried out. The pain was sharp and precise.

"Shall we start again?" he asked, raising his crop.

"One—one!" Harrietta supplied.

He delivered two quick blows, one to each cheek.

"Two—three," Harrietta counted.

"Those were for neglecting to address me as 'my lord,'" he informed her.

The word 'no' rose to her lips, but she swallowed it before enunciating.

"Yes, my lord," she mumbled and braced herself for the next one. "Two, my lord."

"Very good. You are a quick study."

He struck her again on the same buttock, which had already been sensitized by the earlier blows.

"Three, my lord."

The position was excruciating. She could do nothing to relieve the awkwardness of it or prevent the dizziness from having her head upside down. She disliked that her backside was so fully exposed to him, her arse at his mercy.

The fourth and fifth blows were delivered in quick succession to the same spot, and Harrietta felt tears pressing against her eyes at the stinging pain. The sixth and seventh were deliberately slow and far from one another.

"Absorb the pain of each individual lash," he instructed her. "Are you enjoying it yet, *ma petite?*"

Enjoying it? *It bloody hurts, you bastard.*

Eight. Nine. Ten.

Harrietta struggled for a normal breath. Her arse was on fire, as if each lash was rupturing her skin. She did not think she could continue with fifteen more lashes remaining. She felt his had softly caressing one buttock.

"Your arse is blushing nicely," he told her.

Then his hand slid between her legs, skimming her quim. Harrietta gasped in surprise. His touch was made all the more tender by the contrast of the throbbing pain of her posterior.

"You are wet," he noted.

And, amazingly, it was true. Her body had responded to the lashing in a way she had not expected!

He reached his hand between her legs again and began fondling her clit. Harrietta groaned, remembering the delicious climax she had enjoyed at his hands the previous night. She wanted that again. But he stepped back to deliver the strongest blow yet.

"Eleven, my lord," she said without hesitation, hoping he would touch her again. She strained to lift her head.

But he only landed the next few blows, each more forceful than the last.

"Now we are approaching the hue I prefer," he commented. "You should see what a lovely red glow your arse has."

To her delight, he began fondling her clitoris once more. Her mind, desperately relieved to have a distraction from the discomfort and the pain, wrapped itself in the warmth of his caresses. An ache of a different sort pulsed between her legs.

He stepped back to deliver two more strikes before returning to pleasure her. His fingers did remarkable things. The desire was heating her body as much as the lashing, and though she was already upon her toes, she lifted herself as high off the gable as she could to allow him better access.

Again, he retreated.

"Nineteen, twenty, my lord!" Harrietta counted.

Only five left, but by now she cared not as much. Lust was flaming through her body. She needed to spend. He struck her once and allowed the pain to sink into her flesh, but though each blow still caused her to clench her teeth, the yearning in her quim was more agonizing. She waited. Would he strike her or caress her next? Would it be his hand or the crop?

The crop.

"Twenty-two," Harrietta groaned in disappointment.

He cleared his throat.

"My lord, my lord!" she added.

"Too late," he informed her. The crop fell against her thrice.

The tears slid down toward her forehead. She waited patiently, stewing in the pain of her punishment and the anguish of unfulfilled desire. Would it be pain or pleasure next?

He chose pain.

"Twenty-three, my lord."

He rewarded her with pleasure. She grunted her approval, shifting her body in rhythm to his strokes. She felt her body racing up a hill, her climax in sight. She was almost at the top, the moment before the delicious descent into ecstasy.

But he stepped back to give her the twenty-fourth lash.

She had endured indescribable pain. Once, when she was young and had fallen off a horse that she should never have attempted riding, she had experienced the strongest and most painful blow to her body. But this —a prolonged pain—felt more intense. Made all the more poignant by the denial of pleasure. She desperately wanted to beg him to touch her. This waiting was intolerable.

Touch me, damn it, touch me.

He delivered her last and final lash, and Harrietta was glad to feel something against her body. She shuddered with relief that the punishment was over.

But would he allow her to spend?

𝒞

STARING AT HER BRIGHT RED bottom, Vale began to regret that
she had struck her as hard as he had, though he had used but a fraction
of the strength he would have applied to more experienced submissives.
He would have gone more lightly on her punishment had he not seen
her conversation with Lovell on the stairs. From her body language, he
could tell she was not repudiating his advances. And it was jealousy—a
sentiment that had not visited his bosom in many years—that leveled the
crop upon her arse.

Emotion should never play a part in a master's application of dominance. That he had succumbed to his jealous feelings worried him. But
she had done better than he had expected. He imagined there might have
been a tear or two stinging her eyes. His sixteenth blow had been harsh,
but one would not have discerned any wavering by the resolution in her
tone when she counted.

And she had been wet. The punishment had aroused her, as it was
meant to. She was straining for his touch now. He stepped up to her
and eyed the lovely curve of her rump. There was a nice roundness to it
and not the scrawny arse that he sometimes saw with women of slighter
forms. With any other woman he would have left her there to consider
her predicament for a while, but he felt compelled to touch her. Fondle
her. Make her cry out in her ecstasy. He wanted that sense of accomplish-
ment knowing he had brought her body such joy.

It did not take long before her body began jerking and quivering at his
hand, straining against the shackles. And he gloried in her climax, fondling her more to ensure as many waves of release flowed through her
as possible. How easy it would have been for him to pull out his cock
and ram it into her quim, now flooded with her juices. The height of the
gable had her rump at the perfect level for him. He was tempted. God, he
was tempted. When he stepped back, he could feel his cock groaning. But
he could not. He told himself it was for her sake, though he wondered if
it might not have been for his own as well.

"You did well, *ma petite*," he praised, rubbing her ankles and wrists as
he removed the shackles. After helping her to her feet, he pulled her over
to a bench and across his lap. Reaching to the floor, he dipped his fingers
into a jar and massaged a salve onto her tender rump.

"This will soothe the burn," he explained, the hardness of his erection pressing against her body while he appreciated her lovely arse.

"Thank you, my lord," she said when he set her back on her feet.

A bell of thick iron rang through the *Cavern*, its solemn baritone echoing through the alcoves.

"Ah, someone wishes to exhibit his submissive," Vale informed her. He removed the collar and leash from the wall. "Come."

This time she did not protest, but he could tell she was not pleased at the notion of wearing the collar. He had no preference himself. Most of the women enjoyed wearing the collar, but for the most part, he had no need of a material device to command his submissives. With Harrietta, however, he was taking no chances.

In the middle of the assembly floor, a ring of lamps on the floor encircled a wooden table. A woman, naked, had already been tied to it. A rope had been wound around her body many times. Her master, a shorter but stout man wearing only a loin cloth and a leather mask, stood near her with his arms crossed. A number of men and women had gathered around the couple. Vale pulled a chair from the wall for himself and had Harrietta sit at his feet.

"We begin," the man in the circle announced. "My friends, you are fortunate tonight. My submissive has confessed a secret desire for her body to be communal property. It satisfies me to share her with all of you."

Vale looked down at Harrietta, who was shifting uncomfortably on the ground in her attempt not to put too much pressure on her buttocks.

"Tell me," he asked her, "have you ever had such a secret desire?"

"No, my lord."

"As you witness this woman, naked for all to behold, her body at our mercy, do you think you will come to share her desire?"

Harrietta considered the question. "I am curious, my lord, but it may be a prospect more titillating in thought than action."

He followed her gaze around the room and noted the different couples. One female dominant had her male submissive servicing her quim with his tongue. The man next to them had two female submissives lying curled at his feet as if they were his bitches. Lovell had his submissive, a young thing barely out of the schoolroom, sucking his cock. Vale noticed with discontent that Harrietta's gaze lingered in that direction.

"First," the man in the leather mask said, "I will have a woman."

A mistress offered her submissive, a redheaded woman with a slender build. The man in leather assisted the redhead onto the table and sat her above the face of the woman bound to the table.

"Pleasure her with your tongue," the man told his own submissive.

Vale heard Harrietta inhale sharply, but she did not turn away. The red-head began to moan and rocked her hips.

"Permission to caress her bosom, my lord?" the redhead asked.

"Permission granted," he replied.

The redhead reached down and began kneading the full breasts of the woman beneath her. It was quiet save for the cries of the redhead and the soft moans from the crowd around them, pleasuring themselves in unison to the women in the circle.

"Touch yourself," Vale told Harrietta.

Her hand moved without hesitation to her mons. Her fingers began rolling her own clitoris. Vale ran his own fingers beneath his nose. The scent of her was still upon him, and the blood coursed strongly to his loins once more. She had a nice light scent. Some women had very heavy and musky scents. Occasionally there was one most foul. He remembered one who smelled of fish that had not been aired. He wondered how Harrietta tasted, if she would be as sweet as she smelled.

"Tell me what you are experiencing."

The lamps on the floor threw just enough light onto her face that he could see a blush coloring her cheeks.

"Arousal, my lord," she answered.

"Would you have an interest in being one of the women up there?"

"Yes, my lord."

"Which one?"

"Both, my lord."

He felt a muscle ripple along his jaw, and he had to close his eyes. But then the image of Harrietta bound to the table, her tongue flicking the quim of another woman, rose in his mind. Then that of Harrietta in place of the redhead. He felt the distress grinding in his groin.

The redhead was now playing with her own breasts and pinching her nipples. He reached a hand down to Harrietta and tweaked one of the extended pebbles. Harrietta moaned, and the motion of her fingers quickened. Her chest rose and fell heavily as the redhead began to tremble in orgasm.

"Do not spend without my consent," Vale warned Harrietta.

"Yes, my lord."

"Now," the man in leather proclaimed, "I will have four men."

One man took his position where the redhead had been, but facing forward so that his cock was aimed at the woman's mouth. Another was between her legs. The remaining two each placed his cock in one of her hands.

"You may spend," they were told, "*on* her but not *in* her. The latter is my privilege alone."

Harrietta watched intently as the four men began to fuck the woman on the table. Vale glanced around the room. Many of the men and women had already spent, some now in a languid stupor. Lovell was pounding his submissive, who was on hands and knees, in the arse. As if sensing eyes upon him, Lovell turned to look at Vale and smirked. Instinctively, Vale reached for Harrietta and drew her protectively to himself.

He had her sit on the edge of his chair between his spread legs and reached his hand over her hip to fondle her clitoris. She sighed with satisfaction, and he allowed her to lean her back against him. Her hair felt soft against his chest, and he was impatient for the opportunity to fist his hand through the silken tresses.

The man with his cock in the woman's mouth was the first to spend. He pulled out and shot his seed over her lips. It splashed across her cheeks. He was followed by the man fucking her quim. His seed sprayed over her abdomen.

"Thank you," the woman murmured.

Harrietta was gasping and writhing. Every time her rump brushed against the inside of his thighs, his cock stiffened further.

"Not yet," Vale told her.

"Then cease your motions, my lord," she said through gritted teeth.

He chuckled. "Then where would the amusement be, *ma petite*?"

She let out an exasperated groan and clenched her hands. He noticed her trying to move herself away from his hand, but he held it in place and intensified his caresses.

"Please let me spend, my lord," she said, her body straining against him, her back arching like that of a bow.

"No," he said firmly.

"Please..."

In the circle, the remaining two men had aimed their semen at the woman's breast. She rubbed the viscous white fluid over herself.

"Ahhh...." Harrietta cried.

"Hold it," Vale commanded.

She shook her head.

"Hold it."

"I cannot, my l—" she protested and her body erupted in spasms. Her cries drew a number of glances in their direction.

He allowed her climax to finish flowing through her before he jerked her onto her feet with the leash.

Back in their alcove he surveyed her in silence. She kept her eyes averted, sensing his disappointment. He went to a table and retrieved a small case wrapped in Chinese embroidery and lined with silk inside. He opened it to reveal two silver balls linked together with a delicate metal chain.

"You will use these," he instructed, "to discipline your body. They are sometimes referred to as Chinese pleasure balls. Lie down."

She lay on her back on the bench with her legs bent at the knees. He took the balls and inserted one into her vagina.

She gasped, "It is cold, my lord."

"Your body will warm them soon enough."

He slid the second one into her fleshy folds, then pulled her to her feet. Her legs nearly buckled when she felt the balls strike against each other.

"Keep them in you for as long as possible," he informed her. "The longer, the better. I, of course, will be able to ascertain the next time we meet in three days time whether or not you have been dutiful in your assignment."

He handed her the now empty case, dismissed her and watched as she walked awkwardly away. When she was out of view, he let out a long ragged breath, wondering if he had to go in search of Lance again tonight. He undid the buttons of his breeches and pulled out his cock. It had wanted her. Wanted to be where his fingers had been tonight. If he had been any other common man, he would have been derided for not knowing what the quim of his own wife felt like about his cock.

As he stroked himself, Vale shook his head. His control of the situation was ebbing. Not a good predicament. And yet he had enjoyed every moment. Enjoyed her arousal. Emboldened by the climaxes he had wrought upon her body. And it fueled an appetite for more. As his wife, she was his in name only, but when she was bent over the gable, she was completely his.

With a grunt, Vale brought himself to spend, pumping his seed into a handkerchief he had grabbed. He leaned his back against the wall as the final shudders worked their way through his limbs. He thought about approaching Harrietta's chambers tonight. How would she react if he chose to exercise his rights as a husband? Would she recoil in horror? Or would she be wet with thoughts of the *Cavern*? Good God, he was in danger of finding himself jealous of himself.

Over his wife? Harrietta Aubrey, nee Delaney? She was no beauty. Possessed no elegance. She was intelligent, but there were women of far superior wit. She was kindhearted. Though charity was quite the mode these days, few would have ventured to visit an orphanage. Or felt a kindred spirit with one of its orphans—and a Negro one at that.

Her heart as well as her mind had an openness he appreciated. And he admired her determination. He remembered when she was about four and ten years of age and had attempted to ride a horse Harold had warned her repeatedly not to ride as it was a temperamental beast and quite above her skills as a horseman. True enough, the horse had thrown her off. Harold had admonished her for proving his point. With tears in her eyes from her bruising landing, she had hobbled back to the horse and, ignoring her brother, pulled herself back onto the animal.

As with the *Cavern*, Harrietta would have her way.

On his way to the stairs leading up to Penelope's balcony, Vale passed the alcove occupied by Lovell and his submissive. Lovell had attached over a dozen clamps to the woman's breasts alone and several to each thigh. He yanked the chains attached to the clamps on her thighs. She emitted a bloodcurdling cry. Vale understood that for some women, the greater the pain, the greater the arousal. But he doubted Lovell's ability to gauge the right amount of pain.

"Worry not," Penelope said, coming up behind him. "She is a whore for pain."

"She is young," Vale replied.

"And virulent."

"Nonetheless, I will keep watch over them."

Penelope sighed. "I would rather you not interfere with my other patrons, Vale."

"Throw me out if you will."

"Then what would become of your wife?"

His spine straightened and he turned sharply to look Penelope full in the face.

She sighed again and retreated. "I have no desire to banish you, of course. But what will happen when you are done with the Marchioness?"

He was unprepared to answer the question for he had been sure he would be able to dissuade Harrietta from *Madame Botreaux's*.

But he would have to redouble his efforts. And he would start tomorrow morning.

CHAPTER ELEVEN

"GOOD MORNING," VALE GREETED HARRIETTA at breakfast the following morning as she made her way to her seat.

Harrietta returned his greeting, sat down, and bolted back to her feet when her tender derriere met the firmness of the chair.

"Something the matter, my dear?" Vale asked with a raised brow, setting down the paper he had been reading.

"No—no, I—I thought I forgot something," she mumbled before sitting down gingerly. "These—these are new chairs?"

"Yes, these possess a higher back."

The new chairs had not the soft cushions of the prior ones, Harrietta thought dismally. It seemed to her that Vale was eying her more intently this morning. Did he suspect something? Had Sarah mentioned something to him? No, she found it difficult the maid would have deliberately attempted to stir trouble. It was probably her own guilt that had her imagining things, Harrietta concluded. Nonetheless, she was relieved when breakfast was served, and hoped it would be a quick meal.

The two silver balls she had been presented last night were lodged in her quim. She had not been able to keep them inside her soon after she had received them. Embarrassed, she had quickly deposited them back into the box he had given her. As she had sat in the coach after departing *Madame Botreaux's*, with the little box in her lap, she opened it and stared at the orbs. This had been beyond anything she had imagined.

Once home, she had attempted to insert the balls into herself. They, along with her smarting arse, reminded her of her "lord" and she had soon found herself aroused by the memory of all that had transpired that evening. With the balls inside her, she had masturbated. The flexing of her vaginal muscles on the balls had added a scintillating effect to her orgasm.

She had debated whether or not to have the silver balls inside of her when she went down to breakfast. It would be horrifying if they should fall out of a sudden. Using a petticoat, she had fashioned a loin cloth for herself that would catch the balls should they slip out of her. It took all her concentration, girding muscles that she had never been aware of, to make it down the stairs and into the dining hall without losing the balls.

"There will be a balloon ascent tonight at Vauxhall," Vale noted as he spread butter upon his crumpet. "If you've an interest in attending, that can be arranged."

Harrietta perked up at the thought of seeing a hot air balloon for the first time. "With Charlotte?"

Vale cleared his throat. "I had thought perhaps you would accompany me."

"Oh...of course."

"If the prospect of my company disappoints you, you have only to say. I take no offense."

"Not at all," Harrietta protested. "I-I should like to attend Vauxhall with you. It has great displays of chinoiserie, does it not? Oh...but I cannot. I am to dine with Mrs. Robertson."

Vale frowned. "Mrs. Olyvia Robertson? She is a friend of Lady Falconet, is she not?"

Harrietta shrugged and spooned a bite of the soft-boiled egg into her mouth. She did not offer up the knowledge that Lord Elroy and his sister would most likely be in attendance as well.

"Another night, then. Perhaps we can see the fireworks," Vale said. "And we should visit Ranelagh Gardens as well. They are currently featuring a traveling menagerie."

"Oh, yes!" Harrietta exclaimed, unable to believe her luck. "I should very much like to visit Ranelagh as well."

"Then it shall be done."

He smiled at her, and she returned it, wondering what she had done to merit such attention from her husband. Briefly, it made her feel even more guilty for her visit to *Madame Botreaux's* last night.

"Would you entertain a simple request of mine, Harrietta?" he asked when she had finished her breakfast and prepared to head back into her bedchambers.

"What is the nature of the request?"

"I wish for you to take a walk with me in the garden. The gardener has planted some new flowers, and I am not enamored of how he has con-figured his selection of flora, but if it pleases you, I will allow the garden be kept the way it is."

Harrietta hesitated, but surely a glance at the garden would prove no long duration.

"I should be delighted," she responded.

He offered his arm, which she took, but it was no easy matter to keep pace with his steps when her body from her abdomen to her thighs were clenched as tight as can be.

"Harrietta dear, are you in pain?" he inquired.

"No!"

The word flew too quickly from her mouth, though perhaps she should have admitted to some pain as an excuse to retire to her chambers.

"Good."

He slowed his pace to accommodate her. In the garden, he pointed out the new plants and explained what had been there before. He ruminated over what might prove a better choice and asked a plethora of questions: did she prefer the delphiniums where the bergenia once grew, how did she find the grey lavender lining the path, were the bushes trimmed to her liking?

Harrietta kept her answers brief. The tiny vibration of the balls were agitating, and it took all her effort to keep her focus off her lower body and concentrate on what her husband was saying to her. The balls were slipping. She could not hold them in for much longer.

"What a lovely spring day," Vale commented. "Perfect for a ride. Shall we take the chaise out to Hyde Park?"

She paled at the notion of riding in an open carriage with the balls bounding inside of her. All the bumping and jarring would be the death of her. Fortunately, the footman arrived to tell them that a gentleman was here to call upon the Marquess. Harrietta could not imagine when she had felt more relieved. Vale excused himself, and she fled back into her chamber—as quickly as one could while pressing her thighs as closely together as possible.

Fortunately, Vale did not approach her again with his invitation for a ride about the park and instead took himself to the bank with his visitor. She wondered at his sudden interest in spending more time with her. Was it because she apparently had her own life to lead? Did he expect her to stay at home pining for him? Had he quarreled with the Countess? She had almost fallen to his charm, like some grateful puppy hungry for attention. If she allowed it, those grey-blue eyes of his would penetrate the armor she had built for herself, the armor she needed to survive in their loveless marriage.

As much as she would have liked to see Vauxhall, she was glad to be having dinner at the home of Mr. and Mrs. Roberts, where Harrietta received more reasons to resist falling for her husband a la his many other mistresses—two of whom Harrietta sat next to at the card tables after dinner. Alexandra introduced her to Mrs. Fiona Springwood and Lady Venetta Drury over Vingt-et-un, which had now become Harrietta's favorite for its thrilling fast pace. There were two men at the table as well. One was clearly flirting with Alexandra, who did not discourage his attentions. When Alexandra left the table, citing she needed some fresh air, the gentleman immediately rose and followed her, leaving Harrietta alone with Fiona, Venetta and Mr. Garetty, an older man who was hard of hearing.

"How fortunate you are, my dear," sighed Fiona, a beautiful woman with dark brown curls and a flawless complexion, "to be married to Dunnesford. He is a fine specimen of a man."

Harrietta kept her gaze on the cards she held in her hands. Was it appropriate for a woman to comment on another's husband in so forward a manner or was such behavior typical among London's *beau monde*?

"Ah, but it is the Countess D'Alessio who has the best of all worlds," commented Lady Drury, who, but for the sneer on her face, would have been quite attractive as well.

"It surprises me that he has been with her thus long," Fiona replied. "Alas, he was with me but three months. But it was a glorious few months."

The corner of Venetta's mouth curled conspiratorially. "Aye, the month we shared might as well have been a twelvemonth for all the tumbling we did."

Fiona leaned in toward Harrietta with glimmering eyes. "The Marquess has the most marvelous cock. I commend you on your choice of husbands."

Harrietta nearly fell out of her seat.

Lady Drury rolled her eyes upward. "Ah, yes. It is most finely shaped. I would I were a sculptor that I might make a mold of it."

"And the taste…the feel of it in one's mouth…divine…"

A flush filled Fiona's cheeks. Harrietta glanced at Venetta, who was smiling at her. The curl of her lips made Harrietta cringe inwardly.

"You must come from a wealthy family?" Fiona asked Harrietta.

"Not at all," Harrietta responded, hoping her feigned nonchalance sounded convincing as she picked up a card Mr. Garretty had dealt her.

"Then how did you come to marry him?" Lady Drury inquired.

"Were you a secret mistress of his?" Fiona added.

"I won him in a game of cards," Harrietta replied casually as she laid down her cards for she had exceeded twenty-one.

Lady Drury narrowed her eyes. "Surely you jest?"

But Harrietta was saved from further conversation by the appearance of Lord Elroy. From the glare he was casting Fiona and Venetta, Harrietta gathered that he had heard enough of what had transpired.

"Lady Dunnesford," he said, "my sister requested your presence for a moment. Would you tend to her?"

He offered his arm, which Harrietta was only too willing to accept. He escorted her away from the card table.

"Those two can be such vultures," he said to her in an apologetic tone. "They are merely jealous."

"I was aware that I would not be a favorite among certain women, but I am glad not to have to be in their company if necessary," Harrietta confessed.

"You handled them with great aplomb," Lovell praised. "My compliments."

They strolled out onto a balcony.

"You said Alexandra needed me?"

"I lied," Lovell revealed. "It was the only way I could think of to extract you from those two fire breathing dragons."

Harrietta smiled. "Thank you. You are a true knight in shining armor."

Lovell bowed. "At your service, madame."

She turned to look at the moon, which had recently risen above the horizon, and leaned against the railing. "'Tis a shame. I rather liked the game of vingt-et-un."

"Do you enjoy cards much?"

"My sisters and I often played whist, but I find vingt-et-un much more exciting."

"Then perhaps you would grace a card table with your humble knight?"

He bowed again, and she laughed. "I should be delighted, Sir Elroy of the Round Card Table."

At Elroy's table, her luck with vingt-et-un was not improved, but at least the company was better. Lovell was affable, courteous, and witty.

And generous. When she had run out of the allowance that Vale allotted her, Lovell offered to front whatever she needed. After a dismal run at the tables, she and Lovell retired to the corner of the room where a harpsichord stood. He performed the variations of Twinkle Twinkle Little Star by Mozart for her amusement. The evening passed quickly, and she found herself reluctant to part ways except that she had a rendezvous at *Madame Botreaux's*.

"Au revoir, mademoiselle," Lovell said to her as he bowed over her hand. "I think I have never enjoyed cards as much as I have tonight, and I have your company to thank for that."

"Well, I am committed to mastering the game of vingt-et-un for I will repay you for what you lent me tonight," Harrietta told him, noting how striking his blue eyes were and how firm the grasp of his hand on hers was. Were she not married, she might consider falling for Lord Elroy.

"Think nothing of it," he replied.

"I insist. I will honor this debt. It would not sit well with me if I do not repay you."

"Then your wish must be my command, my lady," he said with another bow.

He was quite the gallant, Harrietta mused. She turned to leave.

"My lady."

When she turned back around, he took her hand and pressed a small object into her palm. The warmth of his fingers over hers made her flush.

"I believe it be yours," he explained.

Opening her hand, Henrietta saw her golden earring. It was a set that Harold had given to her on the year of her come-out.

"Thank you. I should be devastated to lose it," she said, affixing it back to her ear.

"I am most gratified to be of service…and hope that I may continue to be your humble servant."

The length of his gaze into her eyes surprised her. She studied Lovell more closely. He had spent most of the evening with her and had been amiable but not flirtatious. There was little indication as to whether or not he held any interest in her beyond mere friendship until now. She gave him a small smile, bobbed a curtsy and left.

But could Lovell truly have an interest in her? she pondered after departing the Roberts home. Handsome, wealthy, titled. And virulent. There was something about him that made her a little nervous. A dangerous element. Perhaps a little exciting. He was not the sort of man she expected would take the time to entertain someone like her. Was it because she was now a Marchioness and married to the much admired Vale Aubrey that she should generate such attention? Or was it because she felt a different woman—more of a woman—since becoming a more frequent visitor to Madame Botreaux's?

The Dunnesford carriage carried her home. Not surprisingly, Vale had not returned. After making it known to the servants that she was retiring, she slipped out her usual door and down the street where Charlotte's carriage was waiting. Despite her best efforts, the conversation between Lady Drury and Fiona would not fade into the night. Harrietta knew the women meant to get under her skin for, as Lovell suggested, they were probably jealous, but she could not help but be affected. She could not rid herself of the image of Mrs. Springwood's mouth wrapped about Vale's cock.

But, damn it all, she herself—the wife of Dunnesford—didn't even know what his cock looked like!

"What disturbs you, *ma petite*?"

Standing naked in her usual spot in the *Cavern*, Harrietta snapped to attention. "My lord?"

"Something weighs upon your mind," his lordship replied as he eyed her more closely.

He stood near her, barefoot, in only a pair of black breeches, his mask, and a loose linen shirt. Harrietta gazed at the ridges of his chest and abdomen. She wondered if Vale had such a shapely torso. Her eyes dropped to his crotch. What did this man's cock look like? Would it match the beauty of the rest of his body?

"Only how I might please my lord tonight," she responded.

"A sweet answer, but there is no need for you to lie. If you've no wish to tell me, I will not force it from you. I have no interest in your personal affairs. Recline upon the bench and spread your legs."

She did as told. It amazed her how comfortably she took his orders now.

He inserted a finger into her quim.

"Grasp my finger," he instructed.

She contracted her muscles down there.

"Needs more work," he commented and went to retrieve another box.

Did he honestly expect results so quickly? she wondered, watching him take out two smaller silver balls. He knelt between her legs and pushed one ball, than the other, into her. They were heavier than the ones he had given her before. And different. For a moment they seemed to generate their own motion.

"These are hollow," his lordship explained, "and have in their core another ball inside them."

His head bent low over her mons. He seemed to inhale her fragrance. Then his tongue pressed against her clit, and Harrietta felt her body leaping off the bench. She had never been touched by a man in such a fashion. *By his tongue.*

He glared sharply at her, and Harrietta settled her body back into position. The balls had rocked inside of her when her body jerked, jarring her nerves.

"You are not to spend without my consent," he told her, then dipped his head back between her thighs.

He flicked his tongue against her clit, sending sparks through her stomach. It felt wondrous. Even more marvelous than the touch of his hand. She felt his fingers parting her folds to better access her clitoris, which he teased and tormented. What a remarkable instrument his tongue was! She felt her body simultaneously melting and straining against his touch. And the balls rolling ever so slightly inside had magnified her awareness of her lower body. The flexing of her vaginal walls about them sent ripples of arousal through her. It was almost more stimulation than she could handle.

She would spend before he allowed it. She held the sides of the bench near her head and dug her fingers into the wood. Her body tried to escape his caresses by moving up along the bench, away from his mouth, which was no longer tasting but devouring her. He grabbed her thighs and pulled her back. The back and forth motion only disturbed the balls inside of her more. She tried to think of less arousing thoughts, but her mind was trapped. The sensations too overwhelming.

She came, long and hard, at the mercy of his tongue.

When she opened her eyes, he was standing upright, staring at her with a frown. He grabbed her by the wrists and dragged her back to the center of the room.

"Wait!" Harrietta exclaimed.

He paused and looked at her.

"My lord. Is there aught I can do for you, my lord?" she asked him.

He raised an eyebrow.

"It would seem—have you no wish to be pleasured in return, my lord?"

He seemed to stiffen.

"I should like to pleasure you, my lord. I could—I could fondle your cock. Or place it in my mouth."

"You have not earned the privilege of my cock," he said.

"When—how can I earn it, my lord?"

"You desire my cock much, do you?"

She thought about Fiona and Lady Drury. Flushing, she declared, "Indeed, my lord. I should like your cock."

"You may have it only when I deem you worthy."

Grabbing a long rope, he bound her wrists behind her head. It took some time and quite a bit of rope, but when he was finished, she was suspended from the ceiling like a bird in flight, her legs spread behind her. It was uncomfortable, yet exquisitely erotic. The fiber of the ropes ground against her skin, but she felt secure.

He came to stand at her head. When she attempted to lift her gaze, she found herself staring straight into his crotch. She wondered if he had ever bound a woman similarly and had that woman suck his cock in such a position. She wanted to see his cock again. She had never had one in her mouth. But it was the naughtiest prospect, and she found it titillating. And even her 'lord,' with his cold calm did not seem impervious to the eroticism they engaged in. She could see the outline of his cock bulging in his breeches.

"You have failed," he told her, "to withhold your orgasm. Your disobedience must be punished. If you cannot withstand your punishment, you may signal your desire to quit by holding up your right two fingers. That signal will end your punishment and your tenure here at the *Cavern*. Do you understand?"

"Yes, my lord," she responded, more afraid because his voice quivered as he spoke.

"Now open your mouth."

He inserted a red ball hinged to a black strap, which he tied behind her head. The ball prevented her from speaking and barely fit into her mouth. He reached beneath her for her breasts and fondled her nipples until they hardened.

She stifled a scream when he affixed an ivory clasp to each nipple. Her body jerked in vain to shed the clasps, but they bit into her nipples with the ferocity of a famished pup on a tit. The pain made her head spin. She gritted her teeth and tried to refocus her mind elsewhere, to separate conscience from her body.

But he made that difficult when, walking to the other end of her, he put two similar clasps to the lips of her labia. This time Harrietta cried out in anguish, though the sound was muffled by the ball in her mouth. She struggled against her bonds, desperate to free her hands so that she might pull off the offending items.

"Cease!" he commanded with a swat at her buttocks.

Her struggling had aggravated the silver balls still lodged in her vagina. She stopped and tried to take in slow, long breaths.

"You will adjust to the pain," he assured her.

At the moment, she doubted him. She wanted to curse, even unleash a string of oaths at him, but she was only capable of incoherent grunting. Her jowls felt sore from awkwardly encasing the ball.

His hand reached underneath her, and he stroked her clitoris. Her body wrenched in surprise. Gently, he rubbed her, plying and teasing her clitoris. How was it possible? He was arousing her body, even while the clamps affixed to her continued to smart. In fact, the clasps near her quim only seemed to alert her more to the pleasurable stroking between them. It was a maddening mix of pain and pleasure. And ultimately of arousal.

And as he had said, her body began adjusting to the clasps. She moaned as the familiar waves of bliss began rolling from between her legs through her body. Her head hung between her shoulders and she could only see his two legs. What a quixotic arousal. The ultimate in corporal stimulation. The juxtaposition of the biting clasps with the tender flesh of his fingers working their delightful magic….she felt herself ascending toward that plateau. He had not expressly forbidden her to spend…although neither had he allowed it.

It mattered not. He had stopped his caresses to her consternation. He removed first the clamps on her labia, and then the ones attached to her nipples. But there was no relief, for his arousal had left her agitated. She watched as he replaced the clamps into a velvet pouch. Then he unclasped the ball from her mouth.

But he left her still suspended in her ropes.

"I will return to finish your punishment," he told her. His mouth curled in a wry grin. "Don't go anywhere."

CHAPTER TWELVE

H E COULD HAVE DIED. WHEN Harrietta had said that she wanted to *fondle his cock and place it in her mouth*, his body had roared in silent frustration. And as he had bound her and attached those clamps to her body, he could not rid himself of the image of her rosy little mouth clamped over his cock. His cock had been mere inches from her lips as she hung suspended in the ropes. By the grace of God, Vale wondered who was truly the one being punished.

Did it please his vanity that she wanted his cock? Aye. But it was not her husband's cock that she had wanted. It was that of 'his lordship.' And his pride was checked as easily and as quickly as it had inflated. What a ridiculous mess.

He wondered what Harrietta would have done if he had acquiesced and pulled out his cock. Would she indeed have wrapped her lips about him? Of course. He had never known Harrietta to back down from anything. Had she ever taken a cock into her mouth and down her throat? He felt a sense of jealousy that he might not be her first, that her delectable mouth was not a virginal gateway. He wondered how she would have taken his cock. Imagined his cock thrusting down her throat, her hair falling in unruly curls about her face. Imagined her eyes looking up at him with the sort of worship he had glimpsed when she looked at Harold.

Damn it all to hell, Vale cursed as he ascended the steps to Penelope's balcony.

The proprietress was reclined on her settee, lounging like Dionysus, wearing a shift fashioned in the style of ancient Greece. A young maid knelt at one end of the settee, massaging her feet. A cad stood behind the maid, kneading her breasts.

"Troubles with your wi—your submissive?" Penelope asked as she eyed him through her quizzing glass.

"I've no wish to discuss it," Vale answered, sitting down and helping himself to a glass of brandy, which he threw back with much needed speed.

"Then why have you come here?" She groaned as the maid covered a toe with her mouth.

"To quench my thirst."

He poured himself another glass. Penelope raised an eyebrow.

"She is being punished at the moment," he elucidated.

"Ah. You have not frightened her away yet."

"That is my goal by the end of the evening."

But he was finding his resolve waning. Half of him wanted her to fail, knew she would fail his first test. But part of him wanted her to succeed. Wanted the clamps and the bondage to arouse her. Wanted her to enjoy all that he was doing to her.

The young man was fucking the maid, who continued to suck on Penelope's toes as a cock was buried in her from behind. Vale watched them, his cock beginning to stiffen once more. He rubbed himself through his breeches but then rose to his feet. Harrietta's neck would be sore. The ropes digging into her flesh now. Straightening the mask on his face, he went back downstairs.

The sight of her trussed up in ropes, struggling against her bonds, her legs spread to reveal her womanhood, made his stomach clench. Taking in a deep breath, he closed his eyes and collected himself. Resolve. Strength. Patience. He had never wanted for these qualities in the *Cavern* before.

Picking up his crop, he slapped her across the arse. "Be still."

Methodically, he undid her bonds, then bent her body over the back of the chair. He secured her wrists to a pair of chains on the ground. Then did the same for her ankles. Walking over to the table of accoutrements, he opened another box and pulled out a string of beads. The beads ranged from small to large. He grabbed a small decanter containing an oily element and dipped his fingers into it. Standing behind her, he slid his finger along her nether hole.

Harrietta gasped. "What—what is it you are doing, my lord?"

"Lubricating your arse, *ma petite.*"

He could see the tenseness in her body, but he continued to rub the oil around her puckered hole.

"For what purpose, my lord?" she asked nervously.

"You will soon see."

"I do not think that I like…I would rather you stop, my lord."

He dipped the tip of his forefinger into her arsehole. She inhaled sharply. He waited a moment before pushing his finger further inside.

"No! Stop!" she protested.

"Do you wish to end this?"

Silence. His heard pounded in his chest as he waited for the answer. What was the answer that he hoped for?

She did not respond, so he smacked her left butt cheek twice for her defiance, then pushed the rest of his finger inside. The sound from her mouth was a mix of grunting and shrieking, if that were possible. He rotated his finger inside of her. God, but she was tight. Amazingly tight. It was undoubtedly a virgin arse he had has finger buried inside. He could feel the walls of her rectum pushing against his finger, trying to oust the invader.

"You may put an end to this at any time," he reminded her, and decided at that moment that he hoped she would for his cock was straining painfully against his breeches.

"I hate you, my lord," she mumbled.

"How you feel about me has no bearing," he replied, removing his finger. He went to reach for the beads, coated them in the lubricant, and inserted the smallest of the beads into her rectum.

"We used to apply butter before we found this lubricant," he explained and pushed the second bead into her. "The butter was far too untidy."

Her body twitched in protest. Her head was bent down, and he could not see her face. Were her eyes shut? Would they hold tears? Or would she stare daggers at him if she could?

She would be staring daggers at him, he concluded. He was glad he could not see her eyes.

"*Uuugh*," she groaned when the fourth bead was pressed into her.

"Relax and it shall go more easily," he advised.

He inserted the final bead, wiped his hands, and shoved two fingers into her moist quim. He attempted to feel for the beads from there, which only made her more aware of her fully stuffed arse. Turning his hand palm down, he thumbed her clitoris. At first the discomfort of the beads was clearing paramount, but gradually, the sensations brought about his hand was gaining the upperhand. He stared at her nicely rounded rump, wishing it was his own cock and not the beads that was buried in her.

She began moaning. Pleasure moans. He continued his caresses until her quickening cries indicated she was nearing her climax. He stopped abruptly and stepped away.

"No!" she panted.

"What is it, *ma petite?*"

"Please, my lord, please touch me."

"Why?"

"That I may spend."

"Your spending is what prompted this punishment."

Ignoring her whimper, he went to retrieve the flogger.

𝄞

HER BREASTS WERE HANGING OVER the chair, and he swung the cat-o-nine tails up at them. She cried out, more in shock than pain. He struck at her breasts again. This time she wailed, the blow clearly smarting. He went to stand at her back and began playing with her clitoris once more. She quickly forgot about her punished breasts and turned her mind to the delicious strumming of her clit. The beads in her rectum had lost some of their edge. She had tried hard, flexing and straining, to push the object out of her. It was most unnatural, and she had meant it when she had said she hated him. Surely he could tell that she was not enjoying it, but he would make her submit to it or else have her banished from the *Cavern.*

But now, despite the fullness in her arse, she felt her climax rising in her. It was a testament to his skilled fingers. She had never received such delight before, not even at her own hand. He was the carnal equivalent of Mozart, she decided and briefly wondered if he played the harpsichord at all. With his digits stroking her clit and fondling her quim, he coaxed a heavy pressure to build between her legs. The pressure wanted release.

She groaned in frustration when he stopped his ministrations and instead whipped the ends of the flogger at her breasts again. The lashes were wide strips and felt like a dozen small hands slapping at her. Her nipples and breasts smarted, but the pain did not cut as deep as the crop for he had not applied his full strength. She did not think she could survive if he did.

"I consider this a light punishment," he told her as he dropped the flogger and drove three fingers into her quim while using his other hand to tug and rub her clit.

"Consider yourself fortunate," he continued. "I could have used a dildo in place of the beads. Or my cock. Or that of another. How would your little arse take it if I had a dozen men each take their turn with you? You wished for cock earlier. Perhaps I should grant your wish in triplicate. Your mouth wrapped about one, another in your quim, and the last in your arse."

Harrietta moaned at the thought. The thought of such a scene truly coming to pass frightened her, and yet it titillated her. Would his lordship command her to service other men? Or other women? Could she bring herself to pleasure another woman as she had seen the other night?

He ground his hands into her flesh more fiercely, more rapidly.

"Oh, yes!" she huffed. "Make me spend, my lord, make me spend!"

"You would like that, would you?"

"Yes, yes!"

She could feel her orgasm looming largely on the horizon for her. She braced herself for the most intense, the most exhilarating orgasm to come.

"No," he pronounced flatly as he stepped away.

It was as if the air had been sucked from her lungs. Squeezing her eyes shut, she tried to will her climax to come. But it would not happen.

He picked up the flogger and alternated between her breasts and her buttocks. It hurt, but not nearly as much as being left on the precipice of what would surely have been a magnificent orgasm. He could not have been more cruel had he offered a glass of water to someone wandering the desert and stripped it from them just as the first drop was to fall on parched lips. Harrietta pulled at her chains in frustration. She would do it herself if she could. Pleasure herself until she came. She needed the release. Craved it.

Time and time again he brought her to the edge, but always left her wanting. Her body felt fatigued by the aggravation, the futile exercise, the constant building and waning of tension. She wanted to scream and curse at him, but she did not want him to have the satisfaction of knowing that his torment was having its desired effect. After what seemed an eternity, he ceased his attentions, removed the beads in her anus, and released her wrists.

"I expect better if we should meet again," he told her, devoid of emotion, before dismissing her.

She could not look him in the eye, but she walked away without lowering her chin. Her body trembled inside, and outside it smarted. And for the first time, she wondered if his lordship might not have been right in his assessment of her. Perhaps she was not meant for Madame Botreaux's. She had no desire to repeat what happened tonight. And she hated 'his lordship.'

"My lady."

Turning, she saw the man in the red mask at her elbow.

"You seem to have dropped this," he said and held out her earring.

❧

S OMETHING ABOUT THE WAY THE man in the red mask had smiled sent shivers down Harrietta's spine. The way a devil might smile upon seeing the true nature of a person's soul.

"It was terrible. I loathed every minute of it," Harrietta later told Charlotte of her ordeal with his lordship, not wishing to dwell on the man with the red mask who had found her earring.

"Especially those…those dreadful beads," Harrietta added.

"What beads?" asked Charlotte as she added the finishing touches of paint to her canvas.

"The ones he—he placed in my *derriere*."

"Oh."

The response had such nonchalance that Harrietta wondered if her friend had heard her clearly? Harrietta studied Charlotte's painting of a naked man leaning against a fountain, holding his partially erect cock in his hand as he glanced to where the shadow of a woman stood. Charlotte added a dab of red hue to the flower petals at his feet.

"I am rather partial to those beads," Charlotte admitted as she set down her brush and went to pull a curtain over half the window to eliminate the glare on her work. The drawing room boasted high windows that admitted a good deal of the mid morning light.

"That surprises you," Charlotte noticed.

"I—it is hard for me to imagine that one can derive joy from such discomfort."

Charlotte shrugged her slender shoulders. "I think they may not suit every taste, but I do find anal stimulation extremely delightful. I adore having a cock in my derriere."

Stunned, Harrietta stared into the cup of tea that she had just picked up. How could Charlotte adore such a thing? True that the woman was more experienced, but…Harrietta considered the taboo aspect of that other opening. The forbidden nature—the sinfulness—of it might hold allure, yes. But the actual sensation? How was that delightful?

The clamps affixed to her nipples and her quim had not been comfortable, though they had disturbed her less. Perhaps the beads were meant to be no different. Certainly they had not prevented her from being aroused. Could they, if appreciated properly, enhance one's arousal?

"My greatest orgasm came from a man who penetrated me from behind," Charlotte answered, her eyes closed. She was practically purring.

Harrietta had been quite sure that she would not be returning to *Madame Botreaux's*, but now her curiosity had been culled again. *If we should meet again* had been his words. He had not expected she would return. Had he done what he did to discourage her from returning? To prove his initial assessment of her correct?

"They were a source of discomfort for me," Harrietta said, "but what made it worse was *him*. I do not like him."

"Is he not able to bring pleasure to your body?"

"It is not that."

Indeed not, Harrietta thought to herself. Her body seemed to dislodge its relationship with her mind when it came to *that*.

"There is a hauteur to him," Harrietta elucidated. "As if he knows better than I what is appropriate for me. He rather reminds me of Vale."

How odd but the indignation she felt toward his lordship rather resembled what she felt toward her husband.

"A troubling thought," Charlotte said in sympathy. "I think I shall pay a visit to *Madame Botreaux's* tonight with you."

Harrietta shook her head. "I had not thought to return and had accepted an invitation to attend a soiree hosted by Lady Falconet. I know you do not approve of them, but I find Alexandra and Lord Elroy exceptionally kind. And I owe Lord Elroy a small debt and mean to win back what I have lost to vingt-et-un. Have you played before?"

Charlotte narrowed her eyes. "A debt to Lord Elroy?"

"Oh, he would not have me repay it, but I insisted."

"You know that tongues will wag if you continue to spend such time with them. The animosity between the Elroys and Dunnesford is no secret."

"I know it as well. And Vale did attempt to forbid me to see them, though he has not mentioned it as of late. I think he recognizes that I know the reason for the acrimony and, thus, he could not in good conscience press the matter."

"Still, I would that you would take care in the presence of that pair, Hettie."

"Worry not, my dear. I am quite capable of handling myself, and though my marriage may be in name only, I have no wish to cast shame upon my husband."

❧

SITTING IN THE DARK, VALE waited for her in the carriage. She had a veil over her face—quite unnecessary for it was a moonless night— and hurried from the entrance of *Madame Botreaux's* into her carriage. She stepped into the carriage and sat down next to him. Only then did she realize that she was not alone. She attempted to scream, but Vale clapped his hands about her, covering her mouth.

"Hush, it is I, Charlotte."

She was struggling too frantically to recognize his voice. Pulling her to him, Vale pressed his mouth to her ear.

"Charlotte, it is Dunnesford."

Stopping, she sat up straight. He loosened his hold of her.

"Dunnesford?" she echoed and threw back her veil to look at him. "What are you—how did you? What are you doing here and hiding about in the dark like some common thief?"

Vale leaned back in the carriage. "I requested that you not take Harrietta to *Madame Botreaux's*."

Charlotte lifted her chin. "And I have not."

"But you facilitated her visits. It was your carriage that took her here."

Though there was no light, Vale was sure that Charlotte was flushing from her brow to her bosom.

"What an unkind cousin you are!"

But he was not moved. "Then you do not deny it."

"I…"

"It matters not. I know it to be your carriage and your driver."

Charlotte bristled. "Indeed?"

"I have had my footman following Harrietta for some time."

"You have been *spying* on your own wife? What a wretched thing to do."

She was attempting to shift the attention.

"It was for her safety," Vale explained. "Harrietta does not appreciate that the streets of London differ greatly from the town she grew up in. She is wont to be carefree and risks harm to her person."

"Which is precisely why I have chosen to assist her. For her safety."

"Do not play me for a fool, Charlotte."

"Well, had I not offered her the use of my carriage and driver, she would have found another means of arriving at *Madame Botreaux's*."

That was true enough. He folded his arms. "What has she told you thus far about *Madame Botreaux's*?"

"Why do you wish to know?"

"She is my wife."

"In name only. You yourself have said that she could take a paramour."

"And has she?"

"The men at *Madame Botreaux's* are not exactly paramours."

"What has she said?" Vale pressed again with a calm that veiled his eagerness.

"Only that she is unlikely to return."

Vale inhaled a breath of relief. He did not think he could repeat his performance of last night. He had been fully aware that Harrietta was not enjoying much of what was being done to her, but she had not uttered further protest after telling him she hated him. That she hated him did not trouble him so much, but when she left without a backward glance, the shimmer of tears in her eyes, he had not thought he could feel more wretched. He had wanted to bring her to spend, to grant her the orgasm that she had been denied.

Well, at the least, the effort had succeeded.

"She spoke in no unwavering terms?" he questioned for confirmation.

"She is not with me tonight," Charlotte replied, then hesitated.

"I know where she is," Vale supplied.

"I discouraged her association with the Elroys."

"As did I, but you may leave that concern to me. What I desire from you is that you not aid and abet her reckless ventures."

"There are no dangers here at *Madame Botreaux's*, merely the freedom for men and women to explore the carnal pleasures."

"Wrong. There is, for instance, the—"

He stopped himself for he had been about to reference Lovell Elroy. Charlotte waited patiently for him to finish his sentence, but he did not. Through the darkness, he felt her gaze pinned on him.

"You," she began. "*You are a patron of Madame Botreaux.*"

He could see the wheels turning in her mind and decided he should put an end to their *tete-a-tete*.

"That would be irrelevant if true," Vale said calmly and rose to step out of the carriage.

"I make no judgment of your person, Dunnesford," she hastened to add. "How could I when I myself have long been a patron here, but…is the Countess a patron as well?"

"Charlotte, I bid you good night."

He stepped out of the carriage and was about to close the door behind him but was stopped by her hand.

"If you knew that I had been abetting Hettie, why not confront me earlier?" she demanded. "And why your interest in what she had to say to me?"

He removed her hand from the door. She tried to pull away from him, but he held onto her, holding her gaze fixed in his.

"There will be no more dialogue with regards to *Madame Botreaux's*."

Only until her silence and lowered chin indicated that she understood him did he release her hand. He bid her good night and walked away.

CHAPTER THIRTEEN

L OVELL ELROY TURNED OVER HIS card to reveal an ace.
    "Of all the luck!" Harrietta huffed, shaking her head and tossing
her cards toward him. "That were the third ace with face pairing you
have had in less than twenty minutes!"

"Forgive me," Lovell replied. "What a terrible host I am to have caused
you to lose your last crown. Please allow me to extend a credit that you
may continue to play."

"While it may be true that I could play vingt-et-un all night, I think a
respite will do me well," Harrietta replied.

"Shall I play for you? Perhaps the Sonata in C minor?"

"Oh, yes! I enjoy the allegro but was never able to attain any satisfying
proficiency."

Lovell offered his arm and escorted her into the drawing room. Two
women were gossiping on the sofa, but the harpsichord stood at the other
end of the room from them. Lovell sat down and motioned for Harrietta
to sit next to him. She was enthralled with his skill, his long fingers glid-
ing effortlessly over the keys.

"This is one of my favorite pieces," he said as he began the adagio. "The
grace and tranquility of this movement is quite a variance with the other
movements. One would not think they were paired in the same sonata. It
is a surprising find, and I delight in surprises."

There was something odd in the way he looked at her when he spoke
that she wondered if there was a reference to something else? Not understanding what that would be, she replied, "I like the dramatic quality of
the molto allegro, but the changes from F minor to G minor to C minor
always gave me pause. You play it superbly, Lord Elroy."

"I knew from an early age that the harpsichord was an object I wished to *master.*"

"And you have done it. I wish I could play this sonata."

"I should be happy to teach it to you." He paused. "But we would want for a harpsichord or pianoforte."

"Oh, but there is one in my boudoir. Vale knew that I sometimes attempt to play…"

He had a wistful smile, and Harrietta realized her error.

"Pray, forgive me, I forgot…" She knit her brows.

"On that *note*…"

Harrietta chuckled.

"I must speak how obliged I am that you have chosen to befriend us," he continued, "given the circumstances with your husband. My sister is quite taken with you, but I am sure Dunnesford must disapprove of your association with us?"

"He does not concern himself overly much with me," she revealed, "and I prefer to choose my own friends."

"You are possessed of admirable courage, my lady. I know few women who would have such independence from their husbands."

"Well, Vale is almost like a brother to me, and sisters and brothers must have their disagreements."

"How true. Then, you would not need to seek permission from Dunnesford…"

She bristled at the thought of asking Vale for permission.

"Forgive me," Lovell added hastily. "It was inappropriate of me—"

"We have an agreeable arrangement, Vale and I. He does not attend me, nor I him."

Lord Elroy did not pursue the matter and proceeded with the final movement of the sonata.

"Bravo!" Harrietta clapped when he was done.

"You are too kind. But I think I will enjoy this sonata all the more if I could see you play it. If you think Dunnesford will not object, perhaps you could visit Alexandra and we could avail ourselves of this harpsichord."

He wanted to spend more time with her? she asked herself, studying him more closely. But there was only an innocent, almost bland, expression upon his handsome features. In the quiet corner where they sat, away from most prying eyes, he could easily have made love to her, but he had done nothing to suggest that he had any interest beyond friendship or generosity of spirit.

"But how kind of you, but I wonder that your time might not be better spent than amusing me?" she protested.

"Not at all. It is not often that one finds another with a shared enthusiasm for Mozart. I think, if you will forgive my intimacy, that you and I are kindred spirits. I am sure there is much more we have in common, Marchioness."

☾

"OH, YER GRACE! BE THIS where you live?" Adia exclaimed, looking out the carriage window at Grosvenor Square.

Vale had already attempted to explain that only Dukes were referred to as 'your Grace,' but Adia had yet to grasp the difference between a Marquess and a Duke. She only knew that she had never seen such a magnificent carriage or such stately horses.

"Does the King live here as well?" Adia asked Harrietta after they alighted from the carriage.

Harrietta smiled, but the innocent question made her cognizant of the luxuries they possessed and that Adia would never have.

They had tea and biscuits in the parlor. Adia was full of questions and could barely stop to chew her biscuit. Vale answered all the inquiries with great patience, and Harrietta was reminded of how he had been many years ago. Bethany and Jacqueline had been less close to Vale than she, but he had never been anything but kind to them. Harrietta had suspected Bethany harbored her own affections for the handsome Vale.

Watching him interacting with Adia, Harrietta began to wonder what sort of father Vale would prove. She had no doubt he would be more than competent. He was certainly capable of scolding and being stern when necessary, but also gentle and benevolent. It was hard to reconcile the part of the man she had loved years ago with a man who had entertained as many mistresses as he had. Perhaps in that respect he would not make a good father.

As they wandered in the garden next, Harrietta became sad with the thought of children. She expected she would have children for Dunnesford would need an heir, but she would have preferred a family that was more like her own. She saw in her own father and mother how a man and a woman could be devoted to one another. Not until she was much older did she realize that the marriage her father and mother enjoyed was rather rare—especially among the gentry of England.

"Would you care to pick some flowers to bring back to the asylum?" Harrietta asked, determined to shake away her despondency in the company of such an exuberant child.

"They are much too beautiful to be picked!" Adia gasped.

"I should like for you to have a token of our day together."

"Truly, yer ladyship? Then I will have one of these, may I?"

Harrietta nodded, and Adia plucked a pink carnation before skipping to the next bed of flowers. Vale stepped up next to Harrietta. She had been rather surprised that he had chosen their company when he could have excused himself once he had seen them safely arrived.

"I wonder that I did a good thing in inviting her here," Harrietta confessed. "The asylum will only appear more dismal after she has seen Dunnesford House."

"Perhaps," Vale responded, offering her his arm. "But do you not see the joy in her eyes? Would you deprive her of that?"

She smiled gratefully at her husband. "I dread that she should return to that asylum."

"Mr. Winters has done an admirable job with it. Many orphaned young girls are sent to workhouses or carted to Hoxton."

"And it is terrible! The thought sickens the soul."

He pressed her hand, and her heart ached for another reason. How she wished he could be a constant ogre that she would not feel so confused, indignant at him one day and tender toward him the next.

Plucking a rose that had come into a full and voluptuous bloom, he turned to her and pushed the stem into her hair above her right ear. Her heart began to pound at his nearness, at his fingers brushing her ear. His eyes scanned her face, and then seemed to settle on her mouth. She was rendered immobile by the sense of destiny looming between them. Did he mean to kiss her? Did she want him to when but seconds ago she wished him a tyrant?

"Are these not beautiful?" Adia asked breathlessly, holding up a bouquet of blues, pinks, and yellows.

The moment was gone, and Harrietta knew not whether she mourned its loss or was relieved. She had been, without a doubt, drawn to Vale at that moment. Had felt a yearning and a desire to touch him and to be touched. She did not want or need to have such feelings for him.

Perhaps a visit to *Madame Botreaux's* would clear her head.

CHAPTER FOURTEEN

VALE SURVEYED THE MEN AND women who had chosen to present that night at Madame Botreaux's. The presenters included a
redhead with freckles on her cheeks and arms, a plump one with cher-
ub-like cheeks, a beautiful brunette that he had seen once with Penelope,
and a slender woman with golden curls and a lovely figure. The first sel-
eection was his, but none of the women interested him. He considered
going home and wondered what Harrietta was doing at the moment.
Perhaps curled in the library with a book. She was more literary than
he for his reading of late comprised only the newspaper and resolutions
of Parliament. He imagined her reading *Fanny Hill*. Would she become
aroused as she followed the heroine on her adventures? Would she wish
to touch herself? Would she allow him to touch her?

Earlier in the evening, Penelope had urged him to press on. Her words,
to be exact, were "either go home and fuck your wife or find yourself a
new submissive."

He could not summon up the eagerness that once accompanied the
selection of a new submissive. The promise of a new body. A new scent.
A new voice. He found his mind constantly returning to Harrietta. There
was still so much left undone, so much more to explore. But Penelope
could be an acute woman. There was no sense in his being here at the
Cavern unless he would engage a new submissive. He stepped in front
of the plump one and looked her over from head to toe. She appeared
a little older than the others. She would do as well as any, he supposed.

"You," he said to her.

Then out of the corner of his eyes he saw a flash of red. Harrietta.

He felt relieved. Her return here meant he had not gone too far with
her. He should have been disappointed that his efforts had not succeeded,

but instead he felt…pleased. It would no longer be a dull evening.

"My lord?" the plump one prompted.

"Another night, perhaps," Vale replied and followed Harrietta to their alcove.

She was standing naked in her spot when he entered. He circled her, glad to see there was no bruising of her skin. His strikes rarely produced bruises, though he had once had a submissive who had the most delicate of skin and often turned grayish-purple to his consternation. A superficial mark was acceptable, but he derived no joy from the deep marring of a woman's body.

"You have returned for more, have you?" he inquired.

She stared straight ahead of her and said with the stoicism of a soldier, "Yes, my lord."

"Why?"

"I wish to determine if I might derive pleasure from my discomfort, my lord." She paused. "I am ready for you, my lord."

Was that a challenge? he wondered, studying her lifted chin.

"You are late," he told her. "Bend down and take a hold of your ankles."

She did as told. He smiled at the beautiful rump presented to him and brought his riding crop down upon one luscious cheek.

"One, my lord," she counted.

Pleased, he delivered several more blows in sharp succession. Her voice did not waiver as she shouted out the numbers. He rewarded her by sliding his hand between her legs and brushing his fingers along her quim. To his surprise, she made no sound. He pushed a finger into her slit, and her muscles flexed about his digit. They were stronger. She must have been using the balls.

"Your progress is commendable, *ma petite*," he praised, twisting his finger in her hot flesh. His groin tightened.

Stepping back, he lashed the crop against her arse, alternating cheeks, swiping his arm against the right buttock, then backhanding the other.

"Thank you, my lord," she said when he had finished, her rear a bright shade of red where the crop had fallen.

He detected a different defiance tonight. Less presumption. More confidence. He hesitated. He had no plan for her tonight.

"Stand," he directed. "Cross your wrists behind your back. My voice will be the rope that binds your hands. If you uncross them, you will be punished."

He liked her with her arms behind her for the position forced her bosom forward and her shoulders back. She had a graceful collarbone—one that he could run his tongue along. Her shoulders did not slope as dramatically as other women and were rather masculine in that aspect, but they would provide a nice leveraging handle were he ever in need of holding her. For example, if he were to bend her over the back of a chair and take her from behind, he could a put a hand on her shoulder and push her body further down onto his stiff erection.

His cock urged him to do just that. It was maddening, but if he took her, he would be making a cuckold of himself.

Instead, he pulled over the bench and sat down with legs akimbo. He pulled her down and sat her in front of him, her rear nestled against his crotch. Her scent filled his nostrils, and he breathed it in like he would the flowers in his garden. He liked the way she smelled. He remembered the absence of a strong perfume when he had kissed her for the very first time many years ago. Now she had the means to purchase the finest perfumes, and yet she chose not to douse herself in fragrance.

He gently grasped, then kneaded her shoulders, working his thumbs into her back to loosen the tension below her nape. His hands glided along her shoulders toward her neck and his fingers slid up to the base of her head. Her hair had been pinned atop her head, exposing the skin of her neck. As he caressed her, he sensed her eyelids closing, felt her body melting into him. His cock pressed against her buttock with hardened need, but for now, he wanted to savor the feel of her skin. As soft as silk.

Lowering his head, he pressed into the side of her throat. Her head tilted away to allow him more access. He let the heat of his breath caress her skin before he placed his lips slowly and deliberately on her neck as if he were about to suck nectar from a tree. She shivered at his touch. He tasted of her. To no surprise, she tasted divine. An opium that went to his head. He trailed his mouth down her neck. A low moan rumbled at the back of her throat.

His hands reached around her for her breasts, grasping an orb in each hand. They did not overflow his hands as many other women, but neither were they limp or overripe. He remembered noting that her areolas had a healthy pink hue. Under his palms, her nipples hardened. He rolled her nipples between his thumbs and forefingers and felt her arse wiggle against his crotch. He fondled her breasts tenderly at first, then with more aggression when her lower body began to squirm.

"Make me spend, my lord," she said with heavy breath.

It was not a plea, but a directive. She added,

"I dare you."

(

THOUGH SHE WAS NOT LONG in the world of *Madame Botreaux's*, Harrietta was sure that a submissive was not supposed to dare her lord and master. But she wanted both to exalt in his caresses and provide him a set-down. She could only imagine how self-satisfied he must have felt after their last encounter when she had not returned. She wanted to prove him wrong and prove to herself that she could master this game. She could reign in the impulses of her body.

There was silence. She was desperately curious to see his face. Did it possess a wry grin? Did it frown at her suggestion?

"Making you spend and allowing you to spend are two entirely different matters," he said at last.

"You need not worry of the latter, my lord," she replied. She harbored some doubts of herself, but she hoped her verbal boldness would permeate her confidence.

He snorted, "What *fierté* we have grown in the last few days."

Raising a hand to her head, he threaded his fingers through her hair and yanked her head down so that she could see him from the tops of her eyes.

"How long before you are a quivering puddle of pleasure, *ma petite?*" he asked in her ear.

His words ran down her spine and her heart accelerated. Damnation. Despite her determination, he still managed to send jolts through her body, and she wondered if perhaps she had done a foolish thing in challenging him. She closed her eyes and thought about Vale. Of the smile on Adia's face when he had offered his arm. Her "lord" would not be such a person. She wondered if the man held any values beyond the sensual.

With his free hand, he playfully slapped the underside of one breast, then pinched its nipple.

"A woman's body is a delight," he said as if engaged in a soliloquy. "There are so many ways to pleasure it."

He twisted the nipple until she gasped, and immediately a warm ache ignited in her quim. Letting go of her head, he grasped each side of her midsection. His grip conveyed such power.

"From the smallest and most oft ignored," he continued, nibbling on an earlobe, "to the large and obvious."

Again he slapped a breast. He grabbed both breasts once more and kneaded them into her chest. Her head had fallen against his shoulder when he had pulled on her hair, and she did not attempt to move it.

His hands dropped to her legs, and he pulled them apart.

"This organ here," he noted, flicking her clitoris with his finger, "is most intriguing as it seems to serve no purpose but that of sexual stimulation. It is a divine creation."

He circled the nub with his fingers.

"Have you ever been flogged here?" he asked.

She skipped a breath. Flogged? In such an intimate and sensitive place?

"I take it you did not like the clips I placed on your nipples the other night. What if I were to place one on this dainty piece of flesh?"

He pinched her clitoris, and suddenly, she felt nervous, which only heightened her senses. The thought of the excruciating pain that would accompany a clamp there made her all the more aware—and grateful—for the pleasing attention her clitoris was currently receiving at his hand.

While he continued to fondle her clitoris with one hand, he dropped his other hand to cradle a breast. With his mouth close enough to tongue her ear, he asked her in hushed tones, "How would you like your breasts bound?"

He traced his hand from the bottom of one breast to the top of the other, and whispered, "I could bind them gently with silken ropes or tightly with ropes of hemp."

He squeezed a breast, and she felt the ache in her quim throb with the pressure.

"Either way, they would protrude nicely for my mouth to devour them," he continued as he tugged at a nipple. "Have you ever had your breasts serviced properly?"

He had asked her a question, but she had lost herself in the image of his hot, firm mouth on her breasts. She could only imagine how wondrous it would feel if it resembled the slightest what she had felt when he had tongued her quim. Would he do that again?

She summoned her mind back and replied shakily, "No, my lord."

"A shame."

His other hand stroked her fast moistening slit. He slid two fingers into her. A ring—one set with a gem—bumped against her folds. She had never noticed a ring on him before, but then, her attentions were usually focused elsewhere.

"Shall we try the pleasure balls again?" he inquired. "Or let us pursue something different."

Reaching over to the table of accoutrements, he selected a dildo, which he slid against her wetness. The waves of delight rolled from her loins, through her abdomen, and down to her toes. Parting her nether lips with two fingers, he pushed the head of the dildo into her. She groaned, but the ache inside of her needed the pressure from within. He pushed the instrument further into her. The walls of her cunt grabbed the mock penis with greed.

With the dildo half lodged inside of her, he began to fondle her clitoris. Harrietta closed her eyes, opening them only occasionally to see the profile of his chin. She could do this, she told herself. She could contain and master her body. The ripples of pleasure were growing, a wave collecting strength, but she kept it at bay. He worked the rest of the dildo into her. Now it was buried inside of her to the hilt.

"And this be only the smallest one at my disposal," he commented.

The thought of a larger one alarmed her, but if there was too much pain, she was less likely to spend. She won either way. The hard part was trying to remember to keep her wrists together as if they were bound.

Slap.

Harrietta jumped at the touch of the crop on the inside of her right thigh. A few more inches to the left and he would have caught her where it would truly hurt. She wondered if that was where he was headed. Would he strike her quim? But he tapped his crop in the same spot while continuing his ministrations of her clit. The combination of fear and arousal amplified all that she was feeling. She clenched her stomach to prevent the rush of sensations from overpowering her.

Whack.

A stronger blow from the crop. The feel of the dildo expanding her cunt, the increasing aggression on her clit, the sense of vulnerability accented by the crop...she had never experienced such a deluge of sensation...she was close to spending.

She tried to twist her lower body slightly to free her clit from his constant molestation, if only for a few seconds of relief, but he struck her thigh harder for her attempt. His cock—a real cock—felt hard as stone against her, and she wondered briefly how it would feel to have two cocks inside of her.

As if reading her mind, he told her, "Move again and you will have the largest dildo up your arse. The whole cavern shall know your situation by the screaming that will ring through the rafters."

She groaned. She could spend in an instant. Her climax dangled tempt-ingly close. A devil in angel's guise. She gulped for breath as she began to writhe against his body, wishing she could sit immobile for the feel of him only excited her more. His leg alongside hers. His hard chest sup-porting her shoulders. His arms wrapped around her body. She fought the desire to fall over the precipice, but his assault on her sensations had no reprieve.

For what seemed an eternity she dangled on an edge, balanced as if on the point of a fulcrum. The worst agitation her body had ever experi-enced. Her fingers had dug deep grooves into her palm. She gasped for air and either she would no longer be able to breathe or she would finally relent and allow her orgasm to claim her like the inevitability of death.

And then the heavens appeared.

"Spend, *ma petite*. Spend."

Her body wrenched forward. A cry tore from the depths of her as her body shook uncontrollably. The dam had broken, and wave after glorious wave swept through the whole of her body, bringing tears to her eyes. The spasms nearly felled her from the bench, but he held onto her as he speared her orgasm to completion. She shuddered for a long time afterwards, a residual wave of pleasure shooting through her like the last flashes of lightening in a storm.

Her limp body lay against his chest. It was only until after her panting and the trembling in her limbs had subsided did she realize that he was holding her in his arms. The tender cradling of a lover more than a mas-ter. Gently, he withdrew the dildo from her.

"You did well, *ma petite*."

He continued to hold for some time. She felt too exhausted to exalt in her triumph. He stroked her hair with the comforting calm of a parent. The back of his knuckles grazed her jaw purposefully.

It felt like Vale's touch.

CHAPTER FIFTEEN

T HE WOMAN'S CHEEKS WERE TURNING red, making her round
face resemble that of a tomato, but Harrietta held firm.

"That Adia's presence should alleviate some of the work of the other
scullery maids does not trouble me," Harrietta informed Mrs. Stewart.
"I have reviewed the budget for the household servants and find there is
ample funds to retain Adia, who will not require a significant wage as we
will be providing her room and board, though I am determined that she
will earn what is fair. I will not take advantage of an orphan."

Harrietta felt slightly awkward sitting behind the writing desk of the
room that Vale had set up for her needs. Till now she had very little use
for the room save for one she wished to pen a letter to her family. She
thought of Harold issuing commands to his troops. She would do him
proud in her own little way.

"But I have no place to put her," Mrs. Stewart protested.

"Adia is a small child. I should be happy to survey the servants' quarters
with you to identify a suitable place for Adia."

Mrs. Stewart bristled and glanced at the doorway as if searching for a
means to escape a conversation she clearly did not relish. Relief lighted
her eyes when she saw the figure clad in embroidered silk.

Harrietta, too, looked to see her husband standing at the threshold. He
had not been present for breakfast, much to her disappointment for what
had transpired last night at Madame Botreaux's had only increased her
eagerness to see Vale this morning. As always, he looked impeccable. He
must have just returned home for his three-cornered hat was still upon
his head and he held his ivory-handled cane in hand.

"Pardon my intrusion," he said. "I meant only to apologize for my absence at breakfast this morning."

Harrietta smiled at him and was thrilled when he returned her smile with equal warmth, a warmth that made his eyes sparkle.

"Mrs. Stewart and I were discussing the addition of—" she began.

"It would be a waste to hire additional hands that would not be required," Mrs. Stewart addressed to the Marquess. "Especially hands that are untrained—"

"We could train Adia in little time," Harrietta defended. "She is a bright girl."

Mrs. Stewart turned imploringly to Vale, who was now leaning his back against the doorframe, his lids half-lowered as if bored.

"Why look to me?" he asked her. "It would seem the Marchioness has made her decision."

"But—"

"The reigns of this household are in her hands now, Mrs. Stewart, and I have no wish to clarify that point a second time."

Mrs. Stewart looked down at her folded hands. "I understand, my lord."

"Good."

"And I think a change of drapery in the library is due," Harrietta added. "I have examined a few bolts of fabric that I think will do nicely."

"Very well, my lady," Mrs. Stewart said.

"That is all."

With relief, Harrietta watched Mrs. Stewart. She would have preferred to be on good terms with the housekeeper, but absent that, she wanted her commands to be carried out. She had prepared herself for a long battle, had envisioned herself bearing down for a siege, and Vale's appearance had cut short that battle.

She gave him a grateful smile, then jumped to her feet. "Can we fetch Adia now?"

"Now?" he echoed.

"I know Mrs. Stewart will despise me for thrusting Adia into her hands so soon, but I think Adia will be thrilled!"

He hesitated, but she knew he was going to humor her.

"Come," she said, grabbing his hand. "I need only my hat and gloves and I shall be ready."

Returning his hat to his head, the Marquess allowed his wife to pull him back down the hall with the eagerness of a child about to visit the confectionery.

(₆

A S HARRIETTA PREDICTED, ADIA WAS more than pleased to leave the girls' asylum and have the opportunity to live in a grand house. She thanked her benefactors profusely the entire carriage ride form the asylum back to Dunnesford House. Vale left Adia with Harrietta, who was only too happy to take the girl to the haberdashery to see what was needed. Though he would have been pleased to be in the company of the two, he perceived he would only be in the way.

He therefore took himself to Pall Mall and that sanctuary for gentlemen, Brooks's. He came across William Wilberforce emerging from Boodle's across the street and inquired politely after the man's efforts to abolish the slave trade before entering Brooks's, where he seemed to draw the attention of the other patrons in the subtle manner of averted eyes, curious stares, and the occasional cough. Not in the mood for gambling, he took himself to the lounge. He considered collaring the next man who stared at him to ask what the devil was afoot when he came across Lance Duport.

"A word with you," his friend said without pause and directed him to a solitary sofa in the corner.

Vale sat down in an armchair and lazily propped his feet on a footstool. He flicked open his snuffbox and waited patiently for Lance to speak.

"The betting book has a new entry of late," Lance informed him.

Vale inhaled a pinch of snuff.

"I remarked to one patron that you would find it most amusing," Lance added.

"If that is the case, why do you look so dreadfully cross?" Vale asked his friend.

"Well…it concerns you."

"I gathered that much."

"And…your wife."

Vale paused briefly before closing his snuffbox. "Do you wish for me to read the bet myself?"

Lance sighed. "It is signed anonymous, but the bet is that your wife will make you a cuckold in less than a fortnight hence."

A servant approached to inquire if they desired refreshment. After requesting a claret, Vale turned to Lance.

"Is that all?"

"Is that all?" Lance repeated, confused.

"It has already been done."

"By whom?"

"By me."

Lance shook his head in disbelief. "Surely *you* did not write the bet?"

"I did not," Vale acknowledged. "It were possible this person is a patron of the *Cavern* and has somehow discovered Harrietta. Or some enemy of mine wishing to stir mischief. But, given all that I am, all that I have done, I could not censure Harrietta if she chose to pursue an affair."

"You astound me. I understand that, as a patron of *Madamee Botraeux's* your sensibilities would differ from that of a common man, but you would not be disturbed if your wife took a lover?"

Vale hesitated. At one time, he had thought such a prospect would not trouble him in the least. He was not bothered by what others thought of him as a cuckold, but now the thought of Harrietta with another man was not such a complacent one.

Images of her nestled against his body last night at the *Cavern* flashed before his eyes. The scent of her arousal filling the air about them. Her rutting body grinding against him. The length at which she quivered in his arms. His cock had been as hard as he could ever remember it being. How he had longed to plunge into the space that damn dildo had occupied. To feel the warmth of her womanhood. But her pleasure, her triumph had been paramount. And when she had succeeded, he could not have been more proud.

Who could have written the bet? Did it have to do with the *Cavern* or not at all? Perhaps someone who witnessed Harrietta with Lovell Elroy? Was it Lovell himself?

The thought made him fume. Of all the men in London, she could not choose that man.

And yet it had seemed she was not impartial to her own husband. That day Adia had come to visit. Harrietta had enjoyed his company. And her smile this morning. It had been more than that of a mere friend or a sister. Could she be so duplicitous as to entertain three different men—her husband, a master, and a lover? He found it difficult to fathom. Her venture into *Madame Botreaux's* was not about love. And if she found carnal fulfillment in the *Cavern*, why the need for a paramour?

"You would not call him out if you knew his identity?" Lance inquired.

"I would," Vale answered, "if he dared hurt Harrietta."

And he would not hesitate to blow the man's brains out, Vale concluded.

"You would allow an affair to continue otherwise?"

Vale put a hand to his temple. "If you recall, I had very little thoughts of matrimony. If I had desires to pursue a marriage of love and not convenience, I might not have considered offering the Countess my assistance. But if I am to continue my situation as regards the *Cavern*, it would only be fair to my wife that she be allowed her own…indiscretions."

"Is your marriage one of convenience?"

"My dear Lance, you are beginning to sound like Penelope. I liked you better when your aim was to have a cock stuffed up your arse."

"Mistake me not, I am all for a marriage that requires no dedication on your part, even if the chances of your buggering me again be slim, but I am a friend, Dunnesford. And I think…I wonder if the circumstances might not have changed?"

Vale stared at Lance. Lance did not have to speak the words. He did not have to even had he the courage to speak them. Vale knew what was unsaid.

He was in love with his wife.

CHAPTER SIXTEEN

ISABELLA WOULD BE AT THE Granview ball, and Vale decided it was just as good a place to have a word with the Countess as any. He stood in the vestibule wearing an ivory coat, satin waistcoat, and embroidered stockings. His hair was powdered and clubbed. As he waited for Harrietta, he paced the floor as he considered how Isabella would take what he had to say to her. He had a plan in place that she might continue her façade, but he knew she would be disappointed nonetheless for there was none that could provide the comfort, security and trust that he did.

"My lord."

Vale glanced toward the staircase and froze, hardly able to believe the vision descending the stairs was Harrietta. Her hair, which rose in a modest coiffure above her brow and descended to her shoulder in large ringlets, was unadorned by powder. He was glad she chose not to wear one of those large hats that were coming into vogue. She wore a slight touch of powder and rouge on her face. The wide square neckline of her décolletage showed off her collar impressively as well as the barest hint of the tops of her breasts. He commended himself on a grand choice of gowns and the mantua maker for her execution. Harrietta had long slender arms, made more dramatic by the tight sleeves and voluminous ruffles at the elbow. Her shoulders and the cut of her gown made her waist appear small enough for him to grasp with one hand. White satin shoes peeked from underneath the ornamented hem of her gown, and she carried an oriental fan.

"My dear," he greeted, extending a hand to assist her down the stairs.

"I can hardly breathe for fear my stays will unloosen or that my hair may tumble from its perch," she confessed.

"You need not worry for you will have swept the breaths of all who behold you."

She glanced at him. "Pray do not mock or patronize. I have never before been fixed in such a manner."

If only she knew the truth of what he felt. He wanted to preserve her as one would a porcelain doll while the devil in him wanted to tear every shred of the mountainous attire off her and take her. Instead he raised her hand to his lips.

"If I am insincere, may my soul be damned for an eternity," he said.

It was no easy task to ease her into the carriage, and during the ride to the Granviews, he regretted that her exacting wardrobe made her conversation stiff. But the longer moments of silence allowed him to stare at her. This was what people expected the Marchioness of Dunnesford to look like. Regal. Elegant. Only he knew the true Marchioness. A woman of wild abandon. A woman without pretention. A woman who drove him mad.

"I shan't be able to dance," Harrietta realized with alarm.

Good, he nearly blurted. He would have no qualms summoning the carriage early and taking her home to undress her. It might take hours to undo what three dressing maids had accomplished, but he would relish every second of it.

"You're staring," she told him. "Is it the patch? Has it come loose?"

Vale examined the little star that had been affixed near the corner of an eye. His gaze dropped to her mouth, and his own twitched with the desire to kiss her.

"Everything about you is perfection," he assured her.

She heaved a sigh. "I have never been to a ball of such grand scale. Will the Prince himself truly be in attendance?"

"Perhaps."

"Harold wouldn't believe me if I told him I had met His Royal Highness."

Vale thought of Harold with a smile. "I think he would have been more astounded to learn that we had married."

"But I think he would have been happy," she ventured with a shy glance.

She was right. Harold would have been. Which is precisely why Vale had married her. His debt had been repaid, if posthumously.

"And you, Harrietta, are *you* happy?" he asked her.

His question seemed to surprise her.

"I—as happy as one can be."

There were words she had left unsaid. Perhaps as happy as one can be *if not for...*

He took her gloved hand in his to compel her to look at him. "Know this: I wish for you to be happy, Harrietta. I never would have offered for your hand if I thought that it would have caused you misery."

She lowered her lashes too quickly for him to discern what was in her eyes.

"You have been kind to me, my lord. And to my family," she murmured.

"Is kindness all that you desire, *ma petite?*"

Her eyes widened and her brow furrowed. She seemed in deep thought before she turned the question back to him, "What more could I wish for?"

Much more, Harrietta. Instead he answered, "If you should desire anything, it would be my pleasure and privilege to provide it to you."

He lifted her hand, pushed back the lace edge of her glove, and pressed her naked wrist to his lips. It had an effect on her, he could tell, but whether her subsequent nervousness was because she relished his unexpected attentions or because she preferred he *not* make love to her was unclear. She kept her comments from thence to the ball, who else might be in attendance, how many members of the Royal family he had met, how envious her sisters would be if they could see her gown and how she would have to make them splendid gifts for their come-out so that they might not feel such disparities existed between them. He kept the *tete-a-tete* on light footing as well, inquiring about her day with Adia and what she had planned for the library, though the memory of her wrapped in the red drapes was beginning to raise his cock, so he had to quickly leave that last topic.

The Granview ball held little novelty for him, but it was completely new to Harrietta, and it amused him to see the event through her eyes. He kept her at his side as they greeted the other guests. And when she was introduced to one of the Princesses, Harrietta curtsied with such grace and smiled with such charm, that the Princess commended him on finding such a rare jewel for a wife. Lady Granview also offered her compliments when he finally relinquished Harrietta from his arm that she could speak to Charlotte. And as he watched Harrietta laughing and speaking with animation to his cousin, he suddenly felt he was the most fortunate of men.

《

" **W**HAT IS THIS I HEAR of a bet concerning Hettie in the books at Brooks's?" Charlotte asked him later in the evening as they observed Harrietta on the floor with Lord Granview for the minuet.

"It is a poor attempt at mischief," Vale replied. "I would not trouble myself with it."

He was looking at Harrietta through his quizzing glass, the other swirl of colorful figures merely a backdrop to her presence, but he could sense Charlotte staring at him as if attempting to unearth some deep, dark secret from him.

"She is lovely tonight, is she not?" Charlotte inquired, following his gaze. "I must admit that I had thought her rather awkward when I first met her, but she has adapted to London society in a remarkable way."

"She is a woman of surprising talents," Vale agreed.

"And dispositions?"

When he did not respond, Charlotte continued her baiting. "I understand her to be quite the apt pupil."

"Her dancing has been nearly flawless," Vale supplied. "I detected only one misstep during the contredance."

"And her skills elsewhere?"

"She is only mildly proficient at the harpsichord."

Charlotte bristled with impatience when he failed to supply the answer she desired.

"And in the boudoir?" she finally let fall.

He raised an eyebrow at her. "That would be beyond my knowledge, dear Charlotte."

"How irksome you are! You know quite well."

"I protest I do not," he said truthfully.

She frowned. "But how? You must. I *know you* to be a patron at *Madame Botreaux's*."

"And what does that have to do with the boudoir?"

She stamped her foot, then lowered her voice when her motion prompted glances in their direction.

"You are *he*," she hissed. "The one in the black and silver mask, are you not?"

"What amusing observations you voice tonight, Charlotte," he said placidly. "How many more do you plan to hazard before the night is over?"

"It only makes sense, but I take it Hettie knows nothing of your…your role at *Madame Botreaux's*?"

"Why should she know of anything that I have to do?"

"I take it whoever wrote that bet at Brooks's knows of Hettie's visits to the Cavern."

"Or perhaps they have merely to see her with Lord Elroy," he said wryly as he observed Lovell making a leg to Harrietta for the cotillion. "I think I had best assert my spousal privileges where her dancing is concerned."

"Strange that you have taken such an interest in dancing when you used to find it rather a dull activity," Charlotte observed archly.

He bowed to her. "I, too, have many surprising…dispositions."

But when he went to claim Harrietta for the next dance, she professed to needing a rest and some cool air. He led her out into the gardens and found her a seat on a stone bench sculpted like a Corinthian column and tucked behind some shrubbery. He went to procure for her a glass of lemonade, which she downed without removing the glass from her lips.

"These are the most wretched shoes for dancing," she explained as she removed them.

"But exceptionally pretty," he offered, thinking that all those who had complimented her poise tonight might consider her differently if they saw her in her stocking clad feet.

"Allow me," he said, reaching for one foot and placing it on his lap. He proceeded to massage the arch of the foot through the embroidered silk.

"Ohhhh."

It was a moan that was quite familiar to him. He was glad the length of his waistcoat would cover the bulge that was forming at his crotch.

"Do you think it would be strange if I went without shoes the rest of the evening?" she asked.

Vale smiled. "It might be considered eccentric, but I never considered you one for convention."

Harrietta laughed. "Is that a compliment or a slight?"

"A compliment, m'lady. You may think me at home with these persons considered my peers, but I must say that I felt most at ease in the company of your brother and your family."

"Indeed? You did not find us dull?"

"Au contraire. You, Harrietta, are never dull."

He rubbed the pad of her foot where she would have experienced the most pressure.

"One could become…easily accustomed to such attentions," she murmured.

"Consider it a wifely right, among others."

"Others? Such as?"

"Such as…this."

With her foot still in his lap, he reached over and took her chin between his thumb and forefinger. He pulled her to him and claimed her mouth for his.

Her lashes flew upward, but only for an instant, before her mouth melted against his. She tasted of lemonade and perfection. The supple lips were the softest he had ever known. Softer, it seemed, than when he had first kissed her. The blood pounded in his groin as he moved his lips over hers, taking her mouth tenderly and patiently though what he wanted was to press his mouth against hers with the full force of his unsatiated lust.

What he found most rousing of all was that she was returning his kiss. He was leading the dance, but her lips followed willingly. She was bent quite far at the waist to reach him, but she did not once pull back. He was about to reach for her, to crush her body to his, when a voice rang out.

"Lady Dunnesford!"

It was their hostess, Lady Granview. Reluctantly, he released Harrietta from his mouth. Harrietta quickly slid her feet back into her shoes and wiped the rouge on her lips that he had mussed.

"Ah, Lady Dunnesford," Lady Granview said upon rounding the bush. "My husband said he saw you and Dunnesford come out this way."

She turned to Vale. "Might I borrow your lovely wife for a moment? My sister does love your sense of style and was wondering if you might not advise her?"

"You flatter me, my lady," Harrietta responded, "but I fear I would prove of little use."

"You are modest. In any event, she very much would like to make your acquaintance."

Harrietta glanced hesitantly at Vale. He wanted so much to refuse Lady Granview, but she was the hostess. He smiled encouragingly at his wife and allowed her to be led away by Lady Granview.

After taking several breaths to calm the pounding of his blood in his veins, Vale stood up. He went in search of Isabella. He found the Countess in the Granview library with her arms around Honora. The two of them had clearly just finished displaying their passions to one another. Honora rose upon Vale's entry and gathered herself to give him and the Countess privacy.

"I shall miss you dearly," Isabella said after he had explained his situation to her, "but I understand, of course."

He lifted her hand to his lips in gratitude.

"Your wife is a lucky woman," she added as her eyes brimmed with affection.

"I am the one lucky."

"If not for my Honora, I might find myself wishing to be your wife. Cest la vie, no? Another life, perhaps, then."

There was a knock at the door and Honora's voice could be heard from the other side.

"Isabella, your aunt is looking for you."

The Countess glanced at Vale. "Would you honor me with one last favor? Perhaps you could contrive to appear to have made love to me in here when you leave? Then I shall tell the world of the terrible row that we had and how you were determined never to see me again. Honora will comfort my broken heart, obviously."

"Your servant, Countess."

Before he stepped out of the library, Vale unloosened his cravat. The Countess blew him a kiss. He emerged from the room, feeling as if a new life awaited him.

CHAPTER SEVENTEEN

FIRST VALE EMERGED FROM THE room, straightening his neck-cloth. Then after a few minutes, the Countess emerged, her cheeks flushed, her hair in slight disarray. It was clear to anyone witnessing the two of them what had transpired betwixt them, and Harrietta's heart sank at the thought as she watched first one, then the other make their way down the hall. She did not understand him. How could he have kissed her, acted as if he were enthralled in her presence, but then make love to the Countess?

Their recent kiss had been no simple kiss. Granted, a kiss between them was no new event, but they had, except for the one in the garden prior to her come-out, been a friendly brush on the cheeks. An expression of friendship and brotherly affection. The one in her family's garden had been different, had left her unable to form coherent sentences afterwards, had left her indignant and stupid. But the one tonight had differed even from that one. She had felt his hunger, thought she discerned longing in the manner in which his mouth took hers, completely covering her lips, her tongue, the air between them.

And perhaps it was because for a short span of time, she entertained the hope that something might come of that kiss that she now felt such misery. Her heart had soared too high and her fall was worse for it.

Of course he could make love to two women. He once moved seamlessly from one mistress to another, she had been told. Had had two women simultaneously lift their skirts beneath him, or so she had heard. He was no different than 'my lord,' for whom sex was a pastime—a diversion no different perhaps than riding or hunting.

Irritated at herself for imagining that Vale could be the husband of her dreams, she made her way to the card room. Lady Falconet waved to her from near the back of the room, and Harrietta went to join her, prepared to bury her sorrow in a good round of vingt-et-un.

❂

"A THOUSAND POUNDS?!" CHARLOTTE EXCLAIMED. "Hush!" Harrietta implored as she looked around the corner to see that the two of them were alone in one of the anterooms surrounding the ballroom.

"It dismays me to ask you," Harrietta said, "but I know not where else to turn. It was the most wretched run of luck. I think Lord Elroy and Lady Falconet would not press me for it, but that Lady Falconet says that her banker, upon learning how much she had loaned to me, advised her to discharge all her debts. Apparently she has mortgaged all her property and can ill afford to lend money she does not have."

"How convenient," Charlotte snorted.

"It was my folly, and mine alone. I did not think that such luck could tarry for as long as it has. Lord Elroy was convinced of my progress."

"He was, was he?"

"Charlotte, please do not speak with such ill tenor of my friends. They have been naught but generous."

Charlotte pursed her lips. "I would that I had such money, and I would give it to you even though I loathe the idea of it being handed over to those two, but at best, I would have a hundred pounds. My assets do not provide much liquidity. Have you spoken to Vale?"

"I could not." Harrietta sank into a chair in defeat. "He thinks me a child at times, I am sure of it. And this will only prove his judgment of me."

"Well?"

Harrietta looked sharply at her friend, then sighed. "I have been irresponsible. Oh! I would that I had never come across this cursed game of vingt-et-un. It seemed simple to master, and the game is finished so quickly that I was down hundreds of pounds before I knew it!"

Seeing her friend's tortured expression, Charlotte went to place her arms around Harrietta. "You ought to speak to Vale. A thousand pounds is nothing to him."

"But for him to hand it over to the two people he despises beyond all others? And after he had warned me not to consort in their company?"

Harrietta shook her head. She was devastated with her husband at the moment, but she could not bring herself to humble him in such a manner. Not even if the Elroys had a legitimate reason for their antipathy. There had been times when she had begun to doubt the strength of what Lady Falconet had told her. Times when she saw nothing but a noble generosity in her husband's eyes. But now, feeling the weight of her own broken heart, she could see how Vale might have destroyed another.

"Perhaps I could secure a loan from a banker?" Harrietta realized, lifting her head. "I met a gentleman this evening who was in the banking business. Devil take it, what was his name? Adams. Addison. Or was it Anderson?"

"You cannot select a banker that Vale will know. You must be discreet."

"You're right, Charlotte. How fortunate I am to have you as a friend!"

"I would still counsel you to speak with Vale. I think he has more regard for you than you would believe."

"Ha! I mean no disrespect to you, Charlotte, but the only one who condescends to me more than Vale is 'his lordship' of the *Cavern!*"

Charlotte snapped to attention. "What think you of your master at *Madame Botreaux's?*"

The question surprised Harrietta, for the topic seemed frivolous compared to the predicament they had been discussing.

"He must think highly enough of you to continue," Charlotte noted. "He has parted ways with many women before and spent much less time with them than he has with you."

Harrietta pondered Charlotte's words.

"He must be taken with you," Charlotte supplied.

At first, Harrietta felt flattered that that might be the case, but it mattered little. 'His lordship' was not the one she wished for. But the man she desired would unlikely to ever be hers. And as much as her body responded to 'his lordship,' the potency of the kiss she had shared with Vale dwarfed anything she felt ere now. The surge she had felt in her body, if it had escaped, could have lighted the London sky. What a silly thing she was that she could be so swept away by one mere kiss.

"And you must enjoy him as well?" Charlotte asked with a wry smile. "For you did see him again after last we spoke?"

"Aye, and I expect I will continue to do so."

Why should I not? she asked herself. Although she had entered her marriage with little expectation, she had become muddled of late, and now at least she had regained her clarity. A love-match was not what her marriage was, and *Madame Botreaux's* provided an exciting divertissement to her matrimonial disappointment.

"I think 'his lordship' will be surprised by me, if only because he had set his expectations so low," Harrietta said with a small triumphant smile.

"And I think you may be surprised by him as well, Hettie. A great deal surprised."

Ɔ

AFTER SPEAKING WITH CHARLOTTE, HARRIETTA devised a plan for repaying her debt to Lady Falconet, but she never had the chance to proffer her idea. Lord Elroy had changed the landscape altogether.

"You no longer carry a debt to my sister," Elroy informed her after she had returned to the card room in search of Alexandra. "I have acquired my sister's loans."

At first Harrietta was elated. She was happy that Alexandra was no longer in a precarious financial situation, but then Elroy pulled her to a quiet corner and there was a gleam in his eyes that she had never seen before—not in him, though her memory whispered of a place where she had seen such a gleam. A dark place. And not so long ago.

"Your debt is now due entirely to me."

She had not used her fan all night, but suddenly she felt the need to hide behind it. Collecting herself as her hand fluttered her shield to and fro, she inquired, "And what is the sum that I owe?"

"I believe the total to be no less than two thousand pounds."

She paled. She had not realized it would have added to that much, but alas, money had never been her strong suit, having never had much to concern herself with. The allowance she received from Vale was quite a new thing for her.

"I intend to pay it in full," she declared, "only I have not that much upon me at the moment."

Lovell laughed. "Of course not. I did not expect you to carry such a sum, but have you no accounts where such money has been saved?"

"I am only recently married and mine own family has very little."

"Perhaps your husband could be pressed upon—"

"No! Do not speak of it to Vale. This is my responsibility."

Lovell nodded, then leaned in toward her close enough for her to feel his breath. She wondered that he dared such intimacy in such a public place as the card room.

"There is one condition under which I would consider wiping off the debts," he propositioned.

She felt her pulse quicken. Did she want to learn what that condition might be? Of course she did, and yet there was something in his tone that made her wary of what he might say next.

"You have, my dear Marchioness, certain proclivities that interest me."

Harrietta smiled as if they were having a casual *tete-a-tete* should anyone glance in their direction and wonder what would preoccupy the two of them in quiet conversation.

"Proclivities?" she echoed.

"Yes. You see, I, too, am a patron of *Madame Botreaux's.*"

Her heart stopped. Her fan stopped. She blinked, then began fanning herself with greater speed and force. Her voice nearly cracked when she spoke.

"Madame whom?"

One corner of Lovell's mouth curled, and he stared into her eyes with such penetration that she knew it would do no good to pretend falsehoods with him.

"Come, come," he said, "you need not be ashamed. It is a fine establishment. I have been a patron of hers for many years."

She felt a little relieved, except...

"And this condition you speak of?"

"Ah, yes. You are quick to the point. I like that about you, Hettie."

She started at the familiar use of her name. Though Alexandra had called her by that, Lovell had, until now, been most proper with her.

"I would be willing to erase all two thousand pounds that you owe me if you gave yourself wholly to me for a sennight."

CHAPTER EIGHTEEN

C OULD HE HAVE BEEN MISTAKEN about the kiss? Vale wondered
as he glanced at his wife, seated as far from him in the carriage as
possible and absorbed in thought. He had been convinced that she had
returned his kiss, but she had been distant from him the rest of the evening. Had he offended her? Repulsed her? Studying her furrowed brows,
he would have given a grand sum to know what thoughts occupied her
at present.

"How fare your feet?" he asked her. "We ought procure for you a pair
of shoes that would be less villainous upon your feet."

That perked her interest.

"Yes," she responded. "And I—I had thought a new bonnet perhaps for
riding. I saw a divine style in *The Ladies Magazine*. And I should like to
surprise my mama and my sisters with new bonnets as well when they
come to visit. And…well, I should like a larger sum for my allowance."

He noticed she was fingering her fan nervously.

"But of course. How much more should you desire?"

"Two thousand pounds."

He raised a brow.

"That would buy more than bonnets, my dear."

"Well, entertaining myself has been more expensive than I thought. I
do love to play cards, and I should loathe to borrow from mine friends."

She lowered her eyes, and he could not read her expression. Only
sensed that something was amiss. He had had his share of mistresses who
cost a pretty penny in the baubles they desired, the houses they kept, and
the gowns they wore but a few times before they determined they had
to have a more current fashion. Harrietta had never struck him as one of

those women.

"There is naught I can deny my wife," he said. "I will pay whatever bills you desire and increase your allowance by two hundred pounds that you may amuse yourself at cards."

He gathered she was not entirely happy with his response, but she smiled and thanked him for his generosity. When they arrived at their home, Harrietta wished him a swift good night and could not whisk herself up the stairs to her boudoir fast enough.

"Harrietta," he called when she was halfway up the stairs.

She turned, reluctantly it seemed.

"I am quite fatigued by the evening," she told him before he could speak. "If you require my attention, perhaps it can wait until tomorrow?"

He looked into her eyes, desperate to unearth what had transpired in her that she should seem a different person to him.

"Of course, my dear," he said. "I bid you a good night."

She turned away from him and went up the stairs without a glance back.

&

"MY LADY HAD AN AGREEABLE evening at the ball?" Sarah inquired as she assisted the Marchioness with her evening toilette.

Harrietta managed a wan smile. She had little wish to discuss the particulars, though she could tell that Sarah wished to know.

"I've never seen men and women dressed so extraordinary," Harrietta relayed.

"I think there are none that could have looked as striking as my lady or his lordship."

The most beauteous pair would have been Aubrey and the Countess D'Alessio, Harrietta thought sadly.

"And the dinner was beyond anything I had ever attended," she said to change the subject, listing the delicious soups, the succulent meats, and heavenly sweets.

She managed enough gaiety during her undress, but when she was finally by herself, Harrietta lay across the covers of her bed, pulled a pillow to her chest, and cried. She had seen the hurt in his eyes before she had turned to ascend the stairs once more. She was glad that she had managed to hurt him in some small way, and yet it broke her heart. Indeed, she loved him too much to want to see him pained.

But what right had he to feel pain? He had the Countess. Not satisfied apparently with a mistress, he had wanted his wife as well?

But what right had she to feel angry at him when he had explained his situation before offering his hand? He had offered no illusions of what their marriage was to be.

And yet she had no wish to make him a cuckold. Not in such a public fashion.

Not with Lovell Elroy.

The anonymity of *Madame Botreaux's* was as far as she had been willing to go. But spending a sennight with Elroy at his estate in the country…

Vale would not forgive her.

But to be revealed to the world that she was a patron of *Madame Botreaux's*? That would bring more shame to Vale, surely. She had not thought Elroy capable of such a thing, but the look from his blue eyes— the strange light that shone from them and that made her blood run cold—convinced her that he would.

What a muddle she had made of her life! Harrietta scolded herself. Vale had been right to warn her not to consort with the Elroys. She wondered now if they had purposefully encouraged her card play, enabling her debts, and set a trap by which they could avenge themselves upon Vale. And she had become their unwitting pawn!

Harrietta pushed a fist into her pillow. What a dolt she was!

There had to be a way to escape her predicament. But she had only the shortest of time before Elroy's carriage would come for her on the morrow.

⟨6

GIVEN ALL THE DANCING HARRIETTA had done and the late hour at which they had returned, Vale was not surprised that his wife had not yet awakened though the hour was approaching noon. He had breakfast by himself, and never had such a meal in solitude felt so lonesome. He missed glancing across the table to see the glimmer in her eyes. Missed hearing the delight in her voice. The room seemed less bright, and even the eggs seemed less flavorful without her presence.

He read the paper with half a mind, then retired to his study. How many times had he approached her door and reached for the handle last night? He imagined her sleeping in her bed. Imagined stepping softly toward her. Perhaps he would reach for her, brush a sleeve past her shoulder to caress it. She would stir, a wistful sigh falling from her lips as if in dream. He would sit upon her bed, and lean in to kiss her neck, breathe in the scent of her skin. Would there be trace amounts of perfume left?

But he had not entered her chambers. How could he after the unfeeling statement she left him with last night? As if naught had transpired between them. As if they had not kissed for the first time as true husband and wife. It had left him rattled. He had never seen her look at him the way she had done last night. Part of him wanted to take the steps separating them and carry her to her chambers, willing or no. To force his attentions upon her and show how her husband, Vale Montressor Aubrey, could make her writhe and gasp in pleasure as much as 'his lordship' of *Madame Botreaux's*. The gentleman in him had prevailed, and he had watched her back receding into the hallway with a vulnerability he had rarely ever had to experience.

He considered revealing his identity to her when next she came to visit the *Cavern*. But would she be horrified? Furious? Would she forgive him his deception? Would he lose her?

Finding himself too restless to sit any longer, Vale took himself for a walk in the garden. Adia was in a flower bed pulling at the weeds. The little girl looked a world apart from the urchin at the asylum with her hair neatly braided and wound atop her head, a clean smock on her, and real shoes.

"G'mornin', yer Grace," she greeted with a broad smile.

"Mrs. Stewart has you at gardening?" he asked her, surprised.

Adia shook her little head. "She says but 'tis she got no time to be thinkin' of what fer me to do, so I come to find me own to do. I think I'll find some flowers for Mistress Hettie an' surprise her with the new blooms."

"I think she should like that very much. And you must find for yourself a flower or two." He sat down at a nearby bench to watch her.

"You be very kind, yer Grace. You and Mistress Hettie be like a king and queen from a fairy tale. I think often I must be in a dream and pinch myself often."

Vale smiled and plucked a leaf that had fallen onto the sleeve of his coat. Even on a day when he had no place that he had to be, he was dressed to perfection from his polished heels to the broach in his ruffled cravat. He wore a silk robe wrapped at the waist.

"How does a king choose his queen?" Adia asked.

Twisting the stem of the leaf between his thumb and forefinger, he contemplated the appropriate answer for Adia.

"At times, his choice helps form alliances between families or countries," he explained. "And at times...he listens to the dictates of his heart."

"Was that so betwixt you and Mistress Hettie?"

"Not initially," Vale confessed. There had been few children in his life save for Harold's sisters, and he knew not but how to tell the truth with them.

"But yer fond of her now?"

"Yes, Adia," he replied with a softness that surprised himself. "Very much."

Adia smiled. "An' she be fond of you, yer Grace."

"I hope." He cast aside the leaf and prepared to turn the topic to the weather.

"For sure, yer Grace. I did see her blush as crimson as blood after the flower you gives her."

He stared at the girl, but she had turned her attention back to the weeds as if she had not said anything of importance. Was it possible that a child could discern what he could not? He felt hope rising in his breast and was about to ask her more when Charlotte appeared.

"Oh," Charlotte let fall upon seeing him.

"It is a delight to see you as well, cousin," he said in reply to her obvious disappointment at seeing him.

"I thought I might find Hettie here," Charlotte said.

"She may still be in her chambers, having had a long night at the Granview ball."

"Her maidservant said not."

"She left," Adia spoke up. "I saw her with bonnet in hand."

Charlotte's frown fell further.

"Unaccompanied?" Vale asked.

Adia nodded.

Vale turned to Charlotte. "You have some matter of urgency with her?"

"I—I thought perhaps she would wish to take a stroll about the park with me."

"Adia dear, will you tend to the vase of flowers in my study? I believe they are wilting and require fresh water."

Adia was happy to be of use and trotted off to do his bidding. When the girl had left, Vale turned the full force of his gaze upon his cousin.

"You're a poor liar, Charlotte."

She pouted her lips defiantly, but under his hard stare, she relented. "You will not be unkind to her, Vale? Promise me? She is young and new to the ways of the city."

"Have I been...? Nevermind. I've no wish to be anything but kind to Harrietta."

Nonetheless, Charlotte did not answer. She wrung her hands in a manner that worried him.

"Is Harrietta in some trouble?"

"Yes. Only do not blame her. She meant no harm by it!"

"Charlotte, out with it," Vale said, feeling his muscles tense.

"It is that evil pair! That Alexandra woman and her detestable brother!"

He paled but waited for Charlotte to continue.

"Hettie had a run of ill luck at vingt-et-un, and they took advantage of her under the guise of friendship. They loaned her an exorbitant amount for which they now wish to collect upon."

He instantly recalled Harrietta's request for a larger allowance.

"I wish she had come to me with the matter."

"I did press upon her to do such a thing, but she felt too ashamed."

"How much is owed the Elroys?" he asked, though he suspected the amount.

"I thought it to be a thousand pounds, but...I received today a letter..."

Vale took the parchment she held out to him and scanned the contents.

> *My dearest Charlotte,*
>
> *I am undone! Lord Elroy has secured the amount I owe his sister. My debt, in the grand sum of two thousand pounds, lies entirely in his hands and he would have me pay it in full or reveal me as a patron of M.B.*
>
> *What a fool I have been! If I had only listened to Vale. But I have been stubborn and must now meet my Fate.*
>
> *I have no wish to burden you, my dear friend, but either I will find the sum due to Lord Elroy or his proposition to me last night, if I am unable to settle the debt, is to spend a sennight at his estate. I am shamed no matter what I do.*
>
> *I write only to tell you that I would not blame you or Vale if you should disdain me and cast me forever from your bosom. I never meant to bring shame upon my family or my friends, but I will have done it,*

mayhap by the time you read this letter. All this I write to you in confidence, dear Charlotte.

But if I may request a favor of our friendship one last time, it is that Vale learn of my infidelity from you. My only consolation is that while it may anger him that I am to go with Elroy, the pain lies only with his pride and not his heart. Indeed, I am now glad—grateful—that his heart belongs to the Countess!

I will forever treasure the affection and friendship you have shown me, and remain

Forever yours,

Hettie

"Is it not terrible?" Charlotte wailed. "What a monstrous person is Lord Elroy!"

The letter crinkled in Vale's grasp, his knuckles white with rage. He had read the letter through twice. And what angered him the most was the pain he imagined Harrietta to have felt in writing this.

"Our poor Hettie!" Charlotte bemoaned. "What are we to do?"

"We must reach Harrietta before Lovell lays a hand on her," Vale replied with a shiver.

Adia returned to announce that she had refreshed his vase and agreed the flowers were wilting and perhaps a new bouquet would do better?

"Yes, I wish for a large bouquet with a variety," Vale told her. "When did your mistress depart earlier?"

"Early in the mornin', yer Grace."

He swallowed an oath. She had several hours on them. Patting Adia on the head, he went to ring for Francis, who admitted he must not have been up at the time Harrietta stole from the house.

"My gloves and hat," he told Francis. "And pistols."

Charlotte's eyes widened as she watched Vale remove his robe, don a rich purple coat, and strap a sword into place.

"Do be careful, Vale!" she pleaded.

"You had best return home," he advised, "in the event you receive more notices from Harrietta."

Nodding, Charlotte turned to leave.

"You will reach her before she comes to harm?" she asked from the doorway.

"It is Lord Elroy who must need worry of harm," he assured her.

Within minutes Vale was astride his fastest mount and set off on the road that would take him to the Elroy estate. He hoped that Harrietta would be traveling by coach, which would require at least one rest or change of horses at a posting inn. He shuddered to think what Lovell might do with Harrietta.

He had no choice but to reach her in time.

CHAPTER NINETEEN

⊙⊙

THE POSTING INN WITH ITS sparse furnishings and unsettling pro-
prietor, a short balding man by the name of Ezra Miller who openly
leered at Harrietta despite her best attempts to appear disdainful to the
little man, made her further regret her decision to have an affair with
Elroy. She had no friends, she had realized as soon as she had stepped into
the carriage awaiting her in London. Neither Elroy's coachman nor footman seemed to take any interest in her. She had the sense their loyalty to
Elroy exceeded any chivalry they might feel toward her plight.

"Would my lady care for a glass of port?" cackled the innkeeper with a
smile that showed he had two gold teeth.

He had a bottle in hand and a dirty glass, which he set down on the
table before her. Harrietta would have preferred to take a stroll outside,
away from the dank air that clung inside the inn, but she worried if someone should by chance recognize her, though, admittedly, it would be an
unlikely chance. There were more attractive posting inns along this route
than this one.

Sitting down at a wooden table, she rallied herself not to cry, though
a red nose and swollen eyes might be enough to turn Elroy away. She
had put on her plainest gown, an uninspiring brown thing with minimal
lace edging, but realized afterwards that Lord Elroy would likely do as he
wished. Indeed, he need not touch her for there to be scandal.

The innkeeper approached her once more, and she gave him a haughty
look, hoping he would leave her alone. It failed.

"There be a gentleman asking for your company," he informed her
with another lascivious grin.

"It would not be proper for me to visit with him," Harrietta snapped.
"I have neither my abigail nor a chaperone with me."

"But that has not stopped my lady from traveling on her own."

"You impudent little thing," she exclaimed with the emphasis on *little*.

He bristled and glared at her. "He said you would come to him for you are acquainted. He awaits in a room upstairs."

Panic set in briefly. Who could it be? She hesitated, but rose from her chair. Scowling at the innkeeper, she allowed him to lead her up the dark stairwell. He opened a door to a room at the end of the hallway, snorting when she hesitated at the threshold.

"Come in," a voice said.

She stepped inside the room. It was no waiting room but a bedroom. A bed with threadbare sheets occupied the center. A dilapidated chair and table stood next to the bed. Upon the table lay a whip, a cane, and shackles. Her heart began to pound, and she turned quickly back to the threshold, but the innkeeper closed the door before she could protest.

"Well, my dear, I could not wait."

The voice gave her chills. It was Lord Elroy.

He emerged from the shadowy corner, dressed in his riding habit. If it were not for his sinister person, he could be deemed an attractive man. Instead, he appeared the very devil to her.

"The thought of bending you to my will was far too delectable," he continued, advancing toward her, riding crop in hand.

In the hands of 'his lordship,' the crop had been a sensual instrument. But with Elroy, it appeared a malicious tool.

He surveyed her as if he were a wolf assessing its dinner. Harrietta kept her eyes focused on the far wall. She had noticed no other patrons in the inn. If she were to scream, no one would hear. Those that did—the innkeeper and Elroy's men—would not care.

"Look at me," he commanded.

She refused. He grabbed her by the hair and yanked her head back. The force shook askew the bonnet that had been pinned to her hair.

"I gave you an order," he snarled.

She glanced at him from the corners of her eyes. Her heart was beating madly in her chest.

"I see that you are a tigress that needs taming," he noted. "How delightful."

He stepped back and smiled at her. "In less than an hour, I will have you wishing you had never crossed me."

"You are an odious man," Harrietta said. If he would torture her, she would not submit quietly. "I can see now why my husband detests you."

The corner of his mouth curled disdainfully. "He will detest me further when I am done with you. Dunnesford would do well to learn from me the proper way to master a woman. When we are done, you will come to prefer my masterly hand."

"I could never prefer you," Harrietta retorted. "You are not fit to hold Vale's riding crop for him."

Fire ignited his clear blue eyes and for a moment she thought he might strike her. Lifting her chin, she prepared herself for the blow.

"Come, Marchioness," he said instead. "We will be spending a lot of time together in the next few days. Let us be friends."

Grabbing her around the waist, he pulled her to him and crushed his mouth to hers. Harrietta pushed against him, but he held her in a tight vice until she clawed at him, her nails scraping along his cheek. He let her go with a howl and put a hand to his face. She ran for the door, but before she could wrench it open, he yanked her back in the room. Her arm jerked painfully in his grip. His other hand shot toward her neck.

"The sensation of not being able to replenish your lungs," he snarled as he tightened his fingers about her throat, "can be quite evocative. That penultimate breath, before darkness threatens to cloak you, when you are completely at the mercy of your master, when you know not if your next breath shall be your last, is most marvelous. For some women, it has been known to throw their bodies into euphoric spasms."

Harrietta was trying too hard to wrest his hand away from her to listen to what he said. Having no success in disengaging his hand from her throat, her lungs contracting in desperate need for air, she kicked him as hard as she could in the shin. He loosened his grasp enough for her to escape. She pulled open the door and tumbled down the stairs with Elroy but two steps behind her. He caught her as they stumbled into the main room of the inn where she had sat a few moments before. At first he had only her bonnet in hand, but the ribbon strained against her and came undone. But then he grabbed her by the arm.

"But how exciting of you, Marchioness," Elroy said with attempted nonchalance that failed to belie his anger, "to provide me a delicious chase."

Gasping at the harsh manner in which he wrenched one arm behind her—she thought her arm would disengage from her shoulder—she reached for the nearest object in reach. Grabbing the bottle of port that had been left on the table, she broke it against the side of his face. His cry of agony frightened her more than anything till now, but she did not chance to look back. Hurling past the bewildered Mr. Miller, she ran outside and looked around. The road was deserted.

Only the stable boy looked up in surprise. He had with him a mare that he had meant to unsaddle.

"Thank you for retrieving my horse," Harrietta said to him as she grabbed the horse by the mane and mounted the animal.

"But, tisn't yours, m'lady," the lad protested.

Ignoring him, Harrietta urged the horse down the road as fast as she could. Any moment she expected to hear the sound of Elroy or his hench-man behind her. And it was unlikely she would come across someone to help her, but she could not go back. That instinct for survival, older than mankind itself, told her that Elroy was far too dangerous to chance with.

❧

THEY HAD ALMOST BYPASSED THE decrepit posting inn but for the carriage outside. Reigning his horse, Vale dismounted and entered the inn, prepared to offer all the gold he had on him for any information about his wife.

What he did not expect to find was Lord Elroy, his cravat stained purple, his hair sodden on one side, and a glower on his face. Upon seeing Vale, Elroy leaped to his feet. Vale instantly drew his sword. Elroy responded in kind.

"Sir, I protest!" the innkeeper approached Vale.

"Stand aside, lest you wish to feel the tip of my rapier through your gut," Vale warned, his eyes fixed on Elroy.

A bright pink hue caught his gaze, and he looked down on the floor to see with horror a bonnet. Harrietta's bonnet.

"Your wife is a delightful little thing," Elroy told him, seeing the object of Vale's eye. "Much more playful than I expected."

Trying to conceal how much those words made his blood boil, Vale turned his gaze back to Elroy. "I will have your entrails greasing the floor if you laid a finger upon her."

At that moment, Francis and his other footman, Hans, entered the inn.

"Search the inn," Vale ordered them, his sword still pointed at Elroy.

"The Marchioness is gone. She proved a disappointment in the end," Elroy drawled.

Stilling the urge to spear the man, Vale commanded Hans to search the inn and Francis to search the area surrounding the inn. He looked at Elroy more closely, noticing the scratches upon his cheek. His heart lightened at the thought that perhaps Harrietta had fought Elroy. She had too much spirit to succumb so easily to the likes of Lovell.

"I think her weakness a perfect match for you," Elroy said.

"I should have a found a reason to disembowel you long 'ere now," Vale returned calmly, shedding his coat.

"To do so would have required more dominance than you possess," retorted Elroy as he removed his coat.

The two circled each other with swords *en garde*.

"And you derive yours from torturing creatures weaker than yourself. The only means to power for a *coward*."

A muscle rippled along Elroy's jaw. Pushing aside a chair in his path, he lunged toward Vale.

"Creatures like your wife, you mean?" he asked when Vale parried the thrust. "She did scream horribly at the touch of my whip. You have not trained her well."

Vale calmed the rage in his veins. Elroy meant to bait him such remarks. It was of no use to ponder the truth of these statements.

When Elroy received no response, he added, "But there is hope for her, I think, for she did become wet for me. Very wet."

His temper faltering, Vale attacked, but Elroy defended the line.

"Had I known her quim to be such a delight," Elroy said between hard breaths, "I would have seduced her earlier."

They exchanged attacks and parries, their skills fairly matched. They circled one another in the small confines, the innkeeper looking on with consternation but too afraid to intervene. After his one moment of weakness, Vale recovered and concentrated on evaluating the lines of attack preferred by his opponent. Elroy, after a few more attempts to taunt Vale into relinquishing his guard, found he needed to conserve his breath. Both were perspiring.

But Elroy could not resist a final jeer. "Do tell me if the child she conceives has the telltale eyes of an Elroy."

Vale took the opportunity to execute a feint, which Elroy did not detect and thereby allowed an opening. His sword sliced along Elroy's shoulder. Elroy grabbed his wound, but he did not surrender. Hatred burned in his eyes even as his face grew a shade paler.

"I hazard a coward like you, Elroy," Vale could not resist, "to be far too impotent to father a child."

Drawing a wide arc with his sword, he offered Elroy a chance at himself, but parried Elroy's line of attack. Over and over, he allowed Elroy to thrust and lunge at him but managed each time to keep his opponent at bay. Vale could tell the wound was having an effect on Elroy, whose stance had weakened substantially and whose steps lagged.

"I am satisfied that I had a taste of her," Elroy spat.

This time the provocation worked to Vale's advantage, who pressed all of his anger into a vigorous attack. Elroy tried to defend the attack, but he was being backed into a wall. His footing slipped, and Vale pounced. Elroy managed to scuff the top of Vale's hand before losing his blade. Having disengaged Elroy's sword and kicked it from reach, Vale pointed his own at the man's throat.

"I could spear you dead and have no misgivings," Vale told him.

"Then do it," Elroy grimaced. "Or are you too much a coward?"

"I will allow you to live that you may indulge in your disgrace. But you are never to set foot in the *Cavern* again. And if you or your sister should ever speak of or come near Harrietta, I will see you at dawn and dead within the hour."

Hans was waiting with linen. Vale wrapped his hand quickly and put on his coat. He was certain Elroy would no longer pose a threat. The man was a true coward beneath.

"Did you find her?" Vale asked Hans.

The man shook his head.

The duel was over, but Vale felt his heart tightening. There was to be no reprieve for him until he knew Harrietta to be safe.

CHAPTER TWENTY

SARAH ASKED NO QUESTIONS DESPITE the obvious pallor and tremble of her mistress. Harrietta was grateful to be home safe, but she could not be comforted.

"Where is his lordship?" she asked in a weakened voice after she had refreshed herself with a change of clothes—she had a mind to burn what she had worn lest she should be reminded of her horrid encounter with Lord Elroy.

"It is unclear," Sarah answered, offering a cup of tea, "but he left in some hurry with Hans and Francis."

Harrietta had wondered if he perhaps had news of the affair. Perhaps Charlotte had revealed the contents of her letter. Or perhaps Lord Elroy could not wait to trumpet his triumph to the world. But even if Vale knew nothing, she knew she had to tell him everything. She had no wish to keep such an ugly secret from him.

For hours she paced her chambers, waiting for the arrival of the Marquess. She could fabricate no appetite for dinner but did have a glass of sherry to calm her nerves.

And then she heard his steps. She knew not how she recognized the cadence and weight of his tread. Somewhere in her mind, she felt she had often listened for it.

A knock sounded at the door. Harrietta glanced up from her chair and voiced a tremulous, "Come in."

The door opened to reveal the Marquess. He had not changed attire, but Dunnesford was never known not to have handsome clothes. Even with his disheveled hair and dusty boots, he appeared regal and dashing.

There was a silent pause. Harrietta dropped her gaze.

"Harrietta," he said.

Her name sounded forced, and she wondered if fury choked him too much to speak.

"You are safe," he finished.

She rose to her feet, but promptly sank to her knees. Clasping her trembling hands together, she mumbled, "Forgive me...forgive me."

Again, silence. Then she heard him approach her. A hand was cupped under her chin and her face lifted upward. The motion caused a tear to slide from the corner of an eye.

"What is there to forgive, my dear?" he asked hoarsely as he searched her face.

Her chest closed in on her heart. The lack of anger in his tone pained her more. She thought for a moment that she preferred him to rant against her. Did he not know? Would she have to explain it all?

"There is much that needs forgiveness, my lord," Harrietta said, looking away. "I—I have not taken your advice as regards L-Lady Falconet and Lord Elroy. I have been reckless at cards, and owe them a grand sum. T-two thousand pounds. And..."

Having confessed the easier part, she took a breath before launching into the difficult part of her tale of woe.

"I have known for some time of your association with Alexandra and Lovell," Vale said softly.

She glanced in surprise at him.

"Not of your debt," he clarified, "but I knew you to engage in cards with them."

"You knew? But you did not stop me?" She thought of how easily he had acquiesced to raise her allowance to fund her card play.

"I have no wish to dictate your life, Harrietta. Nor," he added, "would I suspect that your headstrong ways would follow my dictates were I to issue them."

Her cheeks burned with the truth of his words. His gaze bore into her with an intensity she had never experienced before, and she could not meet his eyes. Instead, she looked past him and studied the pattern of the silk wallpaper as she said, "And perhaps you know the rest. I suspect you were out looking for me."

Trying to bring back his errant wife, Harrietta chided bitterly to herself.

"I was," he verified. "How is it you managed to return here without passing us on the road?"

"I suspected the nearest inn lay further from London," Harrietta explained. "I rode there and took a post-chaise back."

"Ah."

Vale seemed to struggle with something, a hand clenching, before coercing words through gritted teeth. "Did he lay a hand upon you?"

"I—"

It was no use to deny that she ever meant to have an affair with Elroy, though she thought now she would sooner die than to submit to the villain.

"He did but briefly before...before I kicked him," she murmured.

She heard him sigh with relief.

"And scratched him, I take it?"

She looked at him, blanching. "You—you met him?"

"I saw marks on one cheek and he nursed a wound on the other side of his head."

"Oh, that must have been the bottle of wine I hit him with."

He smiled, his eyes glimmering with amusement. "You will not find yourself disturbed by him again. Nor are you any longer indebted to him."

She frowned. If only she had found a way to address her problem on her own and not have to be saved by her husband!

"I cannot repay you the two thousand," she said, "but I would gladly have you suspend my allowance till that sum is met."

"That won't be necessary. Elroy received not a pence from me, but I made my case rather convincingly, I think."

She looked at him, curious that he still seemed to show little sign of anger. She could only imagine what the encounter would have been like between the two, but she did not doubt that Vale would have prevailed in his purpose.

"I have caused you such trouble with my foolishness," she said, "and perhaps rumors have already begun of me and Lord Elroy...and I am so sorry. I am truly sorry, Vale. I shall not fault you an you choose not to forgive me."

The tears pushed once more upon her eyes, and she bit back the sob that threatened to fly from her throat. He knelt in front of her and took her hands in his.

"It is I who must ask forgiveness," he said, and it seemed his voice quivered as much as hers. "Forgive me, Harrietta. I have been a poor and selfish husband."

"Forgive *you*, my lord?" she inquired, bewildered.

He pressed a hand of hers to his mouth. That was when she noticed his right hand was bound in linen marked by dark red spots.

"You've been hurt!" she remarked in alarm.

"'Tis nothing." When she looked at him skeptically, he added, "I had the aid of my sword to persuade Elroy of my point."

She paled. "You fought Lord Elroy?"

"It's time had come. I am surprised it had not happened ere now."

"Oh!"

"Harrietta! What is it?"

"I feel more miserable than ever to think—to think you had risked your life on my behalf."

"I would have done more, Harrietta. Easily. I adore you, Harrietta."

His gaze locked hers, and she could not look away. Of course he meant he loved her like a sister, because for so long he had been like another Harold to her.

But when he cupped the back of her head and brought her lips to meet his, he kissed her in a most *un*-brotherly manner. She was lost in its power, in the forceful way he consumed her mouth, his lips and tongue roved and absorbed every dip, every crease, every inch of her mouth. His hunger was palpable, as if he had denied his appetite for too long and could not feast enough of her. The air betwixt them grew hot with need and desire. And for a moment, nothing else mattered. Not the tears that were streaming down her, the brininess mingled on their lips. Not the discomfort in her neck from having her head pushed back against her shoulder blades. Nothing but the thrill of his touch. Of him. Her husband.

At last he released her mouth and leaned in to press his lips against her throat. She arched her body toward his, wanting every part of her to touch him, desiring him with every fiber of her being. He responded by clasping her closer and devouring her with his mouth. Pulling the sleeves of her gown past her shoulders, he trailed his mouth there, then back below her collarbone to tongue the crevice at the bottom of her neck. She clung to the lapels of his coat as if she would fall, though his sturdy grasp of her secured her body firmly in place.

His mouth traveled back to hers, and Harrietta kissed him back with all the longing and desperation that had been locked inside of her set free. Her hands circled around the back of his neck as their tongues collided as if dueling for position. For her, they could not kiss enough. She could go on for hours if not for the urgent ache coming to life between her legs. Her hands slid to his cravat and she tried to loosen it. She was unaccustomed to the task, but he assisted her without once taking his lips from hers.

Once his cravat was undone, he tore off the neckcloth and shed his coat. Wrapping an arm around her waist, he molded her body to his. She exalted in the hardness of his cock against her abdomen, and she felt his urgency as well. There was no tenderness, only a raw, maddening desire to have each other. He ripped through the pins on the back of her gown and pulled down the bodice and chemise underneath to reveal her breasts. Cupping one with his hand, he clamped his mouth down upon its nipple. Her quim throbbed in response. Over and over he tongued the hardened nub, suckled it, teased it until she called out his name. He fondled it between finger and thumb, then palmed and squeezed the entire breast.

Her impatience to have their bodies united grew with every caress, every exchange of breaths. She boldly reached her hand below his waist to feel his erection. He groaned as she rubbed his crotch. He grabbed her hand and removed it. Had she offended? Harrietta wondered. Was it inappropriate for her to have touched him? Did he not wish to couple with her?

He stilled the questions in her mind by rising and sweeping her into his arms. He deposited her onto her bed and covered her body with his. The weight of him atop her felt marvelous. Emboldened, she reached for the buttons on his breeches.

"Harrietta," he said, his eyes shining, "there is perhaps a more proper way to make love to one's wife for the first time."

"There is a proper way?" she replied in dismay.

"In truth, I confess a strong desire to ravish you."

"Then ravish me, Vale."

It was a command. Groaning, he fell to kissing her again while his hands roamed her body. She wanted to remove his shirt, but satisfied herself by pulling the hem of it from his breeches and thrusting her hands beneath to caress his chiseled chest. Her fingers grazed his hardened nipples. She then dropped her hands to unbutton his breeches and find his glorious cock. It was as hard as ivory and filled her hand with its warmth and thickness. She felt her wetness pooling between her legs.

"Are you sure you want this, Harrietta?" he asked as he ran his tongue along her jaw and licked her ear.

She had never wanted anything more. "Yes, Vale, yes."

He pulled up the layers of her gown and petticoat toward her waist and bared her legs. She had chosen not to put on her hosiery and kicked off her slippers. Her thighs parted for him, but he would not mate with her. Not yet. He lowered his head and blew upon her hot wetness. Then his tongue reached for her clitoris. Harrietta jumped, but her ache wanted so much to be tended to, and she soon settled into the rhythmic stroking of his tongue against her. How delicious it felt! How familiar! It was as if he knew her body, knew all her sensitive spots. She supposed it was because he was such a skilled lover.

Soon he had her panting and whimpering. Her muscles tightened and she clutched at the sheets below her. Her climax sent her limbs convulsing as his tongue pushed her higher until she knew not wither she came or went. Finally, he eased her down. His caressing became gentle. Closing her eyes, Harrietta allowed the glow to permeate her. She felt him kiss her on the thigh, her mons, her belly. She let out a sigh of satisfaction, but the hunger remained. The hunger to be filled by him.

❧

VALE STARED AT THE BLISS written across her countenance, feeling triumphant for it had been he and not her "lord" from the *Cavern* who had made her spend. It had taken all his resolve not to take her from the start, but he wanted her to spend, to climax over and over again, until she was delirious. Wanted her to know no equal to what she experienced with him.

She opened her eyes and smiled at him. A wondrous tenderness filled his heart, and the need to possess her increased. He put a hand to her waist, wishing the fabric of her gown could be easily torn away. He wanted to feel her flesh, wanted the softness of her skin against him, wanted to worship her body with his hands.

Curling a hand about his arm, she pulled him on top of her. As she gazed into his eyes, it seemed her own reflected stars. She was captivating. He had always known this. Only the tribulations and monotony of life had obscured that truth.

She lifted her hips to him, her desire clear. Quelling the urge to thrust into her immediately, he stroked her quim with his cock, sliding along her wetness, making her moan until she pulled at him with frustration. Only then did he push the head of his cock at her opening. He had to close his eyes at the heat and wetness that engulfed him when he entered her. Heaven help him, he could have easily spent in a minute.

But she had gasped and stiffened beneath him, so he took his time, kissing her until she wrapped a leg about him. A part of him wished he had shed his boots and breeches, but he had no patience. It seemed he had waited his lifetime for this, for her. Plunging deeper, he felt the muscles of her quim grasping him tightly, and he was reminded of the pleasure balls. With a smile to himself, he entwined his fingers in hers and raised her arms over her head. The position reminded him of when she had been suspended from one of the hooks at the *Cavern*.

Rocking his hips slowly, he moved in and out of her. She made the little sounds that all women make. Sounds that could be interpreted as either pain or pleasure—or both. He made a concerted effort to thrust at the angle that produced the most explosive reactions from her, and soon her hips were moving in rhythm to his. He quickened his pace for her. Soon the room filled with the sound of flesh slapping against flesh, of grunting and gasping, of the bed thudding against the wall.

Harrietta let out a cry that could have sent the servants rushing into her chambers. Her body jerked beneath his, awash in spasms, and he pushed himself hard and deep into her. His own orgasm bowled through him with the force of a charging stallion. Letting out his own roar, he bucked against her until his seed emptied itself into her. But to his surprise, the knot in his groin remained. His legs shook uncontrollably, and he gripped her wrists so hard she gasped. A second wave of semen shot from his cock, and only then did his body relax. He collapsed on top of her, his cock still pulsing inside of her. Eyes shut, he briefly wondered if he had been rendered blind by the intensity of it all.

He kissed her neck and inhaled the aroma of desire fulfilled. His heart felt overfull with emotions, and as he rolled his weight off of her and gathered her in his arms, he thought that he could not hold her tight enough. She settled willingly into his body, and all was right with the world.

C

SHE HAD NO WISH TO sever the moment, but she could not help but remember when last they had kissed and the pain that had followed. As beautiful as their lovemaking had been, she could not surrender herself fully.

"The Countess?" she found herself saying, as if reminding him of his duty to his mistress.

He pulled back abruptly, and she regretted in an instant that she had spoken. Why should she care about the Countess? Perhaps it was enough to share his love. She did not think it impossible for a human heart to love more than one at once.

"Harrietta, the Countess is nothing," he said, pained.

"I don't understand."

He let out a breath. "She was never my true mistress. It was but a ruse, a cover for her true affair with another woman."

"A ruse? All this time?"

He nodded. "And it is all at an end. I could not...I could not continue in it. How could I and be truthful to the woman I love?"

"The woman you love?" she croaked.

Lifting her chin, he pinned her with a look that needed no words. This time she could not prevent the sob. The tears flowed with fresh energy—tears of relief, tears of sadness for the unnecessary pain endured, tears of joy.

"Darling, what is it?" he asked in alarm.

She shook her head. "N-Naught but that I love you, too."

He crushed her in his embrace. He kissed the tears on her cheeks and claimed her mouth once more. She trembled against him, unable to fathom so much happiness.

"I think, Harrietta," he said into her hair, one hand protectively holding her head against his lips, "I have always loved you. My heart knew it, but my mind did not."

Harrietta groaned. "But I am a wretched wife! I have made a cuckold of you for surely word shall spread that I met Lord Elroy at the inn. And—"

"Perhaps, but it matters not. Let others think what they will. If I had not been such a wretched husband, mayhap none of this would have come to pass."

Not satisfied, she pressed her lips in a line. "I would that you would punish me instead of blessing me with your love."

A smile formed on his delectable mouth. "If it is punishment you seek, Marchioness, that can most assuredly be arranged."

CHAPTER TWENTY-ONE

ↁ

VALE FOLLOWED HARRIETTA AS SHE made her way to *Madame Botreaux's*. Upon her arrival, she wore her customary mask but did not undress before proceeding down into the Cavern. After he had shed his garments for a simple pair of breeches and his mask of silver and black, Vale walked out onto the balcony where Penelope and Lance were already lounging.

"Your wife has returned," Lance informed him.

"I know it," Vale said with a small smile.

Penelope studied him through her looking glass. "You seem less perturbed by it this evening."

"Ah, Penelope, I regret to inform you—nay, I have no regrets and am pleased to inform you that Lord Elroy will no longer be a patron of yours."

Penelope frowned but received the news better than he expected. "Ah, well, you may have been right about him."

"I was at Brooks's today," Lance informed him. "Simmons told me that it was Lord Elroy who wrote the bet about your becoming a cuckold."

"After tonight, he will have won his bet," Vale replied.

Anxious to attend to Harrietta, Vale did not elucidate and left Lance and Penelope to exchange quizzical glances with each other. He headed down into the Cavern toward the last corner alcove where Harrietta would be waiting.

She stood with her gaze trained to the back. She was wearing a caraco of cotton chintz with elbow-length sleeves, a flounced skirt, and a neck handkerchief—entirely too much clothing, Vale thought to himself. The only part of her that was bare beneath her neck were her forearms. That would change soon enough, he determined.

"You are late, ma petite," he told her.

"Yes, my lord," Harrietta acknowledged, her gaze as straight and direct as that of a soldier.

"Why are you clothed?"

"Henceforth, I will no longer be a patron of *Madame Botreaux's*, my lord."

"Why not?"

"I have my reasons, my lord. I came only to bid you adieu."

He circled around her while lightly tapping his crop against his outer thigh. "I think I can persuade you to stay."

Her gaze dropped in puzzlement, but only for a second. "I thought my lord preferred I did not?"

"I've changed my mind." Standing behind her, he brushed aside a tendril of her hair with his crop. "There is far more for you to explore here."

"Be that as it may, I am done, my lord."

She stepped away from him to take her leave, but he barred her path with his crop.

"I have not granted you permission to leave."

"I am no longer your submissive, my lord."

Vale smiled broadly at her. When she realized the contradiction of her words, she flushed.

"You have said that I am free to choose whether I stay or leave."

"But I have no desire for you to go."

Pressing her lips in a grim line, she pushed aside his crop, but he grabbed her by the arm and yanked her back into the alcove. Beneath the eyeholes of her mask, her eyes flared with indignation. Pinning her to his body with one arm, he circled his other hand to cup her chin. His cock was lengthening against his breeches. He wished there were not the layers of petticoats to separate her rump from resting alongside his thigh.

"Unhand me or I shall scream," she threatened.

"Here in the Cavern, your screams would only indicate the pleasure you are experiencing."

Realizing he was right, she began to struggle against him.

"My husband will see you hanged," she said.

"You would admit to him that you are a patron here?"

Her body sagged as she considered the prospect, and Vale wondered if he should reveal the truth of his identity at that moment, but he had no time to decide. Harrietta had picked up her foot and brought the heel of her shoe down on his foot. Vale cursed but quickly recovered his grasp of her before she slipped away. Grabbing her, he flung her back against the wall and pinned her in place with his body. He thought of how delicious her body had felt under his earlier that day.

"You did not think highly of your husband before," he whispered near her ear. "What makes you think he would come to your aid?"

"He has far too much honor and courage not to," she responded.

Vale felt his chest swell at the pride in her voice. "And are you so sure you wish to be rescued, *ma petite?*"

"Yes," she hissed as she renewed her efforts to free herself.

He bent his head toward hers. She jerked her face away as far as she could, but he ran his tongue along her neck, taking a playful mouthful of her earring and earlobe.

"Prove it."

❧

H ARRIETTA FELT HER HEART THROB. She had not expected this from his lordship, and she wished she had simply sent him a note—or not showed at all. But in their time together, she had felt a strange closeness to him, one that merited at least a goodbye in person. Had she made her second terrible mistake of the day?

"Prove it," her lordship repeated. "Prove that if I were to lift your skirts, I would not find you wet with desire?"

Oh dear, Harrietta thought, trying not to dwell on how his body felt pressed against her, as hard as the wall at her back. She had made love to her husband but a few hours ago. How could she find herself warming to another? Better to escape than to probe the answer to that question.

She struggled against him, but he held her firm. The exertion made her breaths full, and her bosom heaved into his chest. Her legs were trapped tightly between his and hampered by her own petticoats. Was that a sneer upon his lips?

"Admit that you want to be mine," he said. "Admit that no man can pleasure you as well as I. Certainly not your husband."

She looked him in the eye. "My husband fulfills me like no other. But if you think you can do better, you are welcome to prove it."

Ceasing her struggles, she watched him furrow his brow.

"Very well, *ma petite*," he accepted.

When he relaxed his body against hers and bent his head down to her décolletage, she picked up her foot and stomped him on his other foot.

He roared. *"Bloody hell."*

She ran past him, but he shot out an arm and caught a hold of her skirts, causing her to fall forward onto the ground.

"You will be the death of me," he murmured, grabbing her by the wrists and, reaching for a rope, bound them behind her back.

"Help me! Someone help!" Harrietta screamed as she kicked and flailed.

He ripped her neckerchief off and stuffed it into her mouth, covering her mouth with a hand to hold the fabric in place. Then he bent her over the table and straddled her legs. With his free hand he pulled up her skirts and threw them over her, baring her bottom.

"Now, my dear, what sort of punishment do you think you merit for having nearly broken a bone in each of my feet?" he asked, caressing her arse.

Harrietta could only groan. Bound as she was, she was at his mercy. There was naught she could do now but brace herself for the onslaught upon her body.

It began with a smack to her derriere. His hand circled around, and he buried his fingers into the hair at her mons, gently tugging. A finger slid towards her clitoris. She attempted to think about the most mundane matters—what she would wear to Vauxhall, where she might take Adia, what dishes she would request of the cook for dinner tomorrow—but her thoughts could not overcome the sensations pooling between her legs.

Several more blows fell on her buttocks. Her flesh was smarting, but the pain could not eclipse the dread she felt when he slid his hand between her legs and found her wet. Clamping her thighs together as tightly as she could made no difference. He forced his way to her cunnie and drove his fingers into her. Her traitorous body melted into his caresses, yearning for more. He pulled her hips higher, and she knew her pussy lips were in plain view to him. Her petticoats over her head blocked her view, but she sensed he was unbuttoning his breeches. Her body tensed in desire and dismay. She had no way to protest. She did not know that she would if she could.

The head of his cock stroked her slit. She moaned and inadvertently arched her arse higher to allow him better access to her quim. Then he was inside of her, and her legs threatened to buckle completely. Her wetness took him easily. Slowly his hips thrust at her arse. His cock filled her with delicious familiarity. As if it was meant to join with her quim. He took his time. Was it to prolong her defeat and prove his point?

She closed her eyes and bit down on the cloth in her mouth. She flexed the muscles of her cunnie and felt a surge of delight through her loins. He responded by thrusting deeper and harder, causing the pleasant agitation deep inside her to vibrate more intensely. Soon he was pounding her fast and furious. She spent in a whirl of sensations, body seizing against the table, her muffled cries drowned by his grunting.

He pulled her to her feet by her hair. With barely a moment to savor her orgasm, she was dragged to the center of the alcove. He removed the neckerchief from her mouth, and she took a much needed gulp of air. It had been suffocating under her dress. She stood in a daze, wondering what sort of wife she was to have spent at the hand of another man but hours after she had lain with her husband.

As if reading her mind, he said, "There is no shame in giving in to the natural urges of your body. It makes you no less moral, simply more human."

Odd that she should be reassured by his words, but perhaps because she wanted to believe him?

"You are clothed far too much," he noted. "Remove the caraco."

She obeyed but continued to wonder if she should be resisting. Dissatisfied with her pace, he stood in front of her, grabbed the lapels and ripped the garment open, sending buttons flying to the floor. After tossing the caraco, he stared down at her corset and grazed his knuckles over the swell of her bosom. Her heart hammered against her ribs as his languid caress made her cunnie throb.

"Turn around," he commanded.

She did as told, as if it was the most natural order of things for her to comply. She even felt a sense of comfort in his commands.

His firm hands began unlacing her petticoats and corset with practiced swiftness. The petticoats pooled at her feet, and then the corset. Her breasts relaxed from their artificial placement. He reached around her and pinched her nipples through her chemise, eliciting a shooting sensation that went from the tips of her breasts to her clitoris. Just as she was settling into the pleasurable pain of having her nipples roughly fondled, he jerked her chemise down her shoulders and pressed his mouth to the exposed skin.

Have mercy, she silently begged him. He molded his body to the back of her, and his erection pressed itself into the small of her back. Her wetness slid down her thighs, and she was sure he could sense her arousal intensifying.

Abruptly, he grabbed her chemise with both hands and ripped it from her. The garment tore down the middle, baring her breasts, her belly, her legs. She stood in naked glory before him. As she wondered how she would explain the torn chemise to her maid, his lordship walked over to the wall and took the leash and collar from its hook.

This is madness, she thought to herself. How could her heart belong entirely to one man, but her body be in love with the touch of two different men?

He clicked the collar in place about her neck. She followed him as he led her from their alcove and out onto the assembly floor. Leaving her to stand where she had stood to present on her first day at *Madame Botreaux's*, he went to ring the bell. Her pulse began to quicken as men and women began to filter into the common area. There must have been dozens of patrons—all with their gazes fixed upon her. She felt like a prized horse at an auction. One man sitting near the front grinned at her as he fondled his cock. A compulsion to flee filled her even as she felt an arousal mounting in her body.

His lordship stood behind her and whispered, "You asked for punishment. And now you shall receive it, *ma petit*."

The sound of his voice made her groan. Her mind began to clear itself of all thoughts save what was about to happen.

"My submissive wishes to taste the nectar of another's quim," he announced to the onlookers.

"I will offer my submissive," responded a man with a naked woman collared and kneeling at his feet.

His lordship nodded, and the other woman rose to her feet to stand next to Harrietta. Harrietta eyed the woman, a tall one with long dark hair and curved figure. *How am I to do this?* she wondered. She had never been with another woman before.

The woman had smooth alabaster skin, Harrietta observed. As she recalled the few dreams she had had of kissing or fondling another woman, she warmed to the idea of touching another woman.

"Lie down," he instructed the other subsmissive. Then he turned to Harrietta. "Kiss her."

Awkwardly at first but not wanting to embarrass her master, Harrietta knelt down, straddled the brunette and lowered her face. Their mouths touched. Harrietta noted how much softer and more supple the lips of the brunette's were in comparison to those of a man. It was a strange feeling kissing a woman, but not unpleasant. The brunette parted her mouth and Harrietta slipped her tongue into it dark moistness. Murmurs of approval sounded around them.

"Caress her breasts," his lordship ordered.

With both hands, Harrietta took hold of the fleshy orbs. She kneaded them, and the brunette purred. His lordship placed a boot on her back and pushed her body down into the brunette's. Harrietta could feel the points of the other woman's hardened nipples against her own breasts. She continued to dart her tongue in and out of the other woman's mouth while fondling the breasts below her.

"Suckle the teats."

Harrietta bent over the woman's large areolas and engulfed one nipple. The brunette moaned. Encouraged, Harrietta sucked harder as she continued to caress the other breast.

"Permission to touch her, my lord?" the brunette asked his lordship.

"Permission granted."

The brunette wound her fingers into Harrietta's hair and pressed Harrietta's face harder into the breasts until her nose was buried in the ample flesh. Fighting for a breath, Harrietta bit down on the nipple. The brunette squealed in delight and pulled at Harrietta's hair. Harrietta knew to cease her attentions would merit his lordship's anger, but she was not enjoying the current state of affairs. Every time she bit down harder, the woman would wrench her hair so fiercely Harrietta worried her mask would fly loose. There was naught to do but to succumb to the brunette's ministrations.

"Enough," his lordship said finally. "Attend to her quim."

The brunette wore a smug smile as she parted her thighs. Harrietta settled herself on all fours and positioned her face between the woman's legs. Praying that the woman would spend soon, Harrietta dove in. She licked the nub of flesh protruding from its hood. The bushel of hair at the woman's mons tickled her nose, but Harrietta lapped at the quim, which was fast becoming slippery with wetness.

"For arriving fully clothed, you will merit twenty lashes," his lordship told her.

The crop descended quickly onto her rump. Harrietta yelped into the other woman's cunnie.

"As you are occupied, I will have your other submissive count for you."

"One, my lord," the brunette said.

A second blow fell on her other buttock, but Harrietta remained on task.

"Two…three…four…"

Harrietta rolled her tongue over the clitoris, wishing the woman had trimmed her hairy mons. But she could not deny that her own body was responding quite favorably to what was happening. Her own cunnie ached for the same attention.

"Five…six..seven…six…"

Eight! The count is at eight!

But his lordship continued without a word. The brunette miscounted several times. Harrietta felt like biting her, but she refrained. She had been trained better.

Her arse smarted from the extra lashes. The brunette was grinding her cunnie into Harrietta's face. She could sense the woman's orgasm looming. The brunette clamped her thighs about Harrietta's ears, blocking out the sounds of the other patrons mating around them. Her mouth felt sore, but Harrietta wiggled her tongue into the brunette and finally the woman broke into spasms, knocking Harrietta's head about. Harrietta milked the orgasm until the cries and the tremors subsided. Her own cunnie throbbed, wanting the same.

"Well done," his lordship praised, but when she tried to rise to her feet, he pushed her back down onto her knees. "My turn."

The brunette was dismissed, and his lordship unbuttoned his breeches and pulled out his cock. The light in the Cavern was still dim, but she thought the cock was not unlike that of Vale's in shape and size. But before she could examine it further, he had pushed her face at his crotch and stuffed the whole of his erection into her mouth. She began to gag instantly.

"Relax, *ma petite*," he urged gently.

She complied, but it was no easy task taking in his length. She was still surprised that he had finally allowed her to take his cock in such a manner. With the flavor of the brunette still in her mouth, Harrietta tasted the faint saltiness of him. The wiry hairs of his crotch tickled her nose as well, but she minded it less. With his hand fisted into her hair, he guided her mouth up and down his shaft. She unfurled her tongue so that its whole surface could envelope him. Up and down she went, trying to suppress the reflex to gag every time his cock forced itself deeper into her throat.

His grunting came faster. His hips thrust into her face as he pushed her down harder onto his shaft. Then his thighs began to quiver, and she felt hot liquid filling her mouth. She fought to swallow as much as she could, but some of it spilled past her lips and trickled down her chin.

"An adequate effort for your first time," he praised as he wiped the drops from her chin with his thumb.

The distinctive saltiness of his seed remained in her mouth. She glanced around herself but half the patrons were engaged in their own lustful activities. She eyed a woman bounding up and down her master's cock with envy. Her own body trembled with agitation. She had serviced the damn brunette and his lordship. Surely she would merit a reward? In her current state of need, she would have no trouble spending before the entire Cavern. The shyness she thought she would experience before all these witnesses could not dull her desire. Indeed, the thought of spending before so many onlookers thrilled her now.

Helping her to her feet, his lordship walked Harrietta over to a beam that stretched above her head. He tied her wrists to the beam and locked her ankles to the shackles on the floor. But the shackles were a few feet behind the beam, forcing her to bend at the waist with legs akimbo. When he came to stand in front of her, she noticed that he had switched his crop for the nine-tails. She stared at his crotch. Regretfully, he had buttoned his breeches. The taste of him lingered in her mouth, and she hoped to have another opportunity at that cock of his.

What a shameless wanton she had become to crave two different cocks! She wondered if Vale would ever consider a visit to *Madame Botreaux's*. Even as she desired the cock of his lordship, she missed her husband. How thrilling it would be to face her husband in the manner she faced his lordship. To have Vale wielding the lash or the crop. But as she had no notion of whether or not Vale would be receptive to the practices of the Cavern, should she not cast aside her feelings of guilt and enjoy her final night here?

Braving a glance at his lordship, she saw him smile. A knowing smile—as if he read and understood her thoughts. She shivered.

Running the ribbons through his hand, he backhanded the lash against a breast.

"Ahhh!" Harrietta gasped.

His aim was amazing for he had landed all the ribbons on one breast. He did the same to her other orb.

Her cunnie clenched at the pleasurable pain. She kept her eyes to the ground to please him, both dreading and hoping that he would reward her if she should perform to his satisfaction. Another lash at her breasts had her writhing in her bonds. The spectators—some fondling themselves or fondling others—blurred before her.

"Would you consider sharing her quim?" a man from the crowd asked.

"No," his lordship replied to Harrietta's relief.

Aside from Vale and his lordship, she wanted no other man. His lordship delivered a few more blows to her quivering breasts. God, how she wished he would suck on her smarting nipples. Her wetness was sliding down her inner thigh for all to see. She strained for release. The lashing was not nearly as torturous as the pressure building inside of her, hot and agonizing, a kettle roiling with steam.

"Please, my lord…permission to speak?" she moaned in between lashes to her reddened orbs.

"Granted," he said.

"Please fuck me, my lord."

❧

VALE THOUGHT HE HAD NEVER heard such delicious words. He might have been jealous of himself once again, but knowing that, as her husband, he had her heart was enough. He would possess her body and soul soon enough.

She had performed well. Both his heart and his cock had swelled in pride. There would be time to refine her skill in taking his cock into her mouth, and he relished the prospect of teaching her. His cock perked once more at the sight of her naked and bound, arousing the men and women around them. The image of her between the legs of the other submissive would surely stay with him for some time. He wondered if he could ever have enough of Harrietta.

"Fuck me, my lord."

This was no longer a plea but a demand. And he was happy to oblige.

Stepping behind her, he unleashed his cock. They had made love earlier, sweet and affectionate, tender and adoring. As husband and wife. Now he would take her. Ravish her. Forceful and unforgiving. As master and submissive.

He reached around her and teased the swollen nub of flesh beneath her mons. She moaned in delight and rubbed herself into his palm. Sliding his hand further, he was amazed at the gush of wetness he met. Without a doubt, his Hetty was ripe for the picking. He smoothed her fluids over his anxious cock, then rammed himself into her.

She cried out in surprise. Though her wetness allowed his cock to glide into her cunnie with ease, she still felt delectably tight. Her rump curved nicely into his groin and he recalled how they had glowed red for him before. He savored how her hot damp flesh encased his equally hot member, how she flexed and pulsated about him. He could have shot his load then and there. But a practiced master would never allow himself such a luxury without seeing to the needs of his charge first.

Languidly, he withdrew from her, then shoved himself back in. She would have flown free of her bonds had they not been tightly secured. He proceeded to pound her flesh, thrusting his hips in rapid succession. The beam behind her creaked with the force of his motions. Her cries rose high and loud above the din of carnal activity among the other patrons. Her hair came undone. Grabbing her hips, he pushed himself deeper, his cock diving into her womb.

The muscles in his arse clenched tightly as he plunged relentlessly into her until an almost agonizing cry escaped her and her body shuddered violently against him. Her long awaited and well deserved orgasm had come. The boiling heat in his own body surged from deep in his abdomen and rushed up his cock, filling her with his seed. He let loose his own roar but continued to thrust into her, wanting to prolong her spending, wanting her to enjoy her release and feel fulfilled. His head spun and his legs trembled with the force of his own climax. It was as if a star had exploded inside of him.

As her tremors subsided, he finally staggered back and took in a deep breath. Many of the other patrons had spent or were on their way to spending as well—a chorus of desires being met. After pulling up his breeches, he released Harrietta from her bonds, and she collapsed into his arms. He held her tight. If he could have nothing else in the world but this, he would be satisfied. Fate had indeed been kind to him. He had married Harrietta to assuage his guilt—a self-serving motivation. And had found that which had been missing from his life.

But perhaps Fate had also been aware that he had loved Harrietta all this time. Had known from the day he met her, though she was but a babe, that she would be special to him. Only his title, his own prejudices and lack of purpose had obscured the truth.

Closing his eyes, Vale thanked Harold. He owed her brother twice. Once for saving his life. And now for providing him a new one. He wished he could tell Harold how much the young Delaney had blessed his life.

Vale picked Harrietta up in his arms and carried her back to their private alcove. Sitting down, he placed her on his lap and unhooked the collar from her, wondering if she would ever wear such a thing for him again. *Madam Botreaux's* would hold no interest for him now without her.

She placed a hand against his chest. "I should go."

He watched her as she rose to her feet and went to collect her clothing.

"Can your husband compare with that?" he asked, smugly folding his arms.

"He has no need to," she replied.

"Then you intend to return to him?"

"Most certainly. I will cherish my time here at *Madame Botreaux's* and the guidance you have been so kind to share with me, my lord. But it is my husband I long to be with. I desire him more than ever."

Gathering her items, she turned to leave.

He paused, his heart beaming. "Tell your husband that he is a fortunate man, Harrietta. I admit I shall miss the pleasure of seeing you again. Are you certain you will not visit us at *Madame Botreaux's*?"

"Not unless my husband..." She whirled around, the blood draining from her. "How do you know my name?"

His lips curled, but he ignored her question, saying instead. "Would you take with you a token of your time here?"

Retrieving his riding crop, he held it out to her. Harrietta stared at the object. He could see her mind reeling. Her gaze drifted from the crop to his hand, a thin strip of bandage wrapped about it. Her eyes widened.

Gasping, she looked at him, her stare penetrating the dim alcove, seeking the contours of his face. He had noticed that she had never tried to glimpse too much of him, perhaps for fear he would see too much of her. But recognition dawned in her eyes as they stared at his mouth, then trailed to his crotch. "It can't be!" she thought aloud with growing horror. Realizing there was only one way to be sure, she pulled her mask off and threw it aside.

He bowed his head. Reaching up, he untied his mask to reveal the face of her husband.

"All this time?" she cried. "It was you all this time?"

He spoke without the hoarseness he used to disguise his voice. "Forgive me, *ma petite*."

As if needing a place to sit, she looked around her, but all she saw was the bench where she had first spent for him.

"Good God," she moaned. "What must you have thought...? Oh! How could you...? Why did you...?"

"I grant you permission to be angry with me," he said.

"I don't need your permission!" she fired back. "I think I might think you an abominable wretch! I *do* think you an abominable wretch!"

He smiled and presented the riding crop once more. "Then you may have a privilege that no one has ever had here in the Cavern: permission to punish me."

She stared at the crop and hesitated. He could tell she wanted to be furious with him, but could not stay cross with him. He gave her a tantalizing smile. She took the crop.

"You will pay dearly for this," she told him.

He took her in his arms and gazed down at her with a warmth that made her heart leap into her eyes. "I hope for the rest of my life."

His mouth claimed hers. Commanding. Dominating. There would be no question, privilege or no, who the true master was. She sighed into the kiss. He felt a thrill beyond words as he held her. She was his now. All his. His wife. His marchioness to master.

EXCERPT FROM

CONQUERING THE COUNTESS

CHAPTER ONE

❦

"WHO *IS* SHE?" MARVELED PHINEAS Love, adjusting the silken mask he wore to better view the woman wielding the nine-tail. He wished Penelope, the proprietress of *Madame Botreaux's Cavern of Pleasures*, would add more lighting to the dim underground assembly hall where men and women gathered to indulge their prurient appetites. While he understood the darkness helped to conceal the identity of the patrons, it hindered one's ability to fully admire the form of one's part-ner—or partners.

"Lady Athena," supplied Lance Duport. A longtime patron and friend of Penelope Botreaux, Lance had ceased to wear a mask many years ago. He eyed Phineas through a quizzing glass. "My dear fellow, that is a bang-up cravat. Do you think your valet could teach mine?"

Phineas smiled. "You have changed little in the years, Duport."

"As have *you*," Lance responded.

Phineas leaned over the rail of the balcony to observe the patrons who had gathered on the main floor below to witness 'Lady Athena' and the two men chained to whipping posts on either side of her. Though she did not possess the sloping shoulders or slender arms admired by most, she was nonetheless a captivating figure—and for reasons beyond her strange costuming. Black leather boots, of the kind worn by men in the military but for the curvaceous Louis heels, encased her legs well past her knees. Her thin chemise fell over swelling hips, and Phineas believed that if a candle were held to it, the material would prove sheer enough to reveal her full and supple thighs. Her corset, an unusual black damask with gold floral embroidery, was loosely laced in the front, revealing the paleness of her breasts, two swollen mounds with nipples peering over the edge of the chemise. Phineas felt his cock tug at him as he drank in the scintillating curves of her body.

"How droll it is to have you back from your exile, Lord Barclay," commented Penelope, whose rounded figure gave evidence of her affinity for one too many glasses of port.

"Barclay is sufficient," Phineas replied, feeling his jaw tighten as he recalled the five years he had spent on the continent. Devil take it, he had never thought he would miss Yorkshire pudding, but he had.

"I have not had much in the way of an Adonis to feast my eyes upon— not since Vale. Alas, he has not graced our company for nigh on two years." She sighed wistfully. "He used to stand right where you are."

"The Marquess of Dunnesford?" Phineas inquired, turning around to face Penelope. "What induced him to take his leave?"

"He fell in love," Lance answered with a sigh to match Penelope's.

"Dunnesford? In love?" Phineas repeated, incredulous.

Penelope and Lance both nodded. "With his wife."

"The deuce." Phineas shook his head, wondering what other surprises lay in store with his return to England. He turned his attention back to Lady Athena, who alternated between her two submissives with the flow of a choreographed dance. Unfurling her lash, she struck the man behind her between the shoulders, then brought it down upon the buttocks of the man before her. Her strikes were strong and delivered with surprising litheness.

"How long has Lady Athena been a patron of yours?" he asked Penelope.

Penelope aimed her quizzing glass at the woman in question, then brought it back towards Phineas, her preferred subject.

"A twelvemonth perhaps," she replied. "I do not recall your having been so intrigued by a Mistress before."

"All manner of women intrigue me," Phineas responded with a rakish grin.

"You are incorrigible," Lance commented with a shake of his head. "Was it not your entanglement with a woman that forced you from England?"

Phineas remained quiet. He had no desire to revisit the past. Nor did he know or trust Duport well enough to divulge that his affair with a married woman played only a minor role.

"What does it matter?" Penelope admonished. "From what I heard the duel was more than fair. That Jonathan Weston was killed…"

Phineas turned around to see Penelope clearly wishing she could have swallowed her words. He crossed his arms over his chest. "Do you know this Lady Athena?"

She shook her head quickly. "I do not reveal the identity of my patrons, and Lady Athena has never indicated a desire to reveal herself. She does not tarry with any one man for long. I believe tonight she will seek yet another new submissive at the Presenting."

Lance added, "She is one that even you, my friend, will find difficult to conquer."

Phineas raised his brows. "My reputation as a lover must have diminished greatly in my absence."

"Your skills in that vein are of no use with her. She allows no one to bring her to climax."

"Odds fish." Phineas had never heard of such a thing. What was the purpose of coming to Madame Botreaux's if one could not attain that sublime euphoria? This Lady Athena was the most peculiar mistress. He looked over the balcony to see Lady Athena circling one of her submissives. Was it the boots that lent her stalking such an erotic quality?

"I can see your thoughts, Lord Barclay," Penelope said with a small grin. "I will lay you a wager that what you contemplate cannot be done."

Phineas unloosened his cravat with slow deliberation.

"Alas, a work of art gone in a moment," Lance murmured, but his dismay was easily replaced with a new interest as Phineas began to unbutton his shirt.

"Your stakes, madam?" Phineas asked of Penelope.

Both Penelope and Lance nearly drooled as the linen slid down his arms to reveal a chiseled chest.

"My—my word," Lance stammered. "Have you taken up pugilism?"

"I spent most of my time on the Continent in Italy, perfecting the art of the sword."

"*You*," Penelope pronounced. "I wish you to be mine for a full night."

"And if I can seduce the Lady Athena, what is my prize?"

"I must have a piece of this wager," Lance interjected.

Penelope smiled, envisioning her win already. "Name your price."

"Her name," Phineas answered. "I want to know who she really is."

Penelope glanced down in consideration, but after a brief hesitation, she lifted her chin. "I have witnessed Lady Athena for a year now. As delectable as you are, Barclay, she will not change her ways."

"You wound my pride, madam," Phineas replied, covering his heart in mock pain.

"You will have such time until she casts you aside and selects a new submissive." Penelope sidled up to him and tapped his chest with her quizzing glass. "At which time, you shall be mine, dear Barclay."

He captured her hand and brought it to his lips. "I adore a wager that knows no loss for me."

Penelope trembled at his touch and had to take step away from him to breathe.

"And myself," Lance reminded. "I should like to have you for a night as well."

Phineas bowed. Lance, among the finer looking men with his raven black hair and trim figure, would not prove to be the first man he had taken to bed, but he had foresworn men after the disastrous duel that forced his departure from England. However, if he successfully seduced the Lady Athena, Lance would not be a concern, and no woman had yet proven impervious to his charms. His conquests reflected all manner of women from a shy rector's daughter to a frosty matron who disapproved at first of his attentions upon her daughter, then became increasingly envious of her own progeny. Lady Athena possessed the one quality he needed: she was a woman.

Invigorated by the impending challenge, he descended the balcony and prepared himself for the Presenting.

*

GERTRUDE "GERTIE" FARRINGTON APPRAISED THE men and women in the Presenting, a ritual in which new guests and those wishing for a new partner—or partners—presented themselves for selection. She felt formidable in her new garments. Of particular pride were the boots she had designed herself. The mask she wore was cut from the same fabric as her corset. When first she had donned the name and character of Lady Athena a year ago, she had favored a gold mask. Now black was her preferred color.

Her favorite crop resting atop her shoulder at a smart angle, she strode down the line with the air of a general inspecting his troops. Senior patrons selected first, but many of them deferred their position to Lady Athena. Out of pity or respect, Gertie knew not. Nor did she care.

A pretty young redhead in line raised her hopeful eyes, but Gertie passed the woman by. On rare occasions, she had selected one of the fair sex for her submissive, but men spurred her vigor, her anger, in a way no woman could. Gertie eyed a slender young man, one who dutifully kept his eyes cast downward. A good submissive, most likely well-trained, but not willful enough for her. She did not want a man who groveled at her feet too adeptly.

And then her gaze met a pair of intense eyes behind a silver mask. In the dim lighting, she could not discern the color of the eyes, which seemed to capture what little light existed and reflected it back two-fold. They stared at her with unnerving intensity. Feeling as if she might drown in their pools, she pulled her gaze wider and contemplated the whole of the physiognomy. Though his mask covered half his face, the shadows suggested a striking appearance.

The body, too, was beautiful. He stood a head taller than she, and had a pleasing proportion, neither wide and brawny nor long and lanky. She imagined dripping hot candle wax upon the ridges of his chest and land-ing her lash against his strapping thighs. His muscles, sleek but not burly, exposed an aristocratic background full of sport. His calf was well defined, as was the bulge in his breeches.

Conscious that he was still staring at her with unabashed impudence, she raised her brows at him. But instead of realizing his place, he contin-ued to stare. Such defiance could not go unpunished, Gertie thought to herself. She could derive much satisfaction in being the one to admin-ister his punishment. She had seen his sort of arrogance before. Many such men had proven remarkably weak when tied to the whipping post. Would he as well?

Strange, but he seemed to read her thoughts in the way that he looked at her. For the first time since becoming a regular at Madam Botreaux's, she felt herself faltering. Her heart seemed to palpitate unevenly. Walking past him, she spotted a more callow fellow who puffed his chest forward in a display of undue confidence. Just as she was about to select this one, she heard a voice behind her. His voice *felt like velvet*, if such a thing were possible, its resonation low and comforting.

"Afraid, Mistress?"

Gertie could feel the blood pounding a warning in her ears. She turned slowly towards the man with the bright eyes. "It is customary that those in the Presenting line not speak lest spoken to."

"Am I to be punished for it?"

To keep herself from licking her lips at the thought, she pursed her mouth. "Perhaps. You are new here and may merit forgiveness for your first transgression. The decision will lie with your Master or Mistress."

"Are you—afraid—to administer the punishment?"

She stared at him in disbelief. Had he twice called her afraid?

"Consider yourself spared," she responded. The crowd murmured its agreement.

"That fails to answer my query."

She sucked in her breath, then enunciated the difference. "Not afraid. I am *disinclined*."

The corner of his mouth curled. "Ah. Of course."

Of course? What the devil did he mean by that? Did he presume to know her better than herself? Realizing her vexation growing, she took a deep breath and eyed him more keenly. Who was this stranger and why these attempts to insult her?

"Is it punishment you be wanting?" she asked him imperially.

At last he displayed the proper deference by bowing his head. He said in a low baritone, "If you would give it, Mistress."

She shivered for it felt as if his words had caressed her skin. No man in her recent memory had provoked her with such efficacy. She straightened in triumph, but he dashed the cup of victory as quickly from her lips.

"And if you dare," he added. When he looked up, there was a glimmer in his eyes.

If she selected him, then his stratagem prevailed. If she did not, she risked validating his accusations. The great Lady Athena feared no one— even if this man, with his uncanny ability to unsettle her, possessed an air of danger.

Her pride carried the day.

She put the tip of her crop upon his pectoral, lightly at first then with increasing force, digging the point into his hard muscle. To his credit, he did not step back or flinch.

"You will rue your words," she informed him. "Towards that end, I would be much *inclined*."

He bowed his head in acknowledgement. A few patrons around them shook their heads at his foolishness.

Gertie headed towards one of the many arched alcoves that lined the main assembly hall. The stranger followed behind her.

Located at the far end of the cavern, her alcove looked upon the length of the assembly hall. On the opposite end wound the large staircase that led to the balcony of Madame Botreaux. She had once been invited to join Penelope on the balcony but had declined. Gertie had little interest in the other patrons and derived no titillation from watching them.

The furnishing in the alcove consisted of a table, bench and whipping cross. Adorning the walls were ropes, whips, chains, shackles, and a lone candelabra. Gertie indicated the stranger should stand in the center. To her relief, he did as she directed without word. She took a deep breath and began to circle him. Although this ritual was one she always began with after having selected a new submissive, her true motivation was one of procrastination. Why did this stranger compel such uncertainty for her? He waited patiently, his eyes forward as she stalked around him, a panther surveying her prey. He had the elements of a proper submissive, but he was not like any she had known.

"What brings you here?" she asked at last. It was not her custom to engage in dialogue, but she knew not how best to proceed with him.

"I presume the same raison d'être that brings you here," he replied without wavering his gaze. "Mistress Athena."

The smoothness of his voice made her shiver, but the tone irked her. She sensed a veiled taunt.

"I shall call you Hephaestus whilst you are mine," she pronounced with a deliberate smirk for Hephaestus was a lame and therefore grotesque god in Greek mythology, but he only smiled as if he shared in her mirth.

Walking behind him, she eyed the curve of his ass—round, hard and smooth. Delectable. Perfect for the kiss of the lash or for sinking one's teeth into.

"Is my Mistress pleased by what meets her eye?"

*The devil...*Gertie stared at him in disbelief. Who was this man and how did he seem to know her thoughts?

"You are forward," she informed him. "You were not spoken to."

"Forgive me, Mistress," he acknowledged.

"You have been poorly trained."

"That can be remedied."

Her pulse quickened at the thought of learning him the ways of a proper submissive. She could derive much pleasure in bringing him to his knees, but she had the distinct feeling that it would be no easy task. She had never committed herself to any man for considerable length of time—save for the one that she was bound to by law and vow—her husband, the Earl of Lowry. The reason for her patronage at Madame Botreaux's. The stranger before her had presumed that they possessed some shared interest in coming to the *Cavern*, but he could not be further from the truth.

"You shall be punished," she pronounced without indicating whether

or not she intended to provide the remedy he spoke of, "for your trans-
gressions."

She pushed him towards a wooden table along the alcove wall and felt
herself growing warm, an uncommon occurrence. In her time at Madame
Botreaux's, she had observed many an arse, perhaps few as beguiling as his
or accented so well by such tight fitting breeches, but certainly enough
agreeable ones. Why did this one call to her, tugging at some primal urge
embedded deep within her body?

"Let fall your breeches," she commanded.

He did as instructed without the least bit of timidity.

Dear bodkins. She stared at the molded buttocks. Naked, his arse was
even more inspiring. Shaking her head, she forced herself to concentrate
on the task at hand. "Bend over the table."

His arse arched further toward her as he complied.

"You will address me always as Mistress Athena," she told him as she
tapped her crop into her palm in anticipation. "Failure to do so will merit
you at least four lashes, or five, or six. Truly, it depends upon my disposition at the moment."

She fingered the length of her crop. "Do you favor an instrument of
punishment?"

"I favor whatever my Mistress wishes to wield," he replied.

Well answered. But she had no intention of praising him yet. "We shall
start with the crop. If you are as presumptuous as you have been, you will
have the opportunity to taste all of my lovely implements here."

With that, she backhanded one arse cheek. He did not flinch. She
landed another on the other cheek. Still no movement from him. Pressing her lips together, she allowed the pain to sink in for him. Gathering
her strength, she dealt him three successive whacks in the same spot. This
time she heard a small grunt. Even in the dim lighting, she could see the
mark of the crop burning bright where she had struck. She wanted to
reach out and touch him there, caress the wound, perhaps even plant a
kiss.

Swallowing a growl of frustration, she struck him again, and again, and
again, hoping the rhythm would diffuse the strange effect she was experiencing. But the vigorous lashing did not excise her disconcertion. On
the contrary, she felt more flustered. Although he seemed to grip the table
more tightly, he displayed little evidence of the pain he must be feeling.
She unleashed her full strength, but her blows fell on an impassive body.
The only one who seemed to be out of sorts was her. She was breathing

hard from her exertion, and the sight of her crop falling against his arse had only caused her to flush more intensely.

Not knowing quite how to proceed next, she adjusted her mask and told him to don his breeches. "We are done. For tonight."

She was sorry and relieved to lose the sight of his delectable arse beneath his breeches. After buttoning the breeches, he stood erect, his posture emphasizing his broad shoulders.

"Thank you, Mistress Athena."

She nodded even though he faced away from her. He seemed to know the ways of a submissive, though his diligence in abiding by proper behavior was rather capricious.

The ensuing silence made her agitate her crop against her thigh. She let out a deep breath. "You will return two nights hence to this space. If I do not find you here waiting for me by ten o'clock, you are no longer my submissive."

She strode out, not daring to glance back. She hoped he would not return.

CHAPTER TWO

T HE STRIDENT VOICE OF DOWAGER Lowry transcended the
stairs as if she meant to call to someone on the second floor instead
of speaking to her son in the drawing room where she waited. "I do hope
your wife has not selected that dreadful gown of peach for the Bennington ball. Peach is not a becoming color upon her."

Standing alone at the top of the stairs, Gertie glanced down upon the
gown of peach she wore. With her dark brown curls and pale complexion, she had thought the pastel an appropriate color for herself. The satin
gown with its layered lace ruffles at the elbows was one of her favorites
to start the Season. She wore it with matching slippers and had labored
to find the best among her jewelry to accent her attire, finally settling on
her garnet set. Despite her impatience, she had allowed the coiffeuse to
produce curl after curl in a meticulous attempt to create the *Merveilleuse*.
For a brief moment, Gertie considered donning another gown, but they
were late for the Bennington ball as it was, and she had the suspicion that
the most perfect gown would not meet the approval of the Dowager.

"Or that horrid gown of lavender she wore to the Wempole garden
party," Sarah Farrington, her sister-in-law, added.

"Then why do you not impart your sensibilities to her?" Gertie heard
her husband retort with irritation. "Instead you allow me to appear at
these events with an unflattering wife."

"I protest. I have made such an attempt, but alas, it has proven futile."

Gertie recalled Sarah's one endeavor. Her sister-in-law had reviewed
her wardrobe, sniffing at the mediocrity of certain articles and explaining how each gown was unsuited for a woman of her shape and features
before declaring the whole effort to be quite fatiguing and that surely it

was time for tea? Gertie would have gladly taken any guidance from her sister-in-law for Sarah was a beauty of the first order and followed all the latest fashion plates in *The Lady's Magazine.*

"Her arms appear to have grown in thickness," Dowager Lowry disapproved. "I hope you have cautioned her, Alexander, against indulging her appetite too much."

Weary of overhearing more criticisms from her in-laws, Gertie made her entrance into the drawing room. Three pairs of eyes looked her over from head to toe. Alexander and his mother frowned while Sarah smirked upon seeing the gown of peach. Gertie was well aware that she was the ugly duckling among the statuesque Farringtons. Though she knew the Earl to have born more affection for her dowry than her person, she had considered herself fortunate to have acquired a husband who had such fine features. With only a modest countenance and a plump figure, Gertie had been convinced she could only marry a skinny freckled young man or a corpulent wizened man with a gout ailment. Alexander with his golden locks, fair skin, and high cheekbones had appeared a dashing prince.

They had been married three years. The fairy tale had withered soon after their wedding.

Alexander narrowed his eyes at the gown of offense. "Shall we increase your allowance, Gertie, that you may procure a suitable ball gown?"

He asked for the benefit of his mother for he knew the answer. Alexander had squandered the largesse of the dowry and inheritance, most of it upon procuring a new coach-and-four and a house in Berkeley Square—though he considered Grosvenor Square a more fitting address for an Earl—and the remainder at dice, horses, and pugilism. His flippancy with all matters monetary had led his steward to begin consulting with his wife, whom they discovered had a decent head for figures and possessed more common sense. His distaste for such responsibilities trumped his pride, and Alexander was content to have his wife oversee the handling of the estate and household economy, provided he had access to funds when he needed them.

"Perhaps we ought to consider a new dressing maid," Sarah added, raising two perfectly arched brows in her continued inspection of Gertie. "Jane has not done a proper job of disguising the shadows beneath your eyes."

During the first year of her marriage to Alexander, the criticisms from her sister-in-law came in the form of poorly conceived flattery—a la "the bonnet you wear today is much more flattering than the one you wore yesterday." Sarah made no effort nowadays to temper her contempt. Gertie allowed that such a beauty aw Sarah was must easily find fault in lesser mortals and had once quipped to a friend that Sarah should be glad that her splendor shined all the more when standing beside her plain sister-in-law. The angels had blessed Sarah Farrington with locks made from the sun's rays, a swan-like neck, dainty feet and wrists so slender they equaled those of a child. Her nose, like her mother's, was perhaps too sharp in profile, but apart from that, she was flawless.

"Perhaps a little more powder then?" Gertie replied, attempting to view herself in a mirror on the opposite wall.

"We have delayed long enough," Alexander said with impatience.

Sarah had exceptionally discerning eyes, Gertie reassured herself as the Farringtons stepped into their carriage. Jane had received specific instructions to blend away the shadows—the result of an unfortunate series of events from the night before. Even now Gertie felt a warm discomfort as she recalled *him*. Hephaestus she had dubbed him, but the name had done little to achieve what she had hoped. Never had a visit to *Madame Botreaux's* proven so unsatisfactory. She had been in fine form until he had appeared.

The night had progressed from bad to worse when, upon arriving to Lowry House last night, she had discovered that the portico she kept ajar for her surreptitious return had been shuttered. She had stood outside in the dark of night for what seemed like hours contemplating her options. She could knock on the door and wake the servants, perhaps explaining that she had gone for a walk to quiet a restless night, but that would not clarify how the door came to be locked after her. She finally remembered that she had left the window of her bed chamber ajar. She had successfully climbed the vines to reach the balcony of her chambers, but only after scraping a knee and losing a slipper to the bushes below.

"The Henshaws announced the birth of child—a boy," remarked Dowager Lowry as their carriage veered onto Bourdon Street. "The Duchess had been rather apprehensive that Elizabeth would not produce an heir, but I had assured her that her daughter would fulfill her responsibility."

Gertie stared into her hands. She felt the pointed gaze of the Dowager. The Dowager never failed to announce a birth of note—one would have thought her the bloody *Times*—to underscore the fact that she had no grandchild. Gertie felt Alexander shift beside her. She had once told her mother-in-law, despite the delicacy of the matter, that it was not for want of trying. In truth, as much as she dreaded the conjugal act with her husband, she would have liked nothing more than to cradle a babe of her own. Alexander, however, seemed to have lost interest in the past twelvemonth. He had not touched her in some time.

"Gertie, have you been seeing Dr. Fitzwilliam?" the Dowager inquired. "He told me you have not scheduled an appointment with him in over three months. I took the liberty of inviting him over next Tuesday. You will make the engagement at one o'clock, I presume?"

Gertie glanced at Alexander, but he directed his gaze out the window. There would be no help from him on this matter.

"I wonder that his services are needed—or effective?" Gertie returned.

The nostrils of the Dowager flared. "Do you doubt his skill, Gertie? Elizabeth Henshaw was a patient of his."

With an inward sigh, Gertie relented.

Sarah arranged her skirts of midnight blue about her with long slender fingers. "I suppose the benefit of our supreme tardiness is that we are likely to pull straight up to the house, but then we will have missed much of the amusement, and the embarrassment of it all is most difficult to bear. I wonder that that any other woman has to endure sharing a dressmaid with *two* other women? Shall we be forever late to all our events?"

She pinned her accusatory stare at Gertie, who was tempted to respond that most women had not the luxury of a dressing maid at all, but instead she replied, "I think that no one save ourselves shall be cognizant of why we are late."

"It is enough that I am aware!" Sarah snapped.

Gertie looked to her husband, though she knew that he would not defend her or offer that he had acquiesced to her suggestion that they reign in their expenses by releasing some of the servants. She suspected that he had easily agreed in part because dismissing the other maids would have had little impact upon his person. Alexander had been more reluctant to dismiss the groomsman, but when Gertie explained that they had exhausted their credit and that the only possible loan would have to come from Jewish quarters, he had conceded.

Silence pervaded most of the ride to the Bennington residence. Alexander spent the time examining his fingernails, Sarah pouted, and the Dowager stared at Gertie, who had long ceased to attempt a light tete-a-tete with her family. Inevitably, they would find something at fault with her. As Sarah predicted, there was no line of carriages to wait behind when they arrived, and when they were announced, most of the guests were too engrossed in conversation already to notice. Sarah was not often of a cheerful disposition, but Gertie braced herself for what would surely be at least a sennight worth of her cantanker.

Gertie anticipated a long night as her best friend, the Marchioness of Dunnesford, would not be in attendance. The dancing had already begun. Not expecting to dance—Alexander had yet to request a single dance since their marriage—Gertie went to sit beside Mrs. Pemberly, a woman who had befriended her parents before they had passed away.

"Gertrude, how lovely to see you," Mrs. Pemberly greeted with a warm smile that extended to her emerald eyes, which had lost none of their radiance through the years. She patted the spot on the settee next to her. "Ah, you wore that dress last Season, did you not? It is a lovely gown, but I must confess that I think the shade to be less than brilliant against your hue, my dear."

"That would seem to be the prevailing sentiment then," Gertie sighed as she took a seat and watched as a flock of men circled around Sarah for the minuet.

"Indeed?"

"My mother-in-law and Sarah commented upon the same."

"That won't do. I have no wish to be in accordance with Belinda Farrington."

Gertie smiled. Mrs. Pemberly had never been enamored of the Farringtons and had cautioned her father against the Earl of Lowry. It was Gertie herself—or her vanity, rather—and the desire of her father to see his only child married that had sanctioned the match.

"There he stands—across the room," Mrs. Drake, sitting on the other side of Mrs. Pemberly, whispered behind her fan.

Mrs. Pemberly promptly held up her own fan. "The one in white silk? With the gold embroidery?"

"Need you ask?"

One corner of Mrs. Pemberly's mouth curled in almost *naughty* fashion, to Gertie's great surprise. Intrigued by the mystery of their exchange, Gertie looked across the ballroom and immediately discerned what had to be the subject of their attention.

Wearing a magnificent coat that curved away from the front to reveal a gorgeous waistcoat and *very* fitting breeches, he was easily the most beautifully dressed man in attendance. The coat had a standing collar trimmed with embroidery, buttoned pleats, and encased his body with such tightness one wondered how he had fit into it. A deep sapphire of the brilliant cut was nestled in his cravat. He wore his hair powdered, smooth about the forehead with *ailes de pigeon* above the ear. Gertie had never seen the man before. Although his high fashion might have escaped her notice, his features would not. With an intelligent brow, a masterful but not overly square jaw, a straight nose, smooth cheeks, and defined lips, he possessed the perfect blend of fair and rugged beauty. His relaxed eyelids gave him a sense of *ennui*. If he was cognizant that he was the center of much attention, he did not reveal it.

Gertie strained to see the color of his eyes until she realized he was looking at her. She jerked her gaze away. Perhaps he had not been looking at her. He stood across the length of the ballroom and from such a distance it would be impossible to know precisely where he gazed. And why would he choose to be looking at her? Still, it had felt as if he had. Perhaps he meant to return the impertinence of her own stare.

"Who is he?" Gertie asked.

"One who has been on all our tongues the whole of the evening," Mrs. Drake responded.

"What a delicious thought," Mrs. Pemberly quipped.

Gertie gasped. She had never heard Mrs. Pemberly speak in such a fashion.

"Oh, but you must know him, Gertie. He is a cousin to your husband, is he not?"

Gertie furrowed her brows. "I have not met him before."

Mrs. Pemberly nodded. "Yes. He went into exile, as it were, some five years ago, before you were married to Alexander. And then we all thought him dead at the hands of a French count whose daughter Barclay was rumored to have seduced. But you must know Barclay's sisters and brother. Lord Barclay is the eldest."

Mrs. Drake shook her head. "Lady Surrington is the eldest of the brood."

"The Baron Barclay—I supposed he is no longer the Baron then," Gertie said of the younger brother. "He is not only a cousin to the Earl but a neighbor. The Barclay lands borders Lowry. I had forgotten he had an older brother."

"I understand the Farringtons are not overly fond of the Barclays?"

"They do not converse much," Gertie rephrased. She deliberated whether or not to take a second look at the man, and decided against it.

Not to be deterred from her efforts to unearth more gossip, Mrs. Drake asked, "I heard that if there is no heir for Lowry, the earldom would fall to Lord Barclay? Perhaps that is the reason for his return to England?"

"Hush, Pamela!" Mrs. Pemberly interceded. "If Barclay were interested in peerage, why would he have given up his barony to his brother?"

"He could not manage his estate while in exile."

"He has not reclaimed the barony upon his return."

"Because an earldom awaits him!"

"Pamela, you are a ninny. Have you forgotten his repute? Barclay has shown he has but one overriding interest: the *fair sex*. I wish I were twenty years younger that I should be an object of his pursuit."

"You need not be. I heard he courted an Italian countess while in exile, and she had fifty years to her!"

"He has kept his habits then?" Gertie asked for she had heard that Barclay had left England after a duel over a man's wife.

"I should hope so," Mrs. Pemberly responded as she fanned herself more vigorously.

Gertie shook her head and smiled. She rose to her feet. "I think I should look for my husband."

"His years on the Continent have served him well," Mrs. Drake said to Mrs. Pemberly.

Unable to resist any more, Gertie glanced in Lord Barclay's direction, but he was gone.

(6

SHE DASHED BEHIND THE HEAVY damask curtain. Hiding in the Bennington library was not the most dignified activity for the Countess of Lowry, but Gertie would not have anyone witness her tears. Crying did not become her. Her cheeks turned red as apples, the tip of her nose likened itself to a cherry and her eyes puffed pink as the flesh of melons until the whole of her face was a veritable fruit cart.

Lord and Lady Bennington were dear friends, and Lady Bennington had been months planning her first ball of the Season. Gertie did not want the hostess thinking that the event was anything less than a complete triumph with all of her guests. That the evening was proving to be the worst that Gertie could remember was no fault of the Benningtons.

She had gone to seek Alexander in the card room upon suspecting that he might take to hazard, his game of choice whenever he felt short of funds. She had requested to speak to him to remind him that, given their situation, he should limit his gaming. Alexander had turned red with rage.

"Do not *ever* presume to call me away from the tables," he had seethed before stalking back into the card room to, more likely than not, run up more debt.

A little shaken by his vehemence, Gertie had returned to the ball-room to Mrs. Pemberly and Mrs. Drake, both of whom were still on the topic of Lord Barclay. After sitting a while, Gertie had grown restless and decided to seek some air in the gardens, but she had not walked far when she overheard two familiar voices.

"I have not the least interest in Mr. Warburton!" Sarah was protesting.

"It matters not," Alexander had responded. "He has an interest in you."

"But he is *old* and—and *homely*."

"He is wealthy."

"I will *not* marry him."

"As your brother, it is my duty to oversee your interests. We are in a precarious way with funds."

"*My* interests? You mean your interests! Perhaps if you did not lavish your mistress with gifts quite so often, we would not be in such dire straits. That sapphire bracelet of hers must have cost a fair guinea."

The rest of their conversation had continued as if from the end of a long tunnel for Gertie. The words had hit her full and hard in the stom-ach. Alexander had a mistress. She was not surprised by the fact, but the realization was nonetheless painful. Little wonder that he had not sought her bed chambers of late. He had a mistress. A mistress to whom he presented gifts. Aside from his wedding gift to her, a broach that had belonged to his grandmother, she had never received the slightest token from him.

She could not remember if she had stayed to hear the end of their dialogue. Overcome with misery, she had sought seclusion to nurse her wounds. In the quiet of the library, away from the music and merriment, she had sobbed. She had never expected to win her husband's heart, but she had hoped to have a child, a source of pride and joy, someone to bestow the bountiful affection that waited in her own heart. She was sure that a child would take away the despair of her loveless marriage and fill the void with light. But if her husband had no desire…

What a stupid fool I have been, Gertie had chided herself, on the verge of a new wave of tears when she heard a scuffle outside the library door. She dashed behind the nearest curtain.

Two bodies stumbled into the room. Through the slit between the cur-tains, she saw the flash of a familiar midnight blue as the bodies fell onto the sofa not far from where she hid. Her cheeks flamed when she realized the body of the woman writhing below was that of her sister-in-law. The body pinning Sarah to the sofa was that of Lord Barclay.

"Tell me," Sarah said between deep breaths, "how it is we have not met before?"

"You would feign ignorance?" he responded as he pressed his mouth to her neck. "Come, come, we have been neighbors, afterall."

"I had not had my come-out when you left England. I was five and ten, and I think you thought me an awkward little girl then—"

She stopped upon realizing she had revealed her own falsehood. She looked at him with some trepidation, but he only smiled briefly before returning to her neck, which he caressed in slow lingering kisses. She closed her eyes and moaned in delight.

"You have no need to prevaricate with me, Miss Farrington. You were never awkward."

Sarah arched her back and neck, allowing him more surface. "I see that you have lost none of your impudence since leaving England."

"Indeed, I have acquired more during my absence," he murmured into her neck. "I would hazard that you prefer your men impertinent."

Sarah gasped. One of his hands had made its way up her skirts. Gertie flushed. This would not do. She had to find a way out. But she could not tear her eyes from them—from him and what he was doing. There was something masterful in the way he moved with Sarah, plying her body as if he were a puppeteer secure in knowing just how she would react to his every move. No doubt his confidence stemmed from many a practiced seduction.

"Very impertinent," Sarah acquiesced as her gasps quickened.

Gertie marveled at how this Barclay could fondle Sarah with one hand without interrupting the rhythm of his kisses. Imagining what he might be doing beneath Sarah's skirts stirred sensations in her own loins. His ministrations were apparently quite effective for Sarah was panting and moaning, one hand clutching the edge of the sofa with whitening knuckles. Gertie shifted her weight in discomfort. She needed to find a way out for she knew not how long they intended to stay, and though the fullness with which his mouth explored the neck before him mesmerized her, she did not think she wanted to view her sister-in-law much more than she had.

Sarah's moaning became high pitched grunts and wails. She was close to her climax, her eyes shut tight. The two were absorbed enough for

Gertie to slip away. Slowly, she brushed aside the curtain and stepped from her hiding place. Her toe struck the footstool as she dashed towards the door, but she suppressed her cry. Once safely outside the library, she hurried down the hallway and allowed herself a grimace for her poor toe. She found a mirror on the wall and examined how her tears had smeared her powder and rouge.

She also noticed one of her earrings to be missing.

😐

JUST BEFORE SARAH CRIED OUT in ecstasy, Phineas thought he heard something behind him. After gently coaxing the last tremors from her orgasm, he allowed her a moment of peace before moving himself to examine the room about them. He saw no one, but the door was not completely shut and he was sure that he had closed it when they came in.

"What is it?" Sarah murmured as she stretched with the satisfaction of a cat freshly woken from a nap.

"Nothing," he responded. There was no need to alarm her. "I think dinner will be served shortly. We had best return."

It was possible someone had sought to enter the library and he had simply not heard the door open. Sarah had been rather vocal. But then he noticed the overturned footstool. Someone had been in the room.

"When shall I see you again?"

"Methinks your brother bears little fondness for me, madam," he answered wryly as he studied a spot of discoloration on the carpet.

Sarah pouted. "What does that matter?"

It was no discoloration. He bent down and picked up a garnet earring.

"Alexander may be my brother, but I am near twenty years of age and quite capable of deciding whose company I wish to keep."

"No doubt, but I have no desire to find myself in another duel."

He tucked the earring into the pocket of his waistcoat.

"Alexander would never have the courage to challenge you."

Phineas had to agree with her assessment. He had seen enough of Alexander, who was near in age to his own brother, growing up to believe that the Earl lacked much of a backbone. But it had been made clear to him that the scandal of another duel would send him into permanent exile or to a trial by peers. A friend of his who served in the House of Lords had advised him not to test his luck with the latter, saying "If you hadn't made half of them a cuckold by bedding their wives, I would have said otherwise."

Turning to Sarah, Phineas offered his hand. She rose from the sofa and straightened her skirts.

"I will be at Hyde Park tomorrow," she informed him as she patted her ringlets to ensure they had not come undone. "I should be most pleased to see you there—if you are not otherwise occupied."

He brought her delicate hand to his lips. "I will make myself *unoccupied*."

She gave him a broad smile, one that looked odd upon her customarily humorless physiognomy. It amused him at times the women he chose to seduce. With Sarah Farrington, she was as much the seducer as he. Having made eye contact with him, she had immediately thrust up her fan, but her eyes had told him all he needed to know. They had beckoned, and when he had not immediately responded for he had no desire to be part of the group of pups that lapped at her, she had sought him out, conveniently dropping her fan at his feet when their paths crossed in the hallways.

At dinner, Sarah glanced often over her pigeon pie in his direction. She was not the only one to eye him. He was keenly aware that he and not the much touted lobster was the cynosure of the evening. There was not one pair of eyes that did not look his way. One set in particular had caught his attention. The soft green eyes, set in an unremarkable but tender physiognomy of rounded cheeks and supple lips, had studied him from across the dance floor. He had found her familiar, and though he possessed an astute memory for faces, he could not place her.

"When did the Earl of Lowry marry?" he asked of Mrs. Pemberly, who was seated next to him.

"He has been married to Gertie some three years," she replied, clearly pleased to be the source of information for him.

He looked down the table at the Countess of Lowry. She did not appear to be the kind of wife he would have expected Alexander to take.

"I do not think I know her family."

"Well, her family is of the *bourgeoisie* but a good family nonetheless. Her father made quite the profit in the sugar trade."

Ah, that explained Alexander's choice of spouse, Phineas thought to himself. He had known Alexander to be rather vain and would not otherwise have taken a plain woman to wife lest she possessed some other prevailing quality.

"If you ask me," Mrs. Pemberly posited, "I would rate her family above that of the Farringtons. Gertie is far too good for the likes of him."

He studied the elder woman and decided she spoke sincerely and not with any attempt to flatter him with her awareness that the Farringtons and Barclays were not the fondest of relations. Mrs. Pemberly seemed a woman who hesitated not to speak her mind. He returned his attention to that of the Countess, who stirred her soup aimlessly. She sat between Alexander and the Dowager Lowry, both of whom ignored her the whole of the dinner. Phineas recalled seeing the Earl and his wife earlier in the evening. He stood too far to overhear their conversation, but he had seen the livid expression upon Alexander and the forlorn look of hopelessness in Lady Farrington after he had berated her in what must have been harsh terms. Though he knew not her person, Phineas felt a tug of sympathy for the Countess. He knew of few women he would recommend Alexander to. Perhaps Sarah Farrington if she were not already his sister.

The powder and rouge upon Lady Farrington wanted another application, he noticed. His gaze drifted to her garnet necklace, the design of which matched the earring in his pocket.

"I should introduce myself to this new relation of mine," he commented.

Mrs. Pemberly eyed him carefully. "Indeed?"

"The relations between the Barclays and the Farringtons are not as strained as the rumors would have you believe. We converse quite amicably."

"Indeed?"

He looked her square in the eyes and smiled. "Indeed."

She was the first to blink. "Well, you will find Gertie a pleasant and *honest* girl. She is quite refreshing in that regard. You will find no nonsense with her. While she may not be up to snuff with all the *de rigueur* of gentle society, she is extremely *sensible*. I myself have seen her maturation through the years and regard her with as much affection as if she were mine own."

Noting the claws of the lioness, he replied, "You are protective of her."

"I will not see her harmed."

"And you fear that I am a wolf in search of a sheep."

"Though I suspect Lady Farrington is not the type to inspire your predilections, I confess your motives puzzle me."

"A simple desire to acquaint myself with a new member of the family does not satisfy you?"

"Certainly the marital situation of a woman has not stopped you before," she continued without answering him, cognizant of the rhetorical nature of his question. "Dare I presume that you have mended your ways?"

A brash question deserved a brash reply.

"Do you hope that I have?"

Mrs. Pemberly colored, then allowed a grin to creep into her lips. "Fair enough."

The dinner over, Phineas rose to his feet. He turned to Mrs. Pemberly and raised her hand to his lips. "What delightful dinner company you have been, Mrs. Pemberly. I esteem a woman who speaks her mind. I hope that Fortune will grace me again with your presence."

The blush rose in her cheeks once more. She raised a thin eyebrow at him. "I rather think that your sojourn on the Continent was spent not in repentance but in perfecting your charms, Lord Barclay."

"You are a woman after mine own heart," he noted of her ability to compliment and critique in the same stroke.

She fluttered her fan before her with a little more vigor. He offered her his arm and escorted her from the dining hall. Across the room, Alexander was engrossed in a conversation with another gentleman, leaving his wife alone to walk behind him.

Mrs. Pemberly must have noticed the same for she said, "Did you not wish to make the acquaintance of the Countess of Lowry?"

Phineas bowed to his dinner companion and made his way towards the Countess.

"Lady Farrington," he addressed.

She had begun to walk away from the crowd, perhaps attempting to steal away to some haven of solitude, and was obviously startled that someone had called to her. When she turned to face him, he saw that she was not as plain as when seen from afar. Her cheeks had a natural blush, and though her eyes were not the large sparkles of color that graced the physiognomy of her sister-in-law, they possessed more depth. Unlike the shallow waters of Sarah Farrington, the verdant eyes of the Countess intrigued him.

They stared at him in displeasure.

Undaunted, he introduced himself with a bow. "I am Phineas Love, a relation of the Farringtons."

"I am aware that you are a *distant* relation," she replied coolly.

He had the feeling that even though she had to crane her neck to meet his gaze, she was attempting to look down at him. Perhaps she shared the sentiments of her husband towards the Barclays.

"A much belated congratulations on your nuptials."

Her frown deepened. He would have not have been surprised to hear her tell him that congratulations were unnecessary from him as he had not been invited to the wedding.

"Yes," she said, mustering more hauteur into her expression, "I was told you had been banished to France."

Her dislike of him, which was becoming increasingly palpable, amused him, as did most of the disdain people would have towards him. The son of parents who shocked gentle society with their wanton spirit and numerous illicit affairs, he had become immune at a tender age to what others thought.

"You put it harshly, madam. I like to think of my time there as a holiday," he replied. "I had occasion to travel to the Côte-d'Or and would highly recommend the region. The wines there are *par excellence*."

He could tell his impudence riled her.

"Ah, then you will be taking yourself back there?"

He nearly chuckled at her juvenile attempt to rid herself of his company. "I shall be staying in England for some time. I have come across a pursuit of great interest to me."

"Yes, I know," she said wryly.

"You do?"

She faltered, "I mean…naturally you will have missed much of what England has to offer, perhaps not the same quality of wine that you would find in France, but perhaps a rousing game of cricket or warm Yorkshire pudding on a cool winter morning, and certainly friends and family, from whom I will keep you no longer."

She turned to leave. He refrained from specifying that she was now family.

"Before you leave, Lady Farrington," he said, stopping her in her tracks. "I believe this to be yours."

He held out the earring. Her eyes widened upon seeing it. She hesitated, as if she contemplated denying ownership, but it was obvious that her one ear was missing its adornment. When she reached for the earring, he deftly reached for her with his free hand, pulling her closer. Though the nearest guest was not within earshot, he meant his words for her ears alone.

"Next time, feel free to join us, Countess," he murmured as he pressed the earring into her hand.

She burned brightly to the tips of her ears. Grasping the earring, she turned on her heel and hurried away from him.

CAVERN OF PLEASURE SERIES

OTHER WORKS BY EM BROWN

CAVERN OF PLEASURE SERIES
Mastering the Marchioness
Conquering the Countess
Binding the Baroness
Lord Barclay's Seduction

RED CHRYSANTHEMUM STORIES
Master vs. Mistress
Master vs. Mistress: The Challenge Continues
Seducing the Master
Taking the Temptress
Master vs. Temptress: The Final Submission
A Wedding Night Submission
Punishing Miss Primrose, Parts I - XX

CHATEAU DEBAUCHERY SERIES
Submitting to the Rake
Submitting to Lord Rockwell
Submitting to His Lordship
Submitting to the Baron
Submitting to the Marquess
Submitting for Christmas

OTHER STORIES
Claiming a Pirate

Made in the USA
Las Vegas, NV
21 November 2021